Zoë Strachan was born in Kilmarnock in 1975. Her debut novel, *Negative Space*, won a Betty Trask Award and was shortlisted for the Saltire First Scottish Book of the Year Award. In 2003 The Independent on Sunday listed her in their top twenty novelists under 30, and the Scottish Review of Books selected her as one of their new generation of five young Scottish authors in 2011. She has been awarded a Hawthornden Fellowship, the Hermann Kesten Stipendium and a Robert Louis Stevenson Fellowship. She lives in Glasgow with her partner, the author Louise Welsh. You can find out more at www.zoestrachan.com

Negative Space
Spin Cycle

A perfect eye for the small detail . . . the first person voice drifts between past and present with astonishing effectiveness. Int·mate and real.

Scarlett Thomas, Independent on Sunday

St   :han understands and conveys raw emotion. Many read-er   ll connect with this story. *Diva*

st, intimate and powerful . . . You'll find yourself filled an astonishingly vivid sense of what it is like to cope with eath of a loved one. *Iafrica.com*

best queer novels are the ones which queer the landscape, e gay is every bit as apolitical as straight and where gender d exuality are very much like shoes – they fit for as long as e v nt them to. Zoë Strachan's Negative Space is a brilliantly exec ted queer read in the sense that sex is more of an issue than exuality. The L word doesn't even come into it. Strachan writ from the heart – the striving splintered heart. This is not so m ch a gay novel, but a great novel.

Negative Space was nominated for
The Big Gay Read 2006 by Helen Walsh

A werful portrayal of grief. *The Scotsman*

nguage is choice, the milieu is that of the post-art school ives, pubs, the cold familiarity of Glasgow, and the e cold (and beauty) of Orkney. . . . It is the rich and rm process of a person understanding through death how nd why they love, and how and why they love different people in almost precisely the same way.

Paul Wessel in the *Cape Times* (South Africa)

SPIN CYCLE

Strachan follows her prize-winning first novel Negative Space with another well-observed and quietly forceful story about women in emotional turmoil . . . She makes us notice the everyday detail of their working lives, the minor tensions and the camaraderie, the idle chat and occasional pearls of wisdom, and introduces us to a parade of those strange people without washing machines who all get cameo parts while they're waiting for the spin cycle to finish.

Independent on Sunday

Spin Cycle has the noir sexiness of Dance With a Stranger: idiosyncratic individuals, gnarled by bitterness and covetous desire, moments of small embarrassment and mundane realism, the eventual breathless climax . . . A gripping novel, full of twisted psychology and dark, covert obsessions; both murky and dazzling.

Uncut

Pitch-perfect: intelligent construction, unrelenting tension and a redemptive flourish of an ending.

The Big Issue

One of the most gorgeously written books I've read in a long time. Strachan illuminates the failings and dreams of her cast in graceful, probing brush strokes. Each page is wondrous and urgent and leaves you gasping for more. Strachan rocks.

Helen Walsh, author of Brass

Bringing the launderette sub-genre bang up to date, Strachan's three damaged female protagonists are complex, secretive and isolated. A rich, poignant work.

The List

Strachan breathes life into her characters and settings, and there's a warmth to her prose which suffuses reading about them with a sense of intimacy.

Glasgow Herald

The tension never dips, dialogue is perfect. A must read.

Daily Record

EVER FALLEN IN LOVE

Zoë Strachan

SANDSTONEPRESS
HIGHLAND | SCOTLAND

First published in Great Britain by
Sandstone Press Ltd
PO Box 5725
One High Street
Dingwall
Ross-shire
IV15 9WJ
Scotland.

www.sandstonepress.com

The author acknowledges support from
Creative Scotland towards the writing of this volume.

ISBN: 978-1-905207-73-2

Sandstone Press is committed to a sustainable future in publishing, marrying the
needs of the company and our readers with those of the wider environment. This
book is made from paper certified by the Forest Stewardship Council.

Cover design by Guilherme Condeixa
Typeset by Iolaire Typesetting, Newtonmore
Printed and bound in Poland

For
Louise Welsh

0

You wouldn't think that there were still women who could be ruined. Perhaps there aren't any more, but back then, in that university town by the sea, there were. It was quite an old-fashioned place. Luke was quite old-fashioned too. Cast himself as a latter day Dorian or Valmont, sinned the old sins.

He knew how I felt about him, of course. By then I'd stopped even trying to conceal it.

We were sitting on the windowsill of the pool room in the Union. I heard a shriek and traced his gaze to a girl who was celebrating her lucky, winning shot. She brandished her cue in the air, shook hands with her opponent, clinked pint glasses with her friends, all without quite losing her self-consciousness.

Her?

Yes, she'll do, he said.

He gave me twenty pence to stake his claim. A stake which could be raised; he'd honed his technique during his teenage years, his apprenticeship. Better she'd lost, kept quiet. Her taste for games was unlikely to match his.

I'll play you, I said, laying his money on the table. If you want.

You're on, she said.

I have to warn you, I'm not very good.

How about doubles then? You and your pal against me and Diane.

Perfect, I said, smiling at Diane as I went to select a cue.

I'd been striving to develop an epicene quality, in keeping with my tender years. And it was working, to an extent: women found it non-threatening, attractive even, if I'm not flattering myself too much. I indulged it because finally I could. Unlike so many of my peers I was emphatically working class. And so was Luke.

But you're wondering about the girl I was talking to, while he went to the bar to buy tequila all round. Her name was Lucy (short for Lucinda, though she tried not to let on). I recognised her from one of my philosophy options. She always came in late, bells jingling around the ankles of her 14-hole Doc Martens, and sat at the front of the old wooden-benched lecture room, picking her cuticles and trying to bring everything back to Nietzsche even when we'd moved on to Heidegger.

Luke's timing was good. There was still an hour's drinking to be done, but her friends were fading fast, apart from loyal Diane, whose heavily mascaraed eyes, slightly magnified, peered through her specs at me with mistrust. I sensed a little crush on Lucy, who remained high and bright and on a roll. Going by the white-girl braids in her hair, the five silver hoops in each ear, the barbell through her right eyebrow, she was rebelling within her confines. That was the fashion back then; I understand that generic honey blonde and an English-rose complexion are more aspirational now. For him it was enough to know that she'd graduate, swap tie-dye for cashmere, let her piercings heal.

I'm Richard, I said.

Lucy.

Yes, I know. Philosophy 2a.

I thought I recognised you from somewhere. Who's your friend?

That's what everyone asked, I thought, as I watched Luke weave towards us, a brace of shot glasses in each hand. Who's your friend?

1

It was a done deal. Stephie would get off the train in Inverness; he'd collect her at the station. Richard swivelled his chair away from his desk and towards the window. The small ferry was pootling towards the islands with its cargo of day-trippers. At first he'd been surprised to see the people carriers parked at the jetty. All those middle class families posed for photographs by the Aquila Maris. The contents of purses checked and measured into helpings of tea, scones and souvenir stamps from the only part of the country still to require special postage to reach the mainland. In a few hours time the visitors would wobble from the gangplank, ready to be absorbed by their designed-for-safety vehicles. They'd drive along the single track roads, melting into their campsites and caravan parks, leaving the area as peaceful as if their presence had been a mirage.

Peaceful, yes, Richard had felt peaceful too, but now the arrival of his little sister was niggling in his consciousness. 4.30pm tomorrow. He closed his email and looked at the screen for a few more moments before deciding that he felt too unsettled to do more work. He'd get the spare room ready, go back to it later. It was only as his computer sang out its goodbye that he realised that he had no idea how long Stephie intended to stay.

In the supermarket the next day, he selected instant meals and microwave snacks, salads and pulses, rye bread and Mother's Pride. Would she want to gorge herself on junk food or might she be observing some celebrity-endorsed food fad? He skimmed the shelves for products labelled organic and low GI. Was she still a vegetarian? (Had she ever been a vegetarian?) Chocolate. All girls liked chocolate, surely. He even browsed the DVDs, hesitated over a popular horror (his house was isolated, it might freak her out), before finally grabbing a teen flick, a costume drama and the second series of a comedy show he'd never watched but whose catchphrases he recognised when they were regurgitated in the newspapers. At the toiletries aisle he picked up the most expensive bubble bath they had; it was possible that Stephie was recovering from some emotional trauma and would want to spend hours in the bathroom.

And now here he was, shivering by the ticket machines in a T-shirt chosen to announce 'just because I live up north doesn't mean I can't be edgy', watching the jam of people brandishing railcards and jostling each other with rucksacks as they squeezed past the two ticket inspectors. A flicker of eye contact with a tourist, and then Richard looked away. He felt himself blending into the background, hoped that Stephie would notice him the instant she arrived. The mystery wasn't what she ate or liked to watch on television, but why she wanted to come to stay at all. And indeed why her parents (who were, he had to remind himself, his parents too) considered it such a good idea.

'She's got a lot of studying to catch up on,' his mother had typed, ominously. 'She could do with less distractions.'

And so what had been mooted – as far as he was concerned – as a vague plan had taken firm shape despite his protestation that he had a deadline looming and would not be on hand to babysit.

'She's far too old for a babysitter,' the admonitory reply had blinked back in the open email window. 'She can amuse herself.'

When he was Stephie's age he'd certainly been able to amuse himself. He often wondered what he'd do if he could go back and relive that period, usually coming to the uncomfortable conclusion that he'd do exactly the same again. Which didn't necessarily make him a textbook guardian for an impressionable youngster.

'Hey there.' Stephie was standing in front of him, twisting one foot behind the other.

'Hey, hello! Here, let me,' he indicated her wheelie case, which she manoeuvred towards him. It was heavy and swollen, the zip strained, and once again Richard worried how long she was planning to stay. But then women always packed more, didn't they? Make up and so on. It might be an overnight bag, for all he knew.

'When did you go blonde?' he asked, noticing that what he remembered as shoulder length brown hair had been replaced by a crop of mixed highlights.

'Ages ago,' she said, wriggling into the straps of the small day sack she'd been swinging from one arm.

'Right. Well, it's nice. I like it.'

'Got it done in Ayr,' she said. 'Didn't trust the blue rinse merchants at home.'

'Don't blame you. Anyway, car's out here,' Richard said. 'How's your journey been? Hellish?'

'All right,' she shrugged. 'I slept.'

'Well, we've got a bit further to go,' he said, trying not to look at the dark smudges beneath her eyes. Outside the sky had drawn closer and greyer, and the people dressed in vests and shorts looked foolish and out of place. Richard unlocked the door of his battered Ford.

'Nice car. Thought you earned a packet now?'

'Does the job. Nobody to show off to around here anyway.'

'And me bringing all my glad rags just in case.'

'I've explained what it's like.'

'Yeah but none of us have ever seen it, have we? We've never been.'

'I sent jpegs.'

'A jpeg isn't an invitation to dinner.'

Richard pulled up at the give way at the car park exit, shot a glance at his sister. She was looking straight ahead. Seeing rain spots on the windscreen he switched the wipers on, used the movement as an excuse to reach out and grasp her arm.

'You're here now.'

'I'm honoured,' she said. 'So, how much further is a bit?'

'About three hours?'

'Okay.' She turned in her seat and withdrew a pair of sunglasses from the pocket of her jeans. 'I'm going to grab another forty winks. Wake me when it gets scenic.'

5

0

There must, I suppose, have been a point of no return. It would be indulgent to claim it was the first moment I laid eyes on Luke, when it's enough just to say that I met him on the day I left home. I got the bus, which was, as everyone insisted with a frequency that soon became irksome, a long road for a short cut. My parents drove me to the terminus and we said our farewells, much to the interest of the local jakey, who seemed to believe I was going off to war. He broke into a garbled chorus of 'Wish Me Luck As You Wave Me Goodbye', swaying his can of Special Brew in encouragement as we loaded my suitcase and rucksack into the side of the coach. Must've been all the time he spent propped on the bench by the war memorial, or perhaps he'd spotted me at work one Saturday, assumed the white gravestones I was scrubbing were those of my comrades in arms. I twisted round in the back seat to see the cemetery as we left, cricking my neck until I caught sight of the headstones beyond the high wall. Although I was desperate to go, I couldn't help looking back.

It was a tedious bus ride from the 'Leck to Drumrigg, from Drumrigg to Glasgow, from there across to the coast and on. I almost wished I'd allowed my parents to drive me rather than palming them off with promises of mid-term visits. But as the route became less familiar, the boredom was leavened by that sense of anticipation that starts as a delicate throb in your chest then flutters through your stomach, brightening your eyes and refining your senses. Something's coming, I thought, something is on its way. And indeed it was. As the coach grew warmer, an unmistakable smell emerged. Piquant, as though a sloppy puddle of spew lay rank and undiscovered under a seat not far from my own. I felt nauseated, obviously, but worse than that I started to imagine the odour permeating my clothes and skin. A startling flash-forward saw me arriving at university and earning the nickname of Boakboy, which would stick to me like, well, sick, until graduation. Which seemed a very, very long way in the future.

No, this was my New Start, as the posters outside the Job Centre liked to trumpet, and I'd have sold my granny (her mind was beginning to drift, she'd scarcely have noticed) rather than let anything smear its lustre. Boakboy may have been sheer paranoid fantasy, but by the time I reached the city I thought, sod this for a game of soldiers. Gathering my backpack and unwieldy case (veteran of family holidays and that trip to Spain 'before you two were born'), I dragged myself to railway station, where I blew a fair portion of the emergency twenty quid my mother had sneaked into my hand on the train fare. And so I ended up on the same Scotrail express service that Luke joined at Edinburgh Waverley. It must have been fate that brought us together, chance was never so precise.

There were plenty of seats, but loose-limbed and smoky he chose one across the table from me. When he stretched to squash his rucksack into the luggage rack his t-shirt rose, allowing me to glimpse a dark curl of hair above the waistband of his jeans, the very tip of an appendectomy scar. I allowed myself the tiniest of fantasies, of unbuttoning his fly right there and then. As I'd put on my new clothes ready for the journey I'd felt that I was slipping into a new skin, becoming truly me. Sexual experimentation at universities was rife, or so they always said, but my gayness was no untested hypothesis. It was ready to be published and, with any luck, peer-reviewed.

That said, if sitting opposite a pretty boy on the train was my first test of valour, I flunked it. A little half smile was all I managed before inclining my head back towards my book. Excitement prevented me from reading properly. Not at his proximity – it wasn't love at first sight – but at what lay ahead. Although I turned the pages at regular intervals my thoughts hardly touched whatever it was I was reading. One of my course texts perhaps; Sartre or Kierkegaard, a volume more likely chosen for show than enthusiasm. I felt as if an aura of energy was crackling around me, that surely he'd detect.

Are you going to university, by any chance?

I rehearsed the line in my mind, then convinced myself that it was too gauche to ask and looked out the window instead. The grass was the same shade of green as at home, the hills had the same low curves. The ripening fields and scattered sheep were familiar too, though I'd never made this journey before. We sped by a converted mill, a disused viaduct, four clipped thoroughbreds wearing rugs despite the mild weather, and each of these seemed like a sight I'd see going to Ayr to spend my birthday money. Then through the trees which screened it from the track I caught a swift glimpse of a derelict mansion house, roofless, its grey stone façade tainted by fire.

Imagine that burning, he said.

With his words out there already, hanging in the air between us, it wasn't long before I forced out my own line.

Are you going to university, by any chance?

Brave of me to speak, chicken to do so in my deepest, straightest voice. It was as if I'd suddenly got stuck in a lift with Coco from the 6th year (on whom I'd had a stupendous crush), though I couldn't think of anywhere in Leckie that had a lift for us to get stuck in, unless it was a Stannah Stair Lift, and that wasn't exactly what I had in mind. I wanted to impress this person who had sat down opposite me, to coax him into liking me. Revealing too much too soon seemed an unnecessary risk.

Yes, he said. Yes I am.

2

There was no knowing when Stephie might get up. The drive
had taken longer than usual. Long enough to try her patience,
Richard had thought, as they shared a monosyllabic dinner
before watching television for an hour before bed. Ah well, a
good night's sleep and all that. He left the coffee things out on
the worktop in the kitchen, along with a note, then slipped
outside without locking the door behind him, imagining only
belatedly Stephie's anxiety if she discovered she'd been left
sleeping in an open house. He ran up the hill and then down
the curving road towards the old croft jetty. Low lumps in the
ground nearby delineated where rooms and byre had been,
mossy stones pushing through the grass like benign wisdom
teeth. A gnarled tree, still clinging to a sprinkle of spring
blossom, edged its crooked way out of what might once have
been the hearth.

Reaching the jetty Richard slowed to a walk, following it out
over the water. It was narrow and fragile-looking compared to
the new ferry dock, better avoided if the wind was high or the
waves likely to slop over and catch your feet from under you.
On a calm morning though, like this, the smell of salt and
seaweed seemed almost unbearable in its freshness. It wasn't
just a question of clearing your head, or so Richard felt, but
more a sense that the world itself had been cleansed and rested
overnight and was now hopeful about the day ahead. He used
a rusting bollard for his leg stretches, listening to the waves
brushing against the plinths below and thinking of Stephie
sound asleep. How late would he have stayed in bed when he
was her age? Midday, later?

His memory was, he thought, like a series of rooms. Rooms
with white walls and cornices, smooth dusty floors and scuffed
skirting. Each one empty, light filtering through blemished

windows and catching on motes of dust in the stale air. And yet these rooms contained his life; stories written on the plaster in lemon juice, waiting for heat to flow through them, for flames to lick at the picture rails and expose images as charred as the flecks of paper and coal in the grates. He could walk through these rooms, seizing the handles and pushing open the heavy doors, until he reached the final one, where a speckled mirror hung above a high marble fireplace, and if he paused and looked beyond his reflection for long enough Richard knew he would see a chaise-longue with chipped legs and scraps of horsehair leaking from the tattered upholstery. And beyond that, life rippling through the other rooms, illuminating them and making them vivid once more.

As it happened, Stephie rose long before midday, though by the time she was washed and breakfasted and hair-straightened it didn't seem so. Richard watched as she dabbed a spot of blush on the apple of each cheek, then quickly massaged it in. He'd been the same, when he first arrived in the village. Not with blusher admittedly, but changing his top to go out, running his fingers through his hair, checking there were no coffee stains on his trousers. He wasn't sure how long it had taken him to realise that there were no handsome strangers to bump into, no Mermen singing at the water's edge. Nor when he'd started to feel relieved rather than disappointed.

'Will you be okay walking in those shoes?' he asked, nodding towards Stephie's thong sandals, the splay of her turquoise varnished toenails.

'Yeah.'

'It's not as close as it seems in the car.'

'For god's sake Richard. They're dead comfy.'

He supposed his hiking boots weren't strictly necessary for a stroll down the road to the village. Perhaps he'd been too rigorous in adopting the uniform of the countryside; he underwent a makeover whenever he had to attend a meeting in Dundee or London. He was expected to be a geek, sure, but a geek with quirky Japanese accessories and trousers that didn't amount to a social faux-pas. Amazing what a whisper of hair wax could do, a hint of a fin, demi-quiff or side shed enough to reassure his colleagues that although he lived somewhere 'simply hilarious' (to quote Rupe, his commissioning editor), he was in fact capable of tapping in to the aspirations of 'the socially-engaged but seventies-nostalgic post-PC sofa-adventurous consumer' (that from DaCapo's branding strategy consultants).

Richard led Stephie down the hill and past the shingle beach, taking a detour along the new jetty so that he could point to the ferry pulling out of the harbour on Tanera Mhor.

'Not much of a village,' Stephie said, as they got closer.

'Enough people for two pubs. Garage, shop, village hall, church. Public toilets with showers, no less.'

'I'd settle for mobile phone reception.'

'There is down here. I should've said that you might have to go outside the house to speak.'

'Texts?'

'Maybe in the front room. If you're lucky.'

'Okay,' she said, then: 'It's pretty here.'

'Pretty in the sunshine. Come on, there's a good view from up by the war memorial.'

Stephie made Richard pose for a photo with the sea behind him – 'proof for Mum and Dad that you haven't had a sex change or something' – then stood, shifting her weight from one foot to the other and reading the names on the memorial. Richard stooped to straighten the faded poppy wreath from the previous Remembrance Day. After a while, she said, 'I wouldn't have thought so many people lived here.'

'There's surrounding settlements too, and the more isolated crofts. But this,' he waved his hand at the primary school behind him, 'is the biggest place for quite a way.'

'But still.'

'Makes you wonder who was left, doesn't it?'

'How they managed to produce enough men to be killed in the next war,' Stephie said, pointing at the shorter list of casualties for 1939-1945. 'Maybe someone from the Ministry came round and impregnated all the women.'

'Don't be grotesque.'

Stephie stuck her tongue out at him. 'Come to think of it, some of the people here do look pretty similar.'

'Stop it. It isn't easy living here, you know.'

'How do you manage,' she asked, but her words got caught up in the wind behind Richard, allowing him to ignore them as he marched across the road and back towards the shop. He heard the flat patter of her sandals as she ran to catch up with him.

They bought ice lollies and walked back along to the shingle beach. The sun was brighter now, highlighting the peaty hills and glinting off the water. Beyond the headland the islands glowed green. Stephie picked her way across the bigger stones to a huge wooden beam, weathered over the years.

'It's more colourful in the sunshine,' she said, unbuckling her sandals and wiggling her toes in the breeze. 'Still bleak though. Kind of unforgiving.'

'Not when you get used to it. Have you got blisters?'

She examined between her toes. 'Not yet. But I might do by the time we get home. Unless I can go barefoot.'

'I wouldn't recommend it. Too rough, and besides, the cute little baa lambs tend to shit all over the road.'

They watched as a Citroen and then a Renault skirted the bay and drove up the hill, bumping over the bridge then flashing out of sight behind a house. The cars reappeared a second later, sending the gulls flapping into the air as they crawled along the jetty to where the ferry was now docked and waiting for its afternoon seal-spotting cruise. The Citroen disgorged four children with blonde floppy hair, the Renault three more with brown curls. Both sets of parents quickly began the process of stuffing their offspring into brightly coloured sweaters. That done, they were all herded onto the Aquila Maris by old Rab, who would amuse them by leaping around the deck barefoot and shouting about sharks. Just as Richard was trying to formulate an anecdote about local characters, in case the silence between he and Stephie wasn't entirely comfortable, she said:

'Remember the caravan at Maidens?'

'Of course I do.'

'That time you got stung by a jellyfish on the beach and Mum said someone should pee on it.'

'Oh god,' he said. 'I screamed my head off at that, didn't I? More than at being stung in the first place.'

'But we went to the doctor instead.'

He nodded. 'I guess it's cheaper to fly to Spain or the Canaries now.'

'Yeah, and it's probably sunnier there than it ever was in Maidens.'

'That's funny. I remember it as sunny all the time. No, that's not true. There was always that one day when it rained and we all had to stay squashed in the caravan until there was a big row.'

Stephie laughed, concentrating for a second on getting the final melting piece of lolly into her mouth without losing any. 'And then Dad would take Jojo for a walk,' she said.

'So that we'd all end up crammed into a caravan that smelt of wet dog.'

The little ferry parped its horn as it cast off. They watched as it arced out into the bay and disappeared beyond the headland.

'Richard?'

'Uhuh?'

'Why did you come here?'

He sighed. 'I wanted a change.'

'It ain't exactly Vegas.'

'I needed a place where I could really concentrate on my work. The first couple of commissions were lucky breaks. Following them up was crucial.'

Stephie wedged her lollipop stick into a crevasse where the beam had split around a rusting rivet. 'I get that, but why here?'

'I got a good deal on a long term lease for the house. And it's worked out. I got the idea for this project here, as it happens.'

'So what is it then, Virtual Village? I guess lo-fi is in.'

'It's a war game,' Richard said.

'What, like dungeons and dragons, elves and goblins – what was that thing that you used to collect the figures from?'

'Warhammer,' Richard said, with a slight shudder of embarrassment, although he knew a box of little painted figurines was still safe in the attic back in Leckie. 'No, this is real, the Great War. Trenches. Going over the top, that kind of thing. Working title's *Somme*, but that doesn't really fit as the scope's wider. And marketing will probably demand that we change it to World War X-Treme or something ludicrous.'

'And I suppose you don't have to be on the side of good and right.'

Richard hesitated. 'It's a non-linear environment. You can choose your character and storyline. That's the way it works.'

'I see.'

'It's a big project. They've even outsourced the German characters to a studio in Hamburg.'

'Lovely. So all the neo-Nazis can get into it.'

'It's the first world war, you eejit. Didn't you learn anything at school?'

'Not in history. Mrs McGee was off all of the time. Stress, apparently.'

'She was the same when I was there. Except it was called flu then.'

Richard reached for a pebble and started circling it between his palms, increasing the pressure to see if the sandy grey surface would rub off to reveal smooth black stone underneath. Stephie looked out to sea, then behind her to the single track road that wove between the mountains and after twenty miles or so joined the B road south.

'It's so far away,' she said.

'Yes.'

'I thought you liked towns.'

'We grew up in a town, remember?'

'You went away to university in a town.'

'It was in the countryside. By the sea.' He got up, stretched his arms over his head, still holding the pebble. 'We'll have to move, I'm afraid. I've got a few things to get ready for a meeting later.'

'A meeting?'

'A virtual meeting.'

'Right.'

Stephie grabbed her sandals, then hopped alongside him over the stones onto the springy turf. A battered old jeep tooted at them as it rounded the bend and rumbled over the small bridge. Richard raised one hand in salutation.

0

Class bound us together, me and Luke, on our eager first day. Swallowing nerves as we walked up the main street towards campus, our rucksacks packed with soiled, second-hand texts and charity shop threads. The town was all a-bustle. Parents in country tweeds unloaded boxes from Land Rovers and Beemers; smacking kisses and braying voices filled the air. Bright young things monopolised the streets, scattering shy international students like pinballs. I'd read about Sloanes in the magazines my mum brought home from the waiting room at work, and here they were, in pastels and pearls. And with them came the floppy fringed public school boys and their soft leather billfolds. We queued for matriculation behind Torquil and Timmy, registered for Freshers' Week alongside Jilly and Jocasta, and it was scant consolation to overhear that for most of them coming here was second best.

Seduced by the glossy pics in the prospectus, it had been my first choice. Partly, I confess, because it put me in mind of the reruns of Brideshead Revisited on the telly (and, unwittingly, of the wankfests that particular adaptation provoked), but also because of the accommodation policy, which promised an affordable escape from home. Goodbye Leckie, hello world! As Luke and I followed the route marked on the photocopied map we'd received along with our course enrolment details, we saw that the photos hadn't lied: proud crests leapt from lintels and archways, occasionally a street or vennel revealed a sparkling glimpse of the sea or a sudden soar of ruin; sunshine rendered the glass and concrete of the library dazzling; knots of smiling students lazed on patches of grass.

Too good to be true? The same could not be said for the subsidised accommodation that had sealed the deal. Furthest from the lecture halls, furthest from the Union, Herrick House was a lopsided baronial villa flanked by gloomy conifers. Inside, the linoleum-floored hallways gently reeked of damp and old school dinners. The former probably explained by the mouldy patches which could be seen edging up the walls of the common room, the latter odd given that it was a self-catering hall. Here the Yahs were diluted by people who, like me, had a vaguely apologetic tone to their voice and started each sentence with 'Em', as in 'Em, excuse me, but . . .' The ones who, like me, received full grants and were unlikely to complain about grumbling pipes and erratic hot water. What made tired old Herrick absolutely perfect, on the other hand, was that Luke was staying there too. Our surnames were close, so we were assigned the same floor.

Far end of the corridor, take the stair on the left – I repeated what the Warden had barked at us – up four flights to the attic.

So up we climbed, until the final stair spiralled us into a narrow corridor with skylights on one side and numbered doors along the other.

At least the smell's gone up here, Luke said.

Yes, I said, though my nostrils now detected something mildly foosty. I knocked briskly on my door, wondering if I had arrived before my roommate. No reply. As I slipped my Yale into the lock I glanced at Luke, wondering whether to invite him in to see my room, but he'd proceeded along the corridor and found his own door. He seemed to be sneering as he turned and looked back towards me but maybe it was just the light because then he said:

Got any plans for later?

I shook my head, resisting the urge to laugh. Of course I didn't have plans. And so we arranged to go for a drink around six, the nervy lad from the ex-mining town and the prickly youth from the city scheme.

I chose the bed on the left, slumped down on it and shifted to hear it creak. My heart sank as I surveyed my new princedom. Under the eaves, with sloping ceilings and two recessed windows, a chipped wash hand basin by the door that acted as an inverse air-freshener, wicking the faint odour of drains into that corner. But what had I expected: a vase of sweet lilies, a view of the quads, exquisitely tooled panelling? The wardrobes were the oldest and most wooden thing there, and even they were made from veneered tea-chests, or so I noticed as I hung up my clothes.

For a second I felt homesick, if you can believe it, for that 70s semi with its paper thin walls and warm lamps. Here the overhead bulb seemed to be forty watt, heightening the unfortunate effect of the beige emulsion and carpet tiles the colour and texture of out-of-date chocolate bars. The heater, which occupied the wall between the two beds, was an electric bar fire with a meter demanding fifty pence pieces. Both desks were scratched with unknown initials, and I had brought no pictures to pin on the cork board. I placed my prized Oscar Wilde on a bedside table charred along the edges by forgotten cigarettes, as a sign to anyone who might come back for coffee (and, I thought, to my new roommate, whenever he turned up). I was soon to discover that the Complete Works of which I was so proud was little more than nursery reading for my new fellows, who had already rifled a library I hadn't known existed.

As I was arranging my toothbrush in the mug and my toiletries on the shelf, there was a knock at the door.

Yes? I said, swinging the door open and suspecting that I looked like Lurch against the gloomy backdrop of my new home.

Hi, my name's Jo and I live on first floor and I thought wouldn't it be great if all of us got together and went to the Union tonight . . . she paused for breath and flapped some flyers for half price vodka dash at me. So, right, we're going to all meet in the TV room at seven. See you then?

Oh, thanks, I said, already playing the part of someone much cooler and more in demand than I had ever been. But I think I've already got plans.

Oh, she said, peering round me in case I was hiding a roommate who might be more forthcoming at offering steady social support. Well. Next time.

Definitely.

I closed the door and a second later heard a knock, and Jo launching into her spiel once more.

I hoped our self-appointed social convener wouldn't appeal

much to Luke either, but as I arranged myself on the heavy Victorian radiator outside my door at five minutes to six I imagined that he and his roommate had jumped at her invitation. That I was condemned to a first night alone in my dingy beige room. That in a few hours time Luke might mumble at someone, oh, I forgot, I was supposed to go out with this guy I met on the train, and they would laugh and say, never mind. But at nine minutes past six he appeared, and I'm not sure if it's just hindsight that makes me think he'd changed in some subtle way, hardened just a touch.

Having spurned the Herrick night out, we felt we should also eschew the student union. We circled back along Church Street, rejecting a couple of real pubs, full of real ale and real local men; we'd both seen enough of that to last us a lifetime, though in my case mainly from the outside. Of course, even if there had been such a thing as a gay bar, I wouldn't have had the guts to suggest it. I soon discovered the Les-Bi-Gay society and their intense Monday night meetings, at which they populated a corner of the Union with plans for pride parades and endless talk about how desperate they were to cop off with the straight boy or girl on whom they had a crush. And not so long after that I was emboldened to spurn their offers of friendship, mean enough to mock their clichéd concerns.

Just as our walk was starting to seem aimless, Luke pointed down a side street to a corner bar.

Okay, let's just go there. Whatever it's like.

It was faux rustic, with the kind of stone cladding that must once have been fashionable, but the music sounded okay, and there were enough beaten copper tables to suggest it was the kind of pub where young men sound of limb could sit down rather than loiter by the bar alongside the regulars, staring at the portable TV and having the kind of conversation that consists mainly of the word 'aye' repeated with varying intonation. There was a lone man playing the puggy in the corner. I felt grown up, all of a sudden, buying drinks from the twenty pounds my dad said would be more than enough to tide me over until my grant cheque cleared.

Luke sat with his back to the wall, one leg crossed over the other in a louchely effeminate pose I'd never have dared to adopt in public.

Cheers, he said, when I handed him his drink. So, what do you make of it so far?

I don't know, I said. Seems okay.

Hmm.

He raised his hand towards his face then stopped himself, taking a drink from his pint instead.

How's your roommate?

No show yet.

Lucky you.

How's yours, I asked.

Dickhead. Luckily he pissed off with that girl with the screechy voice who came to the door.

Oh yes, I said. Her.

He sighed and I said, Maybe it'll get better. With the roommate.

Well, he called me Jock and went through a whole routine of see you Jimmy jokes. What do you reckon?

Oh my god.

Yeah. I think he thought it was funny.

This might be a silly question, I said, taking a drink of my cider. But do you think he's ever met anyone Scottish before?

Who knows. He's pissed off at being assigned to Herrick anyway, says he's going to request a transfer.

Fingers crossed then.

Yeah. Luke leaned back further, easing his hand into the pocket of his jeans to retrieve his lighter. Why did you come here, Richard?

To open up my world, I said, before I realised that he was looking for a more prosaic answer. I laughed. Oh, you mean here rather than Aberdeen or Glasgow?

You don't have to explain why you didn't go to Aberdeen, he said.

I suppose not, I said. But I looked at the accommodation policy here . . .

Social inclusion, shedding the image of snobbery?

Exactly.

But you'd have managed to get accommodation somewhere else.

Maybe, but here looked prettiest in the pictures.

He smiled at me and said, Fair enough.

I didn't tell him that I used to read about Oxford and Cambridge as well, that I'd sit at my makeshift desk imagining the train journey to the interview. It would be like going back in time as I looked out the window, the trees and hedgerows blending into gentle 50s hues. The fantasy failed me when it came time to actually apply, and instead I listed only Scottish universities. I'd have happily gone to Aberdeen, in spite of the jokes about sheepshaggers, if it got me away from home.

I lied, I said, suddenly. I told my parents I didn't get in to Glasgow but I did. I could have got the bus there, just about.

Would they not have let you go where you wanted?

I don't know. I didn't want to take any chances. What about yours?

What?

Your parents.

Parent. Only got one. Maybe she'd have liked me to stay at home.

Before I could answer he stood up. Don't know about you but I'm starving. Want some crisps?

It struck me that first evening how greedy he was, which shouldn't seem attractive but was. One packet of crisps wasn't enough, he needed two and peanuts as well, though he didn't look as if he had a scrap of fat on him. He had to buy more cigarettes, he smoked so many, and he always finished his drink before me. I hadn't yet admitted to myself that I fancied him, but it was sneaking up on me, that's for sure. He had very dark eyelashes and a more direct gaze than I was used to, and you could see inside his mouth more than seemed usual; his tongue, his teeth. His lips were dry and he had a habit of using the knuckle of his thumb to press them against his teeth to moisten the skin. Sometimes he caught himself with his hand mid air and stopped, as though he'd been told it would only make it worse. It's always the details that slay you.

But he wasn't gay, I was sure of that. When two girls came in to the pub I noticed the way his eyes skimmed over them. They were very dressed up in the way that supposedly cool girls dressed up then. You know: mini-kilts and band t-shirts, a million layers of ripped fishnets and stripey socks, strand after strand of cheap beads. While one girl went to the bar – clomp, clomp, clomp across the floorboards in a break between jukebox songs – the other whipped out a mirror and blinked down on a stick of Indian kohl then drew it out into a flick at the side, blackening her Cleopatra eyes even further. It was quite a dramatic look, though I'd never had a problem with girls doing themselves up like a different species.

Eyeliner, Luke said.

Yes, I agreed. Indeed.

What do you think of it?

Looks better on girls than on Robert Smith.

There was a rattle of coins as the puggy machine paid up at last. The man hunched down to gather his prize, deftly sorting it into the price of a pint.

I meant on girls, you twat, Luke said. He was pressing me a little, I sensed, testing the waters.

It's all right, I suppose. What's your considered opinion?

I like it, he said. I like imagining how it would look smeared all over their faces.

Which might have been a clue, if I'd been interested in picking up on it. I wasn't, and a drink or two later – when he said, come clean Richard, who do you like fucking? – I started spilling my own secrets all over the shop. He wasn't gay, well so what. I wanted a friend far more than anything else. And as I talked, he listened, with just as much greed as he'd approached everything else.

3

Richard drummed his fingers on his desk, listening to Stephie's footsteps padding back and forward in the hallway as she checked herself in the mirror, then clattered back upstairs for something she'd forgotten. He realised that he should probably give her some money and rushed to find his wallet, hoping it wasn't obvious that he was trying to speed her progress.

'Thanks,' she said. 'And they've got magazines in the shop at the garage?'

'Yes. Scottish Farmer, Top Gear, the usual.'

'What?'

'Oh yeah, and some celebrity crap. Size zero shockers, footballing love rats, ohmygod look at her camel nose . . .'

'It's camel toe, get it right. Want me to pick you up a copy of . . . whatever it is you lot read?'

'No thank you Stephie,' he said, resolving to package up his collection of Men's Health for recycling.

'Ah well, guess there's not much call for it up here. Do I need to take a key?'

'No, I'll leave the door unlocked,' he said, manoeuvring her towards it. 'Chances are someone'll give you a lift back.'

'I'm not insane, Richard.'

'No, it's okay. The only people that stop are locals.'

She stared at him. 'Well, as long as you're sure. Personally I'd rather walk than get in a car with a potential psychopath.'

Even after he'd closed the front door behind her he had to wait a couple of moments before settling at his desk, in case she came back. He reckoned she'd be gone for an hour and a half, maybe longer. On a day like this, who wouldn't scramble down to the beach and look at the water lapping over the stones, washing them from dull to gleaming? You could stand and count every seventh wave, letting the need to hurry ebb with the tide.

Which was, he thought, part of the problem. He adjusted the angle on his drawing board, as if that would make all the difference to the large sheet of paper affixed to it. 'Passchendaele', it said along the top, in red marker, then underneath it, enclosed in a blue circle: 'Lead in to Ypres 3'. A diagram of the scene was pinned to his corkboard, from which he began to construct flowcharts offering play options: Desertion → Pursuit by MP/escape (where to?); Mad Jack → hero/fool (death/ glory). Subsets tracked possible player responses to events: 'Tank sticks in mud', 'Gas alert'.

Some time later the phone rang and Richard grabbed it, thinking of Stephie, telling himself that she'd got tired and wanted collected but unable to stop himself imagining that something had happened, that she'd been hit by a car and was being rushed to hospital. Instead of the sombre tones of a policeman, he was greeted by a far more laconic voice.

'Rich . . . how's tricks?'

'Fine Rupe, and you?'

'Marvellous. Just back from the Shanghai expo and I think we've got a bit of a buzz going already.'

'That's great.'

'Yup. Listen, we've got the rendered images for the characters from Solange. She's done fantastic things with whatsit, sub-surface scattering on the skin tone. You'll adore them.'

'Sounds brilliant,' Richard pushed his chair over towards the computer and clicked on his email. 'Can you ask her to fire them over to me just now?'

'She's gone for today but they'll be on the wiki first thing. This is going to be beautiful, Rich.'

'I hope so,' Richard said, noting that he had no new messages and picking up a pen instead. He started doodling, wishing that Rupe would figure out that just because he liked having his name inelegantly truncated didn't mean that everyone else did.

'While I was out there I had a bit of a chat with Tad. He loves what you're doing. Thinks it'll go a bomb all over Europe, if you'll forgive the pun. And if that transfers to the States, well, cross platform could be an option.'

'Do I sense a but, Rupe?' Richard's doodles began to take the form of intensive crosshatching.

'May I be blunt?'

'Only if I can be Philby.'

'What?'

'Nothing Rupe. Just give me the bad news.'

'The bottom line is that poofing about in the trenches is all very well, but concerns have been voiced that there need to be a few girls in there.'

Richard put down his biro and started to massage his forehead. 'How's the female character looking? The one who's fighting in disguise.'

'Really cool, in a butch kind of way. But our target group for this one's predominantly male. Are you with me, Rich?'

Richard swallowed a groan. 'I think so.'

'What you've done so far is splendid. Fab. But what came up when I was running through it with Tad was, how about working in the potential for leave?'

'Leave?'

'R & R, if you catch my drift. Maybe earned by success in fights and puzzles, maybe just as a wildcard, well, you know what you're doing. Can you come up with something by early next week?'

'By something you mean . . .'

'Basically we're looking at a whole new level here. A townscape with a few fleshpots, a chance for those infantrymen to go wild . . . Nothing that dilutes your original vision of the game of course, just a little boost to the fun quotient, okay?'

'It's fun already, Rupe.'

'Yeah but Rich, ask yourself this: is there such a thing as too much fun? Do they make another Halo because you just can't get any more fun than the others? Do they buggery. And that's exactly what we're talking about. Total sandbox.'

Richard picked up his pen again and wrote the word 'sandbox' on his pad, then circled it for emphasis. He could feel his heart rate quickening. 'It would be unpredictable,' he said.

'That's the whole fucking point, Rich. You invent the town, they do what they want there. Anything goes.'

'I don't know.'

'Can you handle the coding?'

'Yes. I think so. It's just . . .' Richard heard a muffling on the line, imagined Rupe putting his hand over the receiver and mouthing the words 'bloody creatives' to whoever was nearby.

'Come on Rich. Total sandbox. How cool is that?'

'Pretty cool, I guess.'

'You said it.' Rupe chuckled. 'Sex'n'drugs'n'Vera Lynn songs.'

'Vera Lynn's Second World War.'

'Thank Christ for that. Soundtrack would be ghastly otherwise. One last thing, Rich.'

'What?'

'Give the mappers plenty to come back to when we're tinkering with the mods.'

What a joy that was going to be, Richard thought, imagining playing the game and discovering handfuls of secret – and probably semi-pornographic scenes – embedded in it. Scenes which DaCapo could express open-eyed surprise at when their attention was drawn to them by the appalled parents of underage players.

'Sure, Rupe.'

'Great. Well, cheerybye. That's what you lot say up there, isn't it? Cheerybye Rich.'

'Cheerybye,' Richard echoed, returning the phone to its cradle.

He typed a name into Google, punctuated with a brisk tap on the return key. He was conscious that if someone was watching, it would seem as if he was conducting part of his research, pinning down some vital snippet in order to complete the Ypres build up. Except that the results that popped up didn't have anything to do with the war, and besides, he knew them almost by heart already. A BT sales manager in Hull. An inorganic chemist at the University of North Texas. A lawyer specialising in matters pertaining to fraud and tax evasion. Third place in the under-sixteen Harriers at an interschools competition in Galloway. Nothing new. Nothing about Luke.

He sighed and flipped a fresh sheet onto his board, drew a rectangle in which he scrawled 'LEAVE'. From it he backtracked an arrow to: 'Killed x number of opposing forces/ forced a retreat'. He added 'Medical/wounded', then, scraping the bottom of the barrel, 'Strategic reasons'. There might be some fun to be had with Rupe's fleshpots after all. Richard turned back to his computer, keyed another name into his search engine, clicked on the fourth result down. His old roommate Calum Peterson, now doing postdoctoral research in high energy particle physics. A familiar university crest in one corner of the page, and a picture of Calum looking happier – and geekier – than Richard could ever remember seeing him, despite the onset of male pattern baldness. A photo of a baby, eyes closed, under News. Links to websites devoted to Buffy and the Lord of the Rings beneath those to partner institutions and publications. If Richard had a memory for surnames he'd have searched for other past contemporaries too, exploiting the impunity of the cyber stalker, nudging his way towards some kind of revelation, reassurance of a satisfactory life ahead.

0

Another day in paradise, Luke said, as we walked through campus, ready to sign up for our classes. And although perhaps it's impossible to recognise an idyll if there isn't a note of unease to throw it into relief, the shady groves and glistering spires seemed intact. We skirted round them on cobbled paths, past those photogenic archways and vennels, until we reached a prospectus-perfect quad. The faint strain of the choir drifting through the chapel walls was almost de trop, like an overcoordinated outfit. Stephanie when she'd waved me goodbye; lips and nails painted peach, matching plastic hairband restraining her first spiral perm.

The mild, early October evening lulled me. Being used to the truly nerve-wracking process of crossing the secondary school playground with its uneven asphalt and myriad no-go areas, I felt entitled here, as though I'd done my penance in advance and could now reap the pleasures. (Me, who'd stuttered my way through the open day at Glasgow, too shy to ask the way to theatre studies.) The central sundial showed it was already gone half four, but we dawdled to the seminar room where we were supposed to meet our new teachers and colleagues.

There I found the wood-panelling absent from Herrick, alongside fleur de lys picked out in gilt and a sombre portrait of a man with an incredibly beaky nose. An ex-professor, I deduced, from his ostentatious gown and the Greek lettering on the spines of the books the artist had posed him beside. His successor, Professor Mendelssohn – whom I recognised from his smiling, avuncular photo – was splashing Makedonikos into glasses and tipping olives and cubes of feta into rustic pottery dishes, trying to avoid soiling his flapping sleeves. What a contrast with the agonising half hour I'd spent with my shy new roommate Calum, in a sixties maths room that was all scuffed lino and dusty blackboards, sweaty cheddar and boxes of Bulgarian Rouge. This was more like the thing, I thought, striking forward.

Welcome, called Professor Mendelssohn, or at least I assumed that's what he said. It was, quite literally, Greek to me.

Hello, I croaked.

Ah, he said, Classical Civilisation, I presume? Yes well, do help yourselves to wine.

And with a swish of his gown he was gone. We followed his instructions, grabbing full glasses of yellowy white, and I tried to figure out the etiquette for olives. They were being eaten, detritus was accumulating in the dish provided, yet nobody was spitting the stones into their hands.

Marvellous! I heard Mendelssohn exclaim to another eager new recruit, though perhaps eager is the wrong word, for this boy was suave and calm and unselfconscious. A heavy wave of hair rippled over one temple, and he stood with effortless posture in an expensively rumpled shirt.

Marvellous, the Prof reiterated. And did you manage over to Crete as well?

Of course he had, of course.

More wine? I asked Luke.

Definitely. He half-closed one eye as if at the onset of a migraine and handed me his glass. I waited while Dr Brownlee – who was rather classical looking, with his aquiline nose and loosely curling crop – served another new student who was wearing a similar shirt to the first and boasted equally privileged bone structure. Dr Brownlee replaced the bottle on the table, obviously not seeing me lurking alongside him. Congratulating myself on my social skills, I inclined the bottle towards a girl wearing glasses with smart, fine frames.

Orange juice for me, she said, confirming my suspicion that she was serious. I smiled as I poured her drink, couldn't decide what to say.

So, she said, taking a delicate sip. One or two?

Sorry?

Are you taking one or two?

Oh, just one, I said, refilling my own glass and thinking that

the wine must be an acquired taste; but then, the only stuff
I'd had before was fizzy and came in strawberry or peach
flavour.

And is that course one or course two?

I didn't know there was a choice, I said, feeling slightly
muddled as she handed me a copy of her course outline, a
sheet of paper divided into Greek I and Greek II.

Oh, I said, I'm not doing Greek, I'm doing Classical
Civilization.

Ah, she said.

What about you, I asked. One or two?

Two. I have an A Level and one's for beginners.

I didn't ask what Classical Civilization was for, suspecting I
knew the answer already.

You couldn't do Greek at my school, I said. For Higher, I
mean.

Really, she said, her eyes darting away from me, seeking out
her intellectual equals.

Anyway, I said. I'd better take this over to my friend. Good
luck.

Yah, she said, distractedly.

I walked back towards where Luke was sprawled on a low
chair, looking intently at two preppy Americans who were
comparing grade point averages. They were hideously Ralph
Lauren compared to his artful scruffiness. My own sartorial
efforts made me look more like a suburban art teacher than the
singer in an indie band. I had the t-shirts and the faded red
Converses, but my cords sagged rather than clung, and my
Harris tweed from Oxfam whiffed in warm weather. I'd often
wondered where all those Harris tweeds came from; was there
a point in the past when that's what everyone wore, or did
Oxfam collate them for sale only in Ayr? Luke seemed far
more insouciant, though when I'd chapped on his door earlier
he'd been buffing his shoes to a sheen. A pair of oxblood
winklepickers, bought second-hand, they required elaborate
cosseting to ensure the scuffing on their toes was kept in check
and they were heeled in good time. But despite the gleam of
glacé leather, it was the white glimpse of his collarbone under
his skinny navy blue shirt that caught the eye. It's funny what

you remember, isn't it? A glaring flash of flesh in the electric light of a stuffy seminar room. But maybe it was just me that was dazzled.

As I handed Luke his drink, soprano vowels leapt over the hubbub, some striking banality followed by a peal of loud laughter.

Is it wrong of me, he said, to really, really want to punch these people?

Of course not, I said, though I'd never punched anyone, apart from when I was a child and my big cousin swivelled my Rubik's cube – ridiculous I know – and I knew I couldn't figure out how to line up all the coloured squares again. I hid on the top bunk where my sister couldn't see me and carefully peeled and replaced the bright stickers but they wouldn't stay stuck and I had to hide the evidence of my cheating at the back of a drawer.

I've had enough of this, Luke said, draining his glass in one go. Want to head?

The laughter was growing louder, the wine hadn't run out, and even the Prof looked animated; by then he was talking to a strikingly blonde boy in a tweed jacket that had clearly never seen the inside of a charity shop. I gulped down my own drink, not quite managing to finish it.

The air was cooler outside and the little street lamps blinking into life around the university buildings looked wan against the dusk sky.

A brush with our betters, I said.

Well, we've got a choice, Luke said, as we approached the less than picturesque student union. We can stick it out, or we can go and cower in the corner, doing computing science with all the other sad fucks.

I laughed, though I'd given serious thought to computing science, the idea of which brought back happy memories of typing programs into my cousin's Amstrad, watching as it followed my coded instructions to cascade colours across the screen or work out simple arithmetic problems. As it was, I hadn't been able to abandon maths. The school-instilled notion was still with me that languages were for girls, English was for poofs (and girls), and modern studies was for thickos.

There were some normal folk there as well, I said.

You, me and about a half dozen geeks and wallflowers.

It's always the quiet ones you have to watch, I said.

I don't know about you, he said, but that's not quite the niche I want to carve for myself.

4

When Richard emerged from his workroom the table was set and a garlicky warmth filled the kitchen. As soon as Stephie saw him she said brightly, 'G & T?' and proceeded to spring ice cubes out the tray with determined slithery thunks. Slivers of lemon were fanned out on a chopping board. Six thirty on the dot. She must have been waiting, or perhaps she'd started without him.

'Thanks.'

They clinked glasses and he suggested sitting outside. He would usually have gone for a run after such a long stretch at his desk, but having left Stephie to her own devices all afternoon he realised it wasn't an option. The glow the evening light cast over her face seemed to blend away her dark circles more effectively than the kind of make-up women spend a fortune on (cheaper variations of which were now strewn along the bathroom windowsill).

'So, how did you get on exploring the hotspots then?' Richard asked, taking a sip of his drink. It was too strong, which he chose to take as evidence of Stephie's unfamiliarity with home measures rather than the opposite.

'Yeah, okay,' she said. 'You were right about the lift. Old guy picked me up at the beach. And do you know what, he wasn't even coming this far. After he dropped me he turned and went back the way we came.'

'Uhuh? What did he look like?'

'Like an old guy.'

'Can you be any more specific?'

She frowned. 'Like Gandalf. But with slightly less hair and a Glasgow accent.'

'That'd be Rab. He's a bit of an old hippy. Does the boat trips. You should go sometime.'

'Not much fun on my own,' she said. 'I saw you at your desk. Peeked in the window but you were engrossed. How's the work going?'

Richard hadn't been aware that she'd seen him, and tried to shake the feeling that he'd been caught with his hands down his trousers, or something equally undignified. Recalling the conversation with Rupe, he said, 'You know, I don't think I want to talk about it. But thanks for asking.'

'Oh well. I probably wouldn't understand what you were on about anyway. As long as you're not stressed out about it.'

'Just the usual. But gin helps.' He raised his glass to her again and she smiled.

'I'm going to get my head down tomorrow,' she said, clinking her glass against his again and taking a drink. 'Study schedule all drawn up in felt tip pen. Can't promise I won't get a bit wound up though.'

'Well, it's a good place for thinking.'

'Oh yeah?'

'Look,' he gestured towards the mountains in the background. 'Or there,' he nodded at the sea and the islands. 'How much therapy would you need to get that kind of perspective?'

'So everyone's small compared to a mountain? Deep, man.'

'Well . . .'

'Come on. If it was that easy there'd be a massive big branch of the Priory in your front garden.'

Richard shrugged. 'Everyone's different.'

'And while we're on the subject,' she said, 'What makes you so sure that I've got thinking to do? Apart from the studying, that is.'

'Otherwise you could study in the college library or your bedroom at home.'

'Your old bedroom. It was bigger than mine so I moved in. Mine is now the computer room with sofa bed. Though I don't know who's going to sleep on it, given that you don't ever come and visit.'

'You've come here.'

'Would you rather I went back?'

'No,' he said. 'Look, I'm making a mess of this. I'm glad

33

you're here. Glad you felt you could come. There's nothing wrong with a change of scene. It worked for me.'

'Unless it means you can't go anywhere else. In case it all comes flooding back. Whatever it is, which let's face it I don't know, because nobody thinks to tell me fucking anything.'

Stephie drained her glass. Richard started to speak then took a bigger mouthful of his own drink, felt it slipping home. Before he could continue she slid out from the bench and stood up.

'Want another?' she asked.

He rolled the half melted ice round the bottom of his glass.

'Okay. Thanks. But don't tell Mum. Don't want her thinking I've been getting you into bad habits.'

'Like Vouvray and Valium, that classy combo?'

'She never used to.'

'Yes she did. It's just that you weren't there to see it,' Stephie called over her shoulder as she went back into the house. 'But who knows, maybe you're not the only person who can worry her.'

Richard heard the fridge door open, the rattle of ice again. Should he ask what was going on or just let her tell him in her own time? He wondered how much their parents knew. He'd been so assiduous at shielding his own life from them when he was Stephie's age, though that had only made things worse in the end. Or was he just being selfish, assuming that his sister's messes couldn't be as desperate as his own, that they could have been more easily hidden had she chosen to play her cards close to her chest.

'So, what's for supper then, domestic goddess?' he said, instantly worrying that he'd hit too flippant a note.

'Ooh, hark at her. Supper? Whatever happened to tea?'

'I grew out of it when I stopped eating at five o'clock. And less of the faux queen stuff, if you don't mind. It doesn't suit you.'

'Sorry,' she said quickly, as if she'd taken his comment to heart. 'This evening we'll be having a simple supper – not, heaven forefend, tea – of roast vegetable lasagne with a green salad and garlic bread.'

'You've been busy.'

'Yeah, well, it's no problem. I like cooking. I broke a bowl though.'

'I heard. Doesn't matter. Ikea's only about three hundred miles away.'

'And,' Stephie said. 'There's only one condition.'

Richard smiled. 'There's a dishwasher, in case you hadn't noticed.'

'I didn't mean the dishes. Anyway, let's go in, it's getting midgey out here and my crispy topping must be crisp by now.'

Richard had almost forgotten how pleasant it was to have someone cook for him, and that together with the wine relaxed him, but Stephie's words lurked at the back of his mind. Their parents were worried about her studies, there might be nothing more to it. He must have looked pensive; as Stephie spooned another wedge of lasagne onto her plate she said, 'Look on the bright side, at least you know I don't have an eating disorder.'

'I thought they were passé anyway.'

'What would you know? Wee poof like you, stuck up here in the back of beyond?'

'I'm not completely out of touch you know,' he said, hating her for a second for using the word, even as a joke.

'Oh, that reminds me. There's some mail from you from Mum. Junk I guess but I promised I'd pass it on.'

'Thanks.'

After they'd eaten she presented him with a bundle of slightly dog-eared envelopes, and Richard leafed through the advertising offers for gold cards and interest free credit, until he stopped at one with a familiar crest on the franking mark. His failure to graduate hadn't stopped the university alumni office getting in touch now and then to invite him to buy a brick for the new biochemistry building or attend a charity auction. Handwritten address though, that was unusual.

'Anything interesting?' Stephie asked.

'I don't think so,' he said, tucking the unopened envelopes behind the knife block. 'Lovely dinner, thanks.'

'You're welcome.'

'Oh well, a promise is a promise, I guess,' he said, opening the dishwasher and checking it was empty. 'I'll clear up.'

Stephie put Clingfilm over the leftover lasagne and put it in the fridge. He resisted asking if it was cold enough yet. 'That wasn't the condition though,' she said.

'What was it then?'

'Oh, we've had a nice evening and there's a film on telly I want to watch. Let's leave it until tomorrow.'

'You're making me nervous.'

'Don't worry. I just want you to . . . fill in a few gaps for me.'

Richard nodded. It wasn't entirely unexpected, and what difference would it make, really? He spent enough time rehashing the past without an audience.

0

I clambered on to a chair to check the fit of my new needle-cords in the mirror above the sink, reconsidered my T-shirt and replaced it with one that was slimmer against my body.

Very swish, Calum said, looking up from his physics workbook.

Thanks. Hey, d'you fancy coming for a drink? We're just going along to the Earl.

No thanks. The Star Wars Society have borrowed a video projector and we're going to watch the trilogy back to back. Of course you're welcome to come along, but I'm guessing it's not really your scene?

Oh I don't know, Empire Strikes Back would have to be in my top ten movies. But I think I'll give it a miss this time, I said.

It's an invalid argument that results in the conclusion that parties are always fun. That a roomful of people should mingle and laugh and dance together as a matter of logical truth, as though they were the best friends in the world. But still I felt a quiver of excitement as I walked along the corridor and knocked on Luke's door. It was answered by Max, the awful roommate. He didn't invite me in.

Hello, I said, trying hard. Is Luke around?

So you're going to the party, he said, his mouth twisting into a surprised little moue. Really?

Behind him I saw Luke swing his legs off his bed, where he'd been lying reading, and reach underneath for his oxblood winklepickers.

Like the shoes, Max said as Luke tied the laces. Is it fancy dress?

Yes, Luke said as he eased his wallet and cigarettes into his pockets. The theme's posh twat.

How droll. Are you sure you'll – he cast his eyes over our clothes – fit in?

I'm hoping not, Luke said. See you later.

Have fun kids, Max called after us. Don't do anyone I wouldn't. Or should that be: don't do anyone I would.

As the door closed this was punctuated with throaty laughter which somehow convinced me that it was meant in reference to me being gay.

Fucking superior cunt, Luke said.

So what's the plan? I said. Pick up a carry out first, then pub?

After the first pint I allowed my expectations to blossom again. They weren't very specific ones, but enough to lend a tingle to the tummy. I'd developed a bit of a crush on a fellow Philosophy student, an auburn haired pre-Raph type who seemed shy of his autumnal hues. I wouldn't have been surprised if he spent his evenings in quiet contemplation, never venturing out, but after the eudaemonia lecture I'd overheard him say that he was going to a party at the weekend. Maybe it was the same party.

Luke and I stayed in the bar until closing time, matching each other pint for pint, then drifted along the main street, following the trace of music until we saw coloured lights pulsing in the windows of a flat above the fishing tackle shop. The entry door was open and on the stairs to the first landing we found a boy in an open-necked white shirt and black dress trousers, sitting on a step.

Excuse me, he said as we squeezed past him.

Yes? Luke said.

Are these my feet?

Oh my god, I whispered.

Yes, I think they are, Luke said, quite kindly.

Very good, the boy said and then, waving his hand in dismissal, Thanks.

His head slumped back against the green-painted wall of the entry and we continued up the stairs. Luke reached out to bang on the door of the party flat – which bore a brass nameplate engraved 'Cowley, Farquarson and Green' – but it opened at the first impact of his fist and we pushed our way through a hall sweaty with people into the kitchen, where we scraped together two mugs and some sticky lemonade to dignify our vodka.

What next, I wondered, lurking by the microwave while Luke went to the bathroom. My shyness was like a badge, an indication of something off-putting, or worse, infectious. At least I had his drink to hold, to prove I wasn't alone. Hoots and shrieks emanated from the front room, the source of the flashing disco lights we'd seen from the street. I deduced that dancing had already started. Resisting the urge to smile like a loon at the pairs and trios hovering at the table or standing guard by the fridge, I convinced myself that standoffish was in. And it's true, friendliness was not the done thing at all. No one introduced themselves, people stood and stared and chatted to their friends . . . but perhaps I've given myself away: there was nobody there that I could call an acquaintance, never mind a friend. My invitation had come courtesy of Luke, via somebody in his literature class. I didn't want him to come back and think that I wasn't worth taking anywhere because I had nothing to say for myself. Spotting a girl struggling to open a bottle of wine with a waiter's friend, I offered to help and attempted some casual chitchat to render myself less conspicuous. After ascertaining that she was studying History of Art and living in halls, I asked where she was from.

My parents live in Chichester, she said, playing along nicely. But actually my mother has family in Scotland.

Oh yes?

They live in Perthshire. Is that posh? I've heard it's posh.

Well, I said, I suppose some of it is.

How funny! She grimaced, as though the existence of a familial bond with posh people strained her credulity, then said, I'm Katie, by the way.

Hello Katie by the way, Luke said, suddenly appearing at our side. I'm Luke. And I guess you've met my friend Richard already.

Hi . . . she said, smiling more at him than at me, but then one of her friends came by and tugged Katie by her glossy pigtails into the front room to dance to some Britpop anthem. We followed them through and I stood beside Luke as he leant against the doorjamb, watching as she twirled, her strappy cheesecloth smock top billowing around her. Pristine white except for an edging of mirrored beads and embroidery, it whispered rather than shouted her desire to be seen as bohemian.

So, he said, his lips close to my ear. What do you think?

I'm not really qualified to say, I replied, scanning the beery boys in their drab t-shirts for a tell-tale flash of auburn hair.

You could venture an opinion.

She's all right, I said. If you like that sort of thing.

Hmm, he said. Maybe I do.

I'd hesitate to say that I had an idea of perfect womanhood, but I made easy aesthetic judgements all the time. Didn't think much of the snobby blondes in their jeans and ankle boots, appreciated the effort of bird of paradise hair and the flicker of heavy lashes. And I just didn't see the appeal of this insipid in-between. Hazy memories of the first night that Luke and I had been out together swirled through my mind, conversations coming back to me as I climbed towards a similar level of drunkenness. Boys, I'd said when he asked what seemed such a mature, daring question. I prefer boys.

That's a very . . . delicate way of putting it.

His eyes had been smiling, and he kept his gaze wrapped around mine for long enough that I hadn't been sure if he was flirting or not. Until he laughed and said,

Well. I prefer girls.

Now, still watching Katie, Luke edged round the dancers towards a couch by the window where there was space for us both to sit. More so when the sole occupant sprang to his feet and enveloped his friend in a laddish sing along to the Happy Mondays.

Mad for it indeed, I commented, as Luke reached out to a shelved recess beside us and withdrew a medical textbook. He extracted papers from his cigarette packet then dug deeper in his pocket until he found a large lump of sticky resin. As he began to skin up a little ripple of curiosity seemed to traverse the room.

Would it be awfy cynical of me to think that this is the party trick I was invited to perform, he said.

Shocking imputation on our hosts, I said. Whoever the fuck they are.

Oh well, he said, first one's just for us I think.

He wasn't a stoner, not really, though since I'd been hanging around with him I'd got a lot more into that kind of thing, liking the masculine chumminess it lent to our evenings, the rambling discourses it provoked. By the time we were finished the second joint I found myself looking at all the boys and girls, their faces drifting past the coloured bulbs and pulse-programmed fairy lights that decorated that bay-windowed room, wondering if you distinguish those who were merely playing and those whose dissolution had struck some deeper seam. I must have wondered this aloud, because Luke was scrutinising their faces too.

The shadows on their skin, he said.

Yes, I agreed. The expression in their eyes.

Something, he said. Some tiny clue that says . . .

I shrugged. I don't know . . . I'm real, I suppose. I feel things.

I think real thoughts, he said. They keep me awake at night.

It wasn't much, but it seemed to me like a connection. Something as valid as the lines we were searching for on the faces of our smooth-skinned contemporaries.

I wonder, he was saying, if Katie there has had many sleepless nights?

He smiled towards her and held out another joint. She was over in a flash, settling herself beside us and chattering away about her boyfriend who'd gone to Durham and how surprisingly rough it was there, and they usually saw each other every fortnight but this weekend was his best friend's birthday, and anyway she couldn't miss Sara's party, now could she?

Is she Cowley, Farquarson or Green? Luke asked.

Katie laughed and said, Green! – as though astonished that we weren't already familiar with Sara – We've been bessie mates since we were about five years old or something. I mean, I just couldn't not come, could I? Even though it means not seeing Adam for absolutely ages.

At first I didn't recognise this elaborate abdication of responsibility for what it was. By now, most of those so-called serious relationships that had seemed the sine qua non of school society were faltering, prey to handsome strangers and one last drink and the light touch of a hand on a tender, ticklish thigh.

Did you know that Richard? Luke said.

What? I'm sorry, I was miles away.

Yeah, good stuff, isn't it?

I nodded and he laughed, patting my shoulder as though I was a child who'd just done something silly and endearing.

Katie was just telling me that we have royalty in our midst.

I looked at the people dancing. Well, I said, I'm sure some of those moves wouldn't be out of place in Annabel's.

You been reading the Daily Mail again Richard? Go on Katie, tell Richard what you told me.

She leaned forward so that she had to lean against Luke's arm and said, You know Guy from Philosophy?

Not to speak to, no.

Oh really? He's sooo nice. Well, he was telling Sara that he's actually like, in line to the throne. Isn't that hilarious?

Mmm, I said.

His family have a massive house in London and an estate in Oxfordshire. Absolutely pots of cash, according to Sara. And don't say anything, promise?

We nodded.

Okay, well I think she's totally hoping he'll ask her out.

When you say in line to the throne, I said, how far down the line is he?

Yah, well obviously he's never going to be like, king or anything. Well, not unless there's some freak accident.

Luke laughed. We can live in hope . . .

Yes, I said. The French had it right, didn't they?

Mind that old Billy Connolly gag about Sawney Bean: in Scotland we don't steal from the rich and give to the poor, we steal from the rich and then eat them? It'd be nice if we could redistribute a little of Guy's wealth.

Or eat him, I said before I realised how it sounded. Luke gave me a nudge in the ribs but Katie didn't seem to notice that my face had turned scarlet.

Well I wouldn't recommend it, she said. Because he's been

given the personal phone number for the Chief Constable of the area.

Luke pulled an incredulous face. Did he really tell Sara that?

Guides' honour, she said, muddling her attempt at a salute. He was joking that if any lecturers gave him bad grades he could get them arrested for drunk driving or something.

What a dick, Luke said. Another drink anyone?

We both nodded and handed him our glasses.

So, does he have a girlfriend then? Katie said, watching as he wove his way in between the dancers and towards the door.

Not that I know of, I said, noticing the way his shoulder blades moved under the fine material of his shirt.

When Luke returned, I watched as Katie gradually got drunker and looser and louder. I wasn't sure what the form was; when to go away and leave them to it, whether to rescue him from her clumsy advances. Perhaps I was underestimating him, how capable he was of laughing in someone's face.

And so I sat there, with not even a glimpse of my pretty lit student to distract me, while Katie nestled up against Luke, all giggles and flicks of her pigtails, absurdly obvious brushes of her chest against his arm. He leant over and whispered to me, Is Calum here this weekend?

Yes, I said. Why?

Just wondered. So's bloody Max. Never mind. I'll take her to the beach. She'll think it's romantic.

I thought of my teenage encounter with Wendy, of other things too, and tried to imagine what it must be like to be so confident in your actions, so ready to take charge. He was going to have sex with her, I was sure, and I couldn't help being jealous. A single slavering snog with a bi-curious show-off in the Union one night, that had been my lot. At this rate I'd end up hanging around the golf course, risking being branded a toilet trader. But now here Luke was, and there Katie was, and I was still sitting there like a spare prick. I got up to leave, she melted into his arms. As I turned to wave goodnight to him, he looked over her shoulder at me and smiled as if to say: look what I can do.

5

Distance and the bevelled glass of the French door made the lights over on the island look as if they were flickering, generated by candles rather than an undersea cable and the wind turbine up by the holiday chalets. There were lights too on the fish pens in the bay, faint green ones that would have invited a far more romantic interpretation if it wasn't for their regular positioning. Stars of the sea, perhaps, or the jewel-like eyes of Sirens. Richard drew the curtain, wondering if even in the dark the salmon heaved into the air, snapping their bodies like whips to shake the lice from their scales.

He sat in his office chair, fingering the envelope Stephie had given him and wishing he kept whisky in his desk drawer, like some film noir hack. Manila, foolscap, something more than just a sheet of paper inside. Almost certainly another appeal, he told himself, despite that handwritten address. The more personal touch; like when that ever-so-friendly-and-charming arts student had telephoned him – his parents having passed on his new number – to conduct a survey on career paths post-graduation. He'd had to admit that he didn't graduate, or did diplomas from other colleges count? Oh well, the student had said blithely, I shan't send you out a card saying how lovely it was to speak to you and could you possibly consider making a small contribution to the library appeal. And Richard had laughed, and said that the library was not his most vivid memory of his student years, realising that he was flirting not with the boy on the telephone but with his past self.

What was it Stephie had asked earlier? Whether he ever wished his brain was more like a computer.

'What,' he'd said. 'So I didn't always forget what I went upstairs to get?'

'No, that the inside of your head was actually laid out like a computer.'

'That would certainly be more logical, Mr Spock.'

'God, you're just wilfully misunderstanding me,' Stephie had paused for a gulp of wine. 'What I mean is, imagine how great it would be if you could look inside your head and see all the files stored there, and just delete all the stuff that clutters things up. Then once a month or whatever you could empty the recycle bin and they'd be gone. All the crappy memories that you can't quite shake would disappear forever.'

'Nice idea,' Richard had agreed. 'But there's always a trace. You might think you've deleted a file, but there's still a shade of it there. Someone could delve in and retrieve it.'

Now he adjusted his Anglepoise, straightened the postcards pinned to his shelf of software reference books, thrust his scattered pens and pencils back into their jam jar. Nestling beside them he found the brass letter opener he'd been obliged to purchase from the village hall car boot sale, at which he'd earned both kudos and notoriety by donating the entire Grand Theft Auto back catalogue plus various other freebies. The old dears manning the stalls were delighted by his generosity, the mothers of the local primary sevens somewhat less so. Richard picked up the letter opener, smoothed its blade with his index finger and used it to slit the seal of the envelope, then probed with his fingers, withdrawing another envelope, white this time, and an abrupt letter from some jobsworth in Alumni Relations explaining that they had forwarded the communication on this occasion only and could not handle any response. Richard wondered about his own response, if he himself would be able to handle it, with or without the aid of p.p. Andrew McMasters.

He couldn't go back to the kitchen to get a whisky without offering it to Stephie as well, without stopping to chat. And then she might notice his agitation, initiate one of those threatened conversations. All of a sudden he remembered the goodie bag from the last industry conference, that it had contained a miniature of Johnnie Walker Black Label. 'For the Japanese,' Rupe had said, knowingly, but to Richard it was something his father used to drink at Christmas and

Hogmanay, a bottle brought out to celebrate family events or football wins, occasions to which Richard felt he had never made a satisfactory contribution. No girlfriend to introduce to his aunties, no manly whoops at Ayr's derby victory. As far as Richard knew the bottle was still in the lurid free laptop bag along with a copy of a book about the Second Life phenomenon that he supposed he should read one day – 'Games within games,' was Rupe's comment on that, delivered with a suggestive nod, as if Richard should already be on the case. A bit late to be proud now, he decided, retrieving the bag from the cupboard. Holding the tiny bottle in his hand, he looked for the first time at the envelope that had been forwarded to him.

He didn't waste time deciding if the handwriting in which his name was scrawled was familiar or not, just ripped the envelope open without the aid of the letter opener, his eyes flicking to the signature before he read anything else.

With best wishes, Calum.

Richard exhaled, telling himself how relieved he was whilst knowing full well that the twinge in his chest was disappointment. Odd that he'd been searching the internet for Calum so recently, but it was habit rather than premonition. Something slightly shameful, like Richard's ghost presence on Friends Reunited, a site he occasionally scanned so as to rank himself amid the successes and failures of those who'd been his peers at school, his gaze filtered through the layers of cyberspace. Calum had searched the internet for him too, it seemed, hoping for an easy email address that hadn't been forthcoming.

. . . wasn't sure if it was the right Richard. If so, it sounds like you've made an interesting career for yourself. As you can see from the headed paper, I never managed to leave uni, for my sins! Anyway, my excuse for getting in touch after so long is that . . .

The whisky was sitting uneasily with the wine Richard had drunk at dinner, and it seemed to him as if the letter comprised of fragments, each one carrying with it a sharply palpable memory: the glow of sunlight on grey stone, the iodine tang of seaweed after a storm, velvet mornings in sweat-stale rooms when his waking thought was an elated, what now?

. . . and I had always meant to drop you a line . . .

Richard felt his eyes swimming. He'd skimmed the letter too quickly, forgotten what had come before.

. . . he asked particularly to be remembered to you . . .

The fragments of memory coalesced into one clear moment, a scene that felt as vivid while Richard replayed it as if it had happened only that morning. Luke had put his hand on Richard's forearm, clasped it tightly and said, 'When I feel hollow, I'd do anything to fill the space inside me. Anything.' And Richard had nodded, the words appealing to his taste for melodrama, making him wish he'd thought to say them first. At the time the sentiment felt as much as though it belonged to him as it did to Luke, and only now could Richard pick away the artifice and taste the kernel of truth. He had buried it deep, ignored it, but that sense of emptiness had never really gone away.

0

We kept walking, Luke and I, along the back road out of town
and right past the Haste ye Back! sign under which someone
had scrawled in Magic Marker: Not fucking likely. It was late
in the autumn, grey and breezy, the sun unwilling to commit to
sweeping the clouds aside, but it felt good to be outdoors and
heading away from the town; an antidote to the surfeit of late
nights and new acquaintances. I watched as a tractor chugged
slowly across a dark brown field, a flurry of birds squabbling in
its wake. The landscape wasn't so different from home, but
without Jojo the dog to drag me along, it soon felt like we'd
been walking for ages.

Are you sure we're going the right way? I asked.

You're like a bloody kid, he said. Are we nearly there yet?

How did you find out about this place again?

Library. The one in town, like, not the uni one. They had a
local history display.

Dark horse, I said.

He shrugged. Went there to do my essay. Escape from dick-
for-brains and all his nobby pals. Calum might be geek of the
week, but you're lucky to have him.

I guess so, I said. What's the big deal anyhow?

Och, I just want to take a look, he said. That's all.

We turned left onto a single track road, where hawthorn
tangled along the barbed wire fences. Cows looked up from
their chewing, resigned eyes following our progress, then a
tumble of heifers kept pace with us for a field's length, nudging
each other as if daring each other to get closer. Luke kept his
distance but I reached out and rubbed one animal's nose with
my knuckles. It tilted its head against my fist then half reared
and skipped back to its companions, as if it was showing off.

Here we go, Luke said, as we approached a T-junction.

Ahead were three red brick cottages, each shaped like a child's drawing of a house: a central door with a window on each side, a chimney poking out from a tiled roof. The first cottage was in good repair, with a valiant attempt at a garden bordering the path to the front door, which had a polished brass letterbox and knocker.

Dream home in the country? I said.

Yeah. Except it looks like the roses round the door have got some sort of blight.

As we walked past I saw that the other two cottages were dingier. The woodwork was painted a municipal dark green that didn't go very well with the brick and as we got closer I noticed net curtains in the windows. There was a small, efficient potato patch alongside one house, and a lean-to full of chopped logs for the fire.

Overhead bulbs, I said.

Yes, Luke said. A Formica folding kitchen table.

One of those fifties fireplaces. With beige tiles.

A gas fire with the ignition switch broken.

Watery mince every Thursday evening.

At five thirty.

I sighed, rather louder than I'd intended, and he laughed.

Do you want to chap the door, like? Pop in for a cup of tea? Leaven the life of the lonely widower with our bright young chatter?

Maybe, I said. If it was that easy.

It isn't. So dinnae go maudlin on me now.

I flicked him the Vickies and he laughed.

Anyway, he said. I think we've established that it's tied housing. So we've got to be on the right track.

We were a whole six weeks away from those lives we now found it so easy to interrogate. I still had a touch of home-sickness too. Breathing quietly so I wouldn't disturb Calum in the next bed, listening to the night wheeze of his asthmatic chest; soaking in the deep, claw-footed tub in the institutional bathroom, suddenly fearing that the lock wouldn't hold as someone banged on the door to tell me to hurry up – these things took their gentle toll. Not to mention always preparing my own meals, toiling down to the basement only to discover that the washing machine was broken again and two more flaccid tangles of lace or satin were pinned to the notice that begged, PLEASE do NOT put wired bras in the wash.

This new road was a little busier, in that another tractor crawled past us and squelched through a muddy rut into a field, and a couple of cars sped past, veering across the central line to save us scrabbling into the ditch. Soon the fencing was replaced by a wall, enclosing mixed woodland.

Step one, Luke said. Stick a wall round the pretty bits so nobody else can enjoy them.

We followed the wall along until we reached a gatehouse. Not some little stuccoed Georgian cottage, but an imposing stone keep with a turret, and a solid metal-studded wooden gate. Which was closed.

Damn, he said softly. On the plus side, it doesn't look particularly inhabited.

Hard to tell from out here, I said, squinting up at the windows in the turret.

Let's keep going, he said, peering round the corner of the wall. He waited until a car passed out of sight then swung his leg over the wire fence and climbed into the field.

Come on.

What is it, I asked, hesitating, then scrambling after him as soon as he started walking.

Wall doesn't go all the way around, it's fence again along here. We can get over and go through the woods.

We picked our way through the overgrown woodland, climbed another fence, and found ourselves on the driveway. From the back the gatehouse looked abandoned, close to derelict, and it seemed hard to imagine that anyone would mind us being there. A smidgen of my new-found sense of entitlement had stuck.

An afternoon stroll, Luke said, as if echoing my thoughts. Nothing wrong with that.

Private? We didn't see any signs.

Bloody hell, he said, tripping in a pothole. This'd wreck the suspension on the Bentley, eh?

Sunlight began to filter through the sprawling trees which flanked the road, and the beleaguered, mossy driveway was soon dappled with light. Birds darted in and out of the hedge-rows and when the wind picked up, russet leaves fluttered down all around us. I had a sense, almost, of time blurring. We rounded a bend and the landscape suddenly opened up. To the right the ground sloped down to a curving river where willows arched towards the water. The grass was shorter on the other side, and a little way away, beyond a couple of small copses of trees, I saw a castle, or a mixture of castle and country house, built from grey stone.

Nice, I said.

He nodded.

What if we meet someone? I asked.

There's no law of trespass in Scotland. And no harm in looking.

We can always apologise. Talk our way out of it.

Of course we can, he smiled. Unless they have dogs.

After a few hundred yards the shabby driveway looped round and over a small humpbacked bridge. Now that we were closer to the castle, I noticed a flashy turret or two that matched the gatehouse, as if the building had been added to and altered by successive generations.

How, I said after a while, can all this belong to someone?

That's the question, he said.

We kept walking. There was nobody around, no cars passed us, and there were no signs of recent activity apart from some bales of straw left piled at the entrance of a field. We got closer and closer to the castle until we were standing at the bottom of a flight of wide stone stairs that led up to a balustraded terrace. A perfect spot for drinks before dinner, or for surveying one's domain with a breakfast coffee. All of a sudden, Luke leapt up the steps, two at a time.

What are you doing? I laughed, hanging back.

He turned to face me.

Didn't I say? The librarian told me that the owners have had to sell up. There's nobody home.

6

Stephie darted towards the sea, and Richard heard her squeal as the icy water splashed up her bare legs.

'You must be joking, it's Baltic,' she shouted back to him, but she continued along the waterline anyway, skipping in and out of the foamy waves as the sea surged forward then dragged away from the sticky sand at her feet.

'What did you expect,' he called. 'The Aegean?'

She ran back over the sand towards him, her cheeks vivid with the exertion. She looked very alive, he thought, his mind stumbling at the strangeness of the observation.

'Okay then,' she said. 'If it's so lovely, why don't you go in?'

'I will.'

'When?'

'In a bit.'

'Nah, that's not good enough. You said it was good for swimming here, and now you're chickening out.'

'I'm not chickening out,' Richard said. 'I'm just doing mental preparation.'

'Yeah right. Go on,' she said, 'I dare you.'

'There are people over there in jumpers. Look, that man's wearing a woolly hat.'

Stephie scanned the beach. 'Yeah, and those kids are in their swimsuits.'

'Children don't feel the cold.'

'Stop trying to change the subject. A dare's a dare, and I dare you to get in that water right now.'

'All right then, I will,' he said, and put the picnic basket down by his feet, then stood on the heel of one trainer and pulled his foot out without untying the laces. Stephie laughed as he wobbled on one leg, stuffing each sock into his shoe.

'I've been neglecting gym duty,' he said. 'Mainly because there isn't a gym.'

'The sea's nature's gym,' Stephie said.

'Happy now?' he said, standing there pale in his swimming trunks, the wet sand squishing coldly between his toes. She nodded and he took a deep breath and ran towards the sea, barely letting the chill of the water register on his calves before he plunged straight in. The breath burst from his body as every inch of skin froze and he started a frantic crawl, his heart racing until he became aware of warmth suffusing his body again. He paused, treading water.

'It's amazing,' he shouted towards the shore. 'Come on in.'

Stephie sat down on the sand beside his clothes so he stretched into breast stroke, swimming towards a horizon distorted by the glare of the sun. He allowed the sensation of moving through the water to consume him, tried to empty his mind of everything bar the tiny adjustments in force of his legs and arms necessary to compensate for the cold.

He's been here since the beginning of term.

No matter how hard Richard pushed his limbs against the water, Calum's letter was still there, nudging into his mind. He'd swum in the sea at university too, with Luke. Once or twice in the summer, rather than as part of the staged Martinmas ritual. Richard remembered a strange feeling of invincibility, somersaulting in the cold salt water to drown the noise of the first wave of UN peacekeepers screaming off the RAF runway on their way to the Balkans. He and Luke, water falling silkily from their goose-bumped skin as they ran from the sea to their towels, feet slithering through the cool sand as they scrambled back into their clothes. The way a pint afterwards felt as though it had been earned.

He asked after you.

Richard slowed his pace, another memory popping unbidden into his mind, a conversation remembered almost verbatim despite the years that had passed. Luke sitting opposite him, his hair wet with seawater, asking, 'She pretty, your sister?'

'Don't know.'

'So she's a bit of a hound then?'

'No-o. Not at all.'

'So she is pretty. Nice tits?'

'How exactly am I meant to answer that? Not only is she my sister, but I'm gay.'

Luke had smiled, a cheeky, provoking smile, and cupped his hands to his chest, where his t-shirt clung to the damp skin underneath. 'Just demonstrate.'

Richard had grabbed a handful of sand and hurled it at him, but it'd caught in the breeze so they both ended up spluttering it from their mouths. As they walked back up the ramp to the promenade, Luke had asked, 'So when'll she come and visit then?'

'With you around,' Richard had said. 'Never.'

Struggling more to swim against the tide, Richard tried to imagine Luke as he might be now. A year shy of thirty, run to fat, prematurely balding. Without that intent, laughing gaze. He looked over his shoulder and realised he was much further out than he'd realised. Stephie was standing again, or at least he thought it was her. Yes, the red of her top, and he was sure he could make out her denim shorts. He waved, but she didn't respond. He tried again, but she seemed to be using her hands to blinker her eyes from the sun. He launched into a fast crawl again, back towards the land.

'You twat,' she said, throwing his towel towards him as he waded out the sea. 'You had me worried for a moment there.'

'I'm sorry,' he said, giving himself a brisk rub down. 'I got a little carried away. The water was nice.'

'Yeah well, even strong swimmers drown.'

'I know,' he said, 'I know.'

They went up onto the headland with the picnic, which had been hastily scavenged from the contents of the fridge and augmented with a bottle of wine. Richard had vacillated between his concern about Stephie's studying and his unwillingness to adopt the role of nanny, but he couldn't get round the fact that it was too rare a day to waste indoors. They'd piled everything onto the back seat of the car and he'd driven them over to the big bay on the other side of the peninsula.

'Is there sheep shit everywhere?' Stephie asked.

'Pretty much,' Richard said. 'It is the countryside. But over there doesn't look so bad.'

They stretched out on the springy grass, turning their backs on the caravan park and facing the sea. Waves swept in and fragmented against the rocks below them, and the children they'd seen earlier were building sloppy sandcastles that dissolved every time the tide flooded their haphazard moats.

'I'm having another Maidens flashback,' Stephie said, unwrapping the egg sandwiches and waving them towards Richard so that he could smell them.

'Yes, but we didn't get wine then,' he said, struggling with the bottle and his Swiss Army knife.

When they'd finished eating Richard lay back and raised one hand to shade his eyes. Clouds lazed across the pristine blue sky.

'You said you wanted me to fill in a few gaps,' he said after a while.

'Mmm,' Stephie said, rummaging in the cool bag. Richard closed his eyes as she withdrew the bottle and heard her splash more wine into her glass, and then his own. Stop, he'd been about to say, I'll have to drive later, but instead he propped himself up on his elbows and took a sip.

'Look over there,' Stephie said, indicating where a yacht with brilliant white sails was scudding beyond the bay.

'Amazing, isn't it,' Richard said. 'It's so still here but only a little way out there's a gale blowing.'

'Yeah.'

He lay back down and looked at the sky again. 'Funny, I never see any shapes in the clouds apart from more clouds. Or cotton wool. Or . . .'

'So I guess what I've been wondering,' she said, 'Is what went on with you a few years ago, when I was still at school.'

'Did you ask Mum?'

'She says it's water under the bridge.'

'It is,' Richard said. He squinted up at Stephie, but she was still looking out to sea, not at him at all.

'Well let's just say I don't like family secrets. Not when I'm meant to be part of the family.'

'Fair enough,' Richard said. He plucked a blade of grass and started to peel it apart, discarding each moist green strip. 'What do you want to know?'

'Why you left uni, why Mum and Dad fell out with you, why you ran away to Dundee and then to here.'

'Anything else while you're at it?'

She sighed. 'I'm not asking for chapter and verse. Just the edited highlights.'

'Well, first of all I didn't run away to Dundee, I went to do a course. Then I got a work placement, then I went self-employed and now I'm here. There's no big mystery. I told you before, I just fancied a change.'

'Yeah, but no friends, no visitors.'

Richard propped himself up and looked at her. This time she met his eye.

'You're not the only visitor I've had you know,' he said.

She turned away again, started poking the ends of her laces into the eyelets of her trainers.

'Look,' she said. 'I don't know enough to figure out what the right questions to ask are. Help me out a little, okay?'

0

We peered through the glass into an empty room, large enough to have been a ballroom. Speckled mirrors faced off above parallel marble fireplaces, and although the plasterwork had yellowed, the wall sconces ringing the room held their gilt.

Mean gits, I said. They even took the light bulbs with them.

Luke reached out, tried the handle on the middle of three doors that led into the room. It didn't yield, of course not, and I had a flash of anxiety as I wondered if there was an alarm. He smiled at me, an open and innocent smile that belied any nefarious intent, scanned the open ground behind him, and tried the handles of the other two doors.

Oh well. He shrugged, as if he hadn't expected success, then vaulted over the balustrade, landing with his knees bent in a barren flowerbed. I took the stairs.

We skirted round the side of the house until we reached a gate. Flecks of rust crumbed off the hinges as I pushed it open. Beyond it was a daisy-strewn drying green with rusted metal posts at each of its four corners, the same as the one at home, except that this was larger and secluded by grey stone walls. A flagstone path bisected the green and led to another gate directly opposite the first one, through which we passed into a courtyard flanked by some rundown outbuildings. We reconnoitred the back door – or servants' entrance, I suppose it was – but it was well secured.

Let's go back, Luke said. This bit's dull.

Kind of sad though, I said. Seeing it all locked up and abandoned like this.

Think of all the poor bastards scuttling back and forwards through that door, hanging out the washing, he said. I wonder if they'd be sad to see it abandoned.

They might be if they lost their jobs.

We retraced our steps across the drying green and back to the rear of the castle. Under two of the little turrets there was a small paved area, partially obscured by unchecked conifers. Luke wandered over to take a look.

I thought there might be a door here, he said, but it seems not.

It was a dank little corner, with two small, grubby sash windows. I pressed my nose up against the glass of one, quickly withdrew when I noticed a large cobweb. Inside was a disappointingly small, square room, completely empty. I was about to suggest we moved on when Luke tried to push one of the windows open. It creaked loudly enough to send a couple of magpies flapping into the air behind us.

Somebody forgot to fasten the lock, he said. Keep an eye out, will you?

Okay, I said, my heart beating faster as I turned to face the stretch of grass in front of the castle. I hadn't realised how elevated it was, what a prime position, green sweeping down to woodland, and in the distance, heavier sky bearing down on the sea.

This might make a wee bit of noise, Luke said, and with another creak, much louder this time, I heard the window shoot up in its frame. He reached under and tried to pull it up further, but it wouldn't budge.

Can you fit through there?

Maybe. I measured my shoulders against the frame. Yeah, no problem. Those bodybuilding steroids haven't kicked in yet.

He turned and made a last scan of the grounds behind us. Okay, he said. You first then.

The opening was mid-thigh height on me. I bent down and leaned in the window, fingertips stretching towards the floor. I might have been slim, but I was also clumsy, and very conscious of Luke behind me as I wriggled through. My hands reached the carpet and I half-crawled, half-slid until my legs and feet followed. For a moment I stood looking at him, his face blurred through the dirty glass so that I couldn't make out his expression. Then he dropped his rucksack through the opening and eased his way after it until he too crumpled into the room. He'd hauled himself upright by the time I held out my hand.

Now what? I asked.

He went over to the door, turned the handle slowly.

It's locked.

Oh.

But it's not a mortise, Luke said. In fact – he squinted along the edge of the door – I think someone's just put a bolt on the other side.

He pushed against the door again.

And, he said, I think you and I might be stronger than their screws.

It wasn't that easy. Putting our shoulders to the door and shoving was no use, so we had to go outside again, find a narrow piece of wood to slide into the gap behind the bolt, and a half brick to whack it with to force the bolt off the other side of the door.

Is there a law of trespass when you're inside a building? I asked.

Of course there is, he said. You need some laws, don't you, or we'd just descend into anarchy.

The door led onto a wide passageway with green glazed tiles from floor up to shoulder height, then whitewash and old metal light fittings above.

Is this below stairs? Luke asked.

I think so, I said.

Funny, I always imagined an understair cupboard, like in my mum's maisonette.

I looked at him.

Not really, he said. I was just kidding.

From there we tried door handles at random, ducking in and out of unlocked rooms. Most of those on the ground floor were sealed or empty, apart from a kitchen which appeared to have been installed in the 1960s and not cleaned much since. We proceeded along the corridor until we came to a large door, which with some hesitation Luke pushed open.

I give you . . . the entrance hall, he said.

Here was wood panelling and stained glass, just like I'd imagined for Herrick House, and surging behind it a host of fantasies of weekend parties and shiny leather riding boots, whisky sloshing into crystal tumblers. We crept up the main stairs, stripped of their carpet, then followed a circuitous route through wistful bedrooms where we savoured the pathos of small abandoned items: a bottle of Timotei upended in an en suite bathroom, three cravats rumpled in a cupboard, coat hangers pinched from the Hydros at Crieff and Peebles. As the bedrooms grew smaller they seemed not so many million miles from rooms I'd known, rooms I'd lived in. The ceilings were higher and there were wooden shutters on the windows, but still. Our voices grew louder and we opened doors with less apprehension as gradually we relaxed, playing at being the rightful heirs.

At the end of the passageway we found another staircase, and descended to the first floor, trepidation returning as we ventured onto the dusty parquet of the ballroom. The mirrors above the fireplaces showed rooms within rooms and I caught myself staring deep into the reflection, as if I might catch sight of ladies in fine dresses and the men in sleek suits who'd whirled them across the floor. I pictured a 1930s heyday, the 50s and 60s spent clinging to the past, then a slow decline into final demands from creditors and shutting off rooms.

They sold everything then, I said.

Mmm. Apparently they couldn't even pay their paper bill, Luke said.

How do you know?

Old Mr Théodas of Théodas & Théodas. Said that when he was a kid he used to bike up here at the crack of dawn every morning to deliver the papers but Lord Whatsit always had some excuse about not settling up. In the end they stopped delivering.

You have been doing your research.

You know me, he said. Enquiring mind.

Or good at charming old men.

Fuck off.

He walked away, out the door, and after a second I followed him, not sure if he was pissed off or just restless and eager to move on. The hallway was dark, except for where a door lay ajar and sunlight poured round it, highlighting a wedge of white paintwork. I went over and pushed it open, entering a drawing room, or at least I suppose that's what it was. Luke was standing by the window, looking out. In the middle of the floor stood one of the rare pieces of furniture not scavenged by the hungry dealers and souvenir-seekers: a chaise-longue with burst upholstery that oozed horsehair and legs that looked as though they had done many years' service as Moggy's favourite scratching posts. A blue ticket, number 574, was Sellotaped to it, and although it was a wreck I was surprised nobody had bought it to restore and sell on. Luke walked away from the window and threw himself down on it, stretching out his legs.

They got The Sun, apparently, he said, which I took as a peace offering.

Bill can't have added up to much then, I said. But I guess rich people are mean.

Yeah, how else would they stay rich? Luke said.

I prodded the chaise with the toe of my trainer, finding the stuffing slightly distasteful close up.

Comfy? I asked.

Not so bad. Look in my rucksack. I've got a surprise.

It wasn't that much of a surprise, given our student-wastrel lifestyle, but it was welcome: a bottle of cheap whisky and two chipped glasses he must have whipped from the kitchen when I wasn't looking.

Do you think we're okay here? I said, breaking the seal on the bottle and dispensing healthy measures.

Okay?

Safe, I mean.

Who's going to disturb us, he said. They're meant to be converting it into a hotel or something but I don't reckon they're going to start work this afternoon, do you?

Cheers then, I said.

Slàinte.

He reached for the bottle and refilled the tumblers which we'd both knocked back in a one-er, then tilted his glass in the light, sweeping amber refractions back and forth across his thigh. The skin around his nails was ragged, I noticed, as though he'd been picking at it. After a while he said,

Tell me something about yourself, Richard.

What kind of thing?

Anything. Something from your past.

I rolled my glass between my palms, trying to think of a story that would paint me, its main character, in a more impressive light.

Okay, he said. Tell me something about where you come from. Your teenage years. The worst thing you've ever done. Whatever.

Truth or dare?

Something like that, yeah.

I don't know if I was trying to show off when I told him about Wendy, whether I thought it would make him respect me more or just make him laugh. But that was the first of a meagre handful of autumn afternoons spent in that corner drawing room, taking turns to sit on the floor or sprawl on the rackety, broken-down chaise-longue. In the end I found plenty to say, and eventually he told me a thing or two as well.

7

Stephie's settling in fine, Richard said when he emailed their mother. Since his sister's arrival he'd found himself caught up in a gradual process of colonisation. Cosmetics sprouted around the bathroom, citrus and bergamot drifted through the house as she bathed or showered. Unfamiliar music blared from the iPod dock in her bedroom. Her bedroom, not the spare room; after only three days it had acquired a new name. Richard chose his words carefully: *She seems to be getting on well with her work.* The promised study schedule was Blu-tacked to the wall in the kitchen, and small piles of notes and books migrated around the room, according to whether she was reading on the couch, note-taking at the table, or sitting on the porch and gazing into space, stirring only when her mobile quivered with an incoming text message. As if to convince himself that she really was working, Richard wandered through to the kitchen.

'Want a coffee?' he said.

'Oh god, I didn't hear you come in. You gave me a fright,' she said. He saw her slip her phone to one side. 'Yeah, coffee would be great, thanks.'

'So how's it going?'

She leafed through an A4 jotter as though it was a flick book. Richard was relieved to see it filled with her sloping handwriting, flashing into bullet points and formulae as she skimmed through the pages.

'Okay, I suppose,' she said. 'Boring.'

He nodded. 'I know the feeling.'

'I thought your work was fun. I mean, you get to play, don't you.'

He waited until the kettle had gone off the boil then moistened the coffee in the filter. 'Sometimes. But there's screeds of code to get through first, and that's where I'm at just now.'

'Well, I'm still willing to bet it's better than endless fucking statistics.'

'Perhaps it is. But it'll all be worth it one day, when you're qualified and practising.'

'Working in the Vodafone call centre more like. You've got to do a postgrad to practise – at a proper university, not a glorified college – and I've already had one false start.'

'Sugar?' Richard asked. 'Good for the brain cells.'

'No thanks.'

He brought her coffee over to the porch table and set it down beside her. Her phone vibrated, rattling against the painted tabletop, but she ignored it.

'You were right to leave nursing though,' Richard said. 'If you didn't want to do it.'

'Don't suppose there are any biscuits left,' Stephie said.

Richard went back to the kitchen, opened the cupboard and shook the tin.

'You're in luck. Last one. Here, catch.'

He threw a Caramel Wafer over to her.

'Ta,' she said, placing it carefully beside her notebook. 'Dad went mental, you know.'

He stood at the door, sipped at his coffee but it was still too hot. 'Yes. Mum said they were . . . disappointed.'

'Every bloody day, I'm not kidding, Margaret's daughter does bank shifts in the private hospital, Margaret's daughter's just back from Sharm el-Sheikh . . it's like Mum's totally fixated on money.'

'Old habits die hard. Dad was lucky to get another job after they closed the pit.'

Stephie blew on the surface of her coffee. 'Just as well. Imagine you going down it. Muddying up your fancy Japanese trainers.'

'Who knows, might have made a man of me.'

'Well, the bottom line is that nursing was a waste of two years. And now I'm still living with them and I can't for the life of me figure out if this course is going to get me anywhere.'

'Psychology sounds great though. Really interesting.'

'Don't patronise me Richard. Just because you got away.'

She grabbed a textbook and skimmed through the contents, then selected a chapter and pointedly started to read. Who invited you here, Richard wanted to say, who said you could barge in to my life with your moods and your outbursts? But instead he closed the door quietly behind him, and went back to his study. He could have said no, he supposed. Claimed he was too busy for Stephie to visit.

Rupe, he wrote, without preamble. *When I said we shouldn't sanitise the trench scenes, I didn't mean we should turn it into a George A. Romero movie. Are the rats mutants? They're larger than some of the soldiers. And has Solange even seen a picture of a bayonet? Some of the infantrymen are 'packing' what appear to be AK-47s . . .*

He heard a knock at the door and minimised the email window.

'Yes?'

The door creaked open and Stephie peered in.

'Here,' she said. 'You have the last biscuit. I don't want it after all.'

'Thanks,' Richard said. As she turned to go he called, 'Stephie . . .'

'Don't worry,' she said and then, pointing at his pinboard, 'What's that?'

'A histogram.'

'Oh right,' Stephie said. 'But what's it a histogram of?'

'It's for one of the levels in the game. Trenches on both sides, Allied and German, No Man's Land in the middle. The gloomy colours on the left hand image indicate poor visibility and an emphasis on stealth manoeuvres, all the red and yellow on the right is meant to show how the look and tactics change if a firefight ensues.'

'Cool. So, gin at six thirty again?'

'Great,' he said, as she closed the door behind her.

He leafed through the designs again. The avatars themselves were shaping up reasonably well, he had to admit. Solange had taken his notes about uniform on board. Although Rupe was allowing him enhanced character input he still wasn't allowed to name anyone and so had to make do with titles: OFFICER,

INFANTRY, COLONIAL, WOMAN. WOMAN's disguise wasn't really going to fool anyone, he reckoned, but never mind. And ever since she'd done the drug dealers in *Favelados* Solange had exhibited rather a tendency to inflate the muscles of black characters to farcical proportions. COLONIAL was meant to be a white-collar man fighting for his motherland. Richard looked at OFFICER again. A slimmer, more subtle uniform, clean shaven rather than stubbly. For once, the art department had broken free of the stereotypical Serb look that had dominated Caucasian characters since Niko Bellic. OFFICER was approaching the young Jeremy Irons that Richard had pictured. He deleted the email he had written and started again.

Hi Rupe. I love what Solange has done with the characters! Fantastic, absolutely spot on. Just a couple of minor concerns about the trench scene . . .

After firing off a revised email rich in subtext, he stretched until his shoulders clicked and walked over to the French doors, throwing them open to a blast of air which, while fresh, wasn't enough to blow away the knowledge that Luke might also be listening to the harsh cries of gulls as he looked out over the sea. To the east rather than westward, back in the university town from which he'd walked away so lightly first time around.

0

Tell me a story. Truth or dare. So I unravelled my memories and found Luke a story, something about back home, about me. And even if I changed the slant to conceal some of my more fragile feelings, what I offered him was true.

Come along, I'd been told. Bring a carry out. Of course they didn't want me there enough to press the point, we were not going to meet up and go to the offy together, hatching plots about where to hide our cache of cider and vodka and black-currant cordial; nothing like that. So few of us were left in Fifth Year that it was hardly worth the bother of excluding anyone apart from the folk that had to go to the Unit at lunchtime. So I jumped at the chance and went to the swing park by the river that night, never guessing how it would end up.

I walked down the cracked tarmac path where I sometimes brought Jojo before school, the path along which my mother and I used to take him at dusk before I got frantic that anyone would see us out together. There was something odd about blurring the boundaries, an implication of sullying a place of innocent activity with something else, something darker. A sweet smell filled the air, from some plant or tree I couldn't name. As I tried not to stumble in the potholes I entertained fantasies, of them laughing at my jokes (what jokes?), slapping me on the back like an old pal, accepting me. Liking me. These idle imaginings soon gave way to something akin to terror as I saw the group, felt the smoke from the fire in my nostrils, heard their laughter drifting towards me. Laughter which made me shrivel inside though who knows if it was directed my way or not. About fifteen of them were gathered in a loose circle: Andrew and Craig already loud and drunk on cheap lager (though what we considered drunk then wouldn't hold a candle to drunk later in life); Aileen and Greg all smug and smoochy, their relationship acknowledged as adult and enviable; a click of girls, whispery and close; Wendy near the fire as if she was cold.

I had no ulterior motive in sitting next to her. She was moody, sure, but there was a gap and it seemed simpler than trying to infiltrate one of the tighter little knots. Besides, we were acquaintances, we'd spoken a few times in Seccy the year before. You had to do secretarial studies or tech, and I'd been off sick so tech was full. I would have got a slagging for it, but luckily Gary Simpson was in the same boat having been suspended, and he wasn't hearing a word against the manliness of learning to touch type. I offered Wendy some of the cider I'd brought and she nodded, gulping it from the bottle in a practised way.

What've you been up to? I asked.

Nothing much.

Yeah, same here. Exams coming.

I'm going to fail.

You don't know that.

Yeah I do, she said, fixing her gaze on the fire. 'Specially my fucking English re-sit. Want some Mad Dog?

I swigged from the pink bottle she offered me, wiping the back of my hand across my mouth afterwards to hide my grimace.

How come?

She shrugged, but after finally spluttering out one sentence about hating her teacher she became verbose, as if she wasn't used to anyone listening. Then equally suddenly she turned snappy, like she was annoyed at her own weakness. I moved on to safer subjects, if whatever song it was would stay at number one, had she heard about Mr Blackie's nervous breakdown. Just as she was becoming animated again there was a shout from Craig, about whether someone I hadn't heard of had managed to get the cock up her. The phrase sent embarrassment shooting from my stomach through my chest.

Fuck off, Wendy shouted, grabbing a stick from the fire and throwing it at him. Red sparks sprinkled where it hit his jeans – Pepes, I think they were – and Andrew started laughing at him and mimicking his whining until everyone else joined in and Craig couldn't retaliate without looking like a dick.

I hate him and all, she said in a low voice, gesturing towards Craig with the neck of her bottle before taking another slug.

So do I. He's such a stupid prick.

I couldn't believe I'd said it out loud, risked her shouting, oi Craig, Richard says you're a stupid prick. We both laughed, and I inched my arm behind her, not around her, just touching her back a little, as though making myself comfortable. She didn't flinch.

The fire died down and it started to get cooler. Wendy was still leaning back, warm and solid against my elbow so that although I had pins and needles in my hand I knew I couldn't move and break the contact. Finally she shifted, and with a soft, apologetic noise sat upright again. My shoulder, released, stopped aching and I flexed my fingers briskly to get the sensation back. I remember, for a split second, feeling disappointed. I admit it. Wendy reached for the cider bottle and held it upside down, scattering the last droplets over the grass.

None left, she said. I'm going home.

Yeah me too. Want me to walk you along?

It was as if someone else had spoken, but the words had come from my mouth.

Okay.

And although I didn't recognise what lay ahead as we got up and scrunched across the weed-scattered blaze of the football pitch, I felt as if my path was all mapped out for me. Looking behind me to check that our departure had been noticed, sure enough there was Craig nudging Andrew, and did I hear the word poof float through the night air towards me or was it my imagination? Andrew caught my eye, and I saw him curl his left hand into a fist, move his right index finger in and out. He was smiling rather than laughing at me, as though we were men together and it was us against them.

As we walked along the path by the river Wendy nudged into me a couple of times, until I got the message and reached for her hand. She held mine tight and pulled me towards her, and I knew I was supposed to kiss her but just kind of froze until the next thing I knew her tongue was squirming unpleasantly in my mouth.

Come on, she said, I'll show you somewhere.

I think she meant to be flirtatious, swinging her hips as she clomped along the path ahead. Even in the dim light I could see her school shoes, thick soled black slip-ons with hefty heels, chafing the backs of her bare ankles. She clambered over the two bar fence then picked her way down under the bridge, where burnt patches and crushed cans and plastic bottles suggested the kind of den I'd have been too scared to use myself. I didn't know what I was doing, but I followed.

8

Richard propelled his wheelie chair towards the French doors and looked out. A flash of blonde hair caught his eye. Although he'd told her to use the landline, he could see Stephie down on the road, her mobile clamped to her ear. He didn't know if she had a boyfriend, he realised, as he wheeled himself back to his desk.

Rupe's leave situation had morphed into an entirely new level, the design for which was taking shape in coloured pen on Richard's drawing board: field hospital, mess unit, village houses commandeered as billets, café bar, outposts for other Allied forces, brothel. Uncorroborated reports from Neil in the office suggested that the Hamburg studio had gone overboard on the Reeperbahn, with soliciting prostitutes and crazy sailors' bars galore. That, Richard thought, probably would constitute dilution of his 'vision'. After months of structuring car chases and drug busts – all featuring walking *Miami Vice* suits who spouted clichés like 'Eat lead, mother-fucker' and pneumatic girls designed to drive powerful motorbikes clad only in bikinis – Richard had been striving towards something a little more serious. Arranged on a large pinboard next to the images Solange had created were his original character notes:

OFFICER is brave sometimes to the point of recklessness and he'll risk his own life to protect his men. The product of public school, he's patriotic and used to an all-male environment. Potential tensions: if he discovers that one of his infantrymen is in fact an infantrywoman or his sense of superiority rubs his men up the wrong way. He may have problems following orders, characterisation should reflect a free-thinker, with the potential to desert if/when he thinks he knows better than his commanders.

Solange – his uniform is tailor-made so he should look more svelte than typical troops: almost, but not quite, dandyish.

How would OFFICER fare in this new environment, created exclusively to give the characters chances to get drunk/start fights amongst themselves and their allies/get laid? Richard began a half-hearted flowchart, starting with BAR and ending in ESCAPE ROUTES FROM MILITARY POLICE. He drew three large question marks after this, and tried to concentrate on plausible options: on foot, in a stolen MP vehicle, on horseback . . . His eye drifted to his in-tray, and possible sources of distraction. An invite to the 'wrap party' for a movie spin-off game DaCapo were about to publish resting on top of a bundle of unpaid bills and other papers. Rupe expected him to go, he knew, and it might be a chance to quiz Neil about what Hamburg was up to. He slid it out and RSVPed by email as directed. Only after he'd hit send did he wonder what he'd do about Stephie, given that the party meant a night in Glasgow.

Now, where the invitation had been, he could see a folded piece of thick white paper; Calum's letter. Richard supposed he should email, express an interest in his former roommate's academic life. Reassure him, because he detected from the tone of the letter that a hint of reassurance was needed. Don't worry Cal, he could say. Water under the bridge. The past is a foreign country and all that. The things we did there were like child's play.

One day perhaps a game would exist that keyed into the memory of the player, and replayed it in the virtual world. You would be able to teleport within your own mind, go back to school to best the bullies who'd reduced you to ill-concealed tears after every PE class. Special powers of strength and speed would guarantee escape from unpleasantness and danger. One night stands could be rejected at the first approach, the objects of unfulfilled crushes become lifelong loves (or the target of cruel rejections). The dead could come back to life. Until the player became as immersed as a Korean teenager in *Lineage* and derived sustenance only from a fridge that automatically re-ordered from a computerised warehouse. Because who was to say that real life consisted of that which took place externally, through clumsy action and resonating error.

Sorry it's taken me so long to write, what with one thing and another . . .

They'd met on the street, Calum said, sometime before Christmas. Richard pictured the last leaves of autumn turning soggy on the pavement below their feet, the dull cast of the buildings as the town eased into winter, the cries of the birds from the rookery by the church. The murmur of the sea growing more persistent, heralding those few weeks without students and holidaymakers when the wind and the ocean whipped at the rough edges of the town with bleak joy.

He's completing his degree, living in one of our new postgrad flats I believe, which must be a step up from old Herrick.

A double Luke emerged, like a distortion in a hall of mirrors: sharing with studious, determined postgrads and chatting casually with Calum in the street, one of the same streets Luke and Richard had walked down together. College Street, for instance, where Luke had punched through one of the windows on an old red phone box, then leant bleeding against a wall and said, 'Don't worry, it'll never come to that.' College Street, where it had come to that, and Luke and his real friends had turned and walked away without looking back once to where Richard was left standing with his parents.

So now Luke had returned – and not just to any university, to that one, where a little wrought iron memorial bench chastened the Philosophy courtyard – and it was no business of Richard's. He too had gone back into education, done another course, selected another life. Richard scrunched the letter up in his fist. He wondered why Calum had bothered writing, wished he'd just carried on watching Buffy and breeding and looking for di-quarks or whatever it was he did and forgotten all about it.

There was a bang and Richard felt the vibration of the side door slamming. He looked at his watch. Stephie was late for her G & T, but then again, she'd been on the phone for a good half hour rather than hard at work. Not that he was exemplary on that score. He smoothed Calum's letter out again, then folded it in half and shoved it and the party invitation into the recycling box on his way through to the kitchen.

'Hello there,' Stephie said. 'How's it going?'

She was wearing a floral crepe top that looked good with her blonde hair and faded jeans, and didn't seem to have the demeanour of someone who had just slammed a door behind her. Perhaps it had just caught in the wind.

'Rubbish,' he said. 'I'm worried they're trying to undermine my original concept for this game. Like the blouse, by the way.'

'Cheers. Primark,' she said, brandishing two avocadoes at him. 'I made a five mile round trip earlier to buy these.' She placed them on the chopping board and selected a knife from his Sabatiers. 'Anyway, tell me about your concept.'

Richard took glasses and cutlery from the dishwasher and began to set the table. 'I pitched this game as exciting because of rather than despite its historical accuracy and they were right behind me. They'd had some bad press and here was a game that they could say actually had educational content. I mean, it'll still be certificate eighteen, but nobody really believes that makes any difference.'

'What kind of bad press?' Stephie pushed her fingers into the flesh of a halved avocado and extracted the stone, then began to strip off the skin.

'A release that was denied a certificate.'

'Because it was too violent?'

'Kind of. It wasn't one of mine, by the way. The Board condemned it on grounds of taste and decency and said that the graphic depiction of mass murder had no redeeming qualities in terms of story, character or morality.'

'Ouch.'

'DaCapo argued that the qualities were aesthetic, but they didn't buy it. And to be honest, it was kind of naïve of them to imagine that *Suicide Bomber* would hit the top of the Christmas charts so soon after the London bombings.'

'Ah, I'm beginning to see how historical accuracy might not ring their bells. Let me guess, the point of that game was to blow things up then die.'

Richard nodded. 'The awful thing is, it was kind of fun to

play. You train as a pilot, then coordinate a squad of bombers, but you get to do the most spectacular bombing yourself. So you delegate them to hit trains, buses, airport security queues, all that, then you go for a really major target like the Houses of Parliament – even the Golden Gate Bridge, which was quite an aesthetic choice.'

'And I guess you're a Muslim,' Stephie said, mashing the avocadoes with a fork. 'Got any chilli left?'

'Hang on.' Richard rummaged in the vegetable drawer of the fridge and handed her a gnarled red chilli. 'No, it was totally equal opportunities. You could also be Far-Right Christian and do abortion clinics and stuff, or an animal rights campaigner, Tamil Tiger . . . there was even a Tibetan Buddhist option. The graphics were awesome.'

'Sounds like there was some kind of moral aspect to it then.'

'Well, not really. You just chose an umbrella cause and blew things up, and as all the characters die so quickly, they're totally two-dimensional.'

He opened a bag of tortilla chips and ate one.

'Oy, leave them until this is finished,' Stephie said, squeezing half a lime in her fist until the juice ran out into the guacamole. 'But you didn't work on this suicide game?'

'No, and I'm not involved in the redevelopment either. They're inverting the concept so that instead of being the bomber you're part of an international squad trying to catch terrorists, but that's always going to be seen as the poor relation of the first game. Rogue copies of which are now collector's items.'

'You should stick to your guns – if you'll excuse the pun – about your historical accuracy.'

Richard smiled. 'You know what else was kind of cool? They did these amazing scenes of heaven or paradise or wherever you ended up at the end. Trance soundtrack and all these little chirpy birds and butterflies and flowers. Or virgins, depending. But I was less keen on those.'

'What about the Buddhists?'

'Reincarnated into a new Lama. Monks come to your village to take you to a big palace amid much jubilation.'

Stephie shook her head and handed him the bowl of

guacamole, then walked out onto the porch with her glass and the crisps. Richard followed her, and they sat side by side at the picnic table.

'It's still warm,' Stephie said, getting up and wandering over to the edge of the patio. She lowered herself onto the slabs where a patch of sunshine remained, waving at the Egg Man – as she'd christened John Anderson who kept the hens – as he walked along the road with an escapee flapping under his arm.

'Fine evening,' he shouted.

'Grand,' Richard called back.

When the Egg Man had gone Stephie looked at him and said, 'Grand?'

'What?'

'Oh, nothing.'

After a moment Richard said, 'Would you be okay on your own here for a night?'

'Why?'

'There's this thing I'm meant to go to, in Glasgow. I'd totally forgotten about it. It's on Friday night.'

Stephie was looking over towards the islands. Someone was out fishing in a little boat, Richard noticed.

'A work thing?'

'Yeah. I mean, if it's a problem I can make an excuse.'

She shook her head. 'Nah, it's all right. I mean, I've got to study anyway.'

He picked up her glass and went inside to refill it. The neighbours' number was written on a piece of paper stuck to the fridge with a magnet; he'd point it out to Stephie. When he went back outside she was standing at the top of the drive, watching a ewe and lamb tilting their heads through the gate to reach a clump of long grass.

'Cute,' Stephie said, going for a closer look. Richard sat back down at the table.

'The things you were asking me yesterday,' he said, but she had crouched down and was murmuring babytalk at the lamb.

'The things you were asking me yesterday,' he said again.

'Hmm,' she said, looking round at him.

'Well, I had this friend, you see.'

'Hang on,' Stephie said, scrambling over the grass and back

to her sunny patch on the patio. 'Do you mean a friend or a *friend?*'

'Enlighten me on the difference.'

'Well, was it just a platonic friendship or something else.'

'Platonic? I suppose it was in a way,' he said. 'Or at least I thought it might be.'

'But this friend was gay, right?'

Stephie took a sip of her wine and adjusted her position to keep her legs in the sun. Richard wondered where she picked up those American inflections, the raised pitch at the end of a sentence, the use of 'right' to signify a question to which she presumed the answer was a forgone conclusion. Television, probably.

'Oh no,' he said. 'He wasn't gay.'

'Dad said he was.'

Richard laughed. 'What does he know? Mind you, scientists haven't given up on the gay gene yet, have they? Maybe Dad knows more about that kind of thing than he lets on.'

'Oh don't be grotesque Richard,' Stephie said. 'Not that I mean what you do's grotesque . . . well, actually it is kind of grotesque because you're my brother, but it would be even more grotesque if it was Dad.' She paused. 'It's a family thing, not a gay thing, right?'

'Hmm,' Richard said. The fishing boat was coming in now, he saw, the sailor rowing in the direction of the old jetty. Hard work, he imagined, although the water wasn't rough. 'So tell me Dad's expert opinion then.'

'You could tell he was queer as soon as look at him.'

'My god, did he say it in a northern accent as well?'

'No, I added that for effect,' Stephie said, getting up and moving back to the table, where she sat alongside him. 'But he did say queer, which I thought was very modern of him.'

'I doubt that he meant it in the empowering we're here, we're queer sense. Anyway, I thought my . . . difficulty wasn't a favoured topic of conversation.'

'I just overheard him talking to Mum about it.'

'Nosey.'

'Yeah, well I felt I'd missed out on all the excitement at the time.'

'You were too busy. O Grades and boyfriends, if I remember correctly.'

'Aye, a heady combination. More crisps?'

Richard nodded, and she went inside. A people carrier passed, bicycles strapped to the roof, a small boy pressing his nose against the glass of the back window. Stephie returned with the bowl, losing a couple of tortilla chips on the way.

'Don't worry,' Richard said. 'It'll be a change for the birds.'

'Anyway,' she said. 'You were telling me about this friend who wasn't gay. How come I didn't meet him but Mum and Dad did?'

'They came up to see me at uni.'

Stephie dipped a chip into the guacamole and crunched it noisily. Richard winced.

'Oh yeah, so they did. And once while they were away I had folk round to the house and someone burned a hole in the carpet and Jason managed to fall through the back door and smash the glass. The row was apocalyptic.'

'I don't remember hearing about that.'

'I'm surprised you didn't hear Dad shouting on the other side of the country,' Stephie said, smiling and shaking her head. 'Mum grounded me and I had to give them half my wages every week for months to help pay for it. Total nightmare.'

'Who was Jason?' As he asked Richard worried that Jason had been Stephie's boyfriend, and therefore a name he should have remembered.

'Oh, just some dickhead from school. But I didn't grass him up.'

'Very noble of you.'

'Yeah well,' she said. 'Want the last crisp?'

'No thanks.'

She shrugged and ate it herself. 'So, did you fancy him?'

She made the question sound schoolish and trite, Richard thought. 'Did you fancy Jason?' he said.

She made a fingers down the throat gesture, then said, 'I'm not trying to do your head in, you know.'

'I know. I'll just go and open another bottle. This one's almost dead.'

'My god,' Stephie laughed. 'Is it a two bottle story?'

'Depends how much you want to know,' Richard said, standing up.

'I'm not going anywhere and you haven't got cable.'

'Captive audience, maybe that's just what I need.'

He went through to the kitchen. They could have a frozen pizza for dinner, he decided, with some of the salad left over from the previous evening. He couldn't have his mum complaining that he hadn't fed Stephie properly. Though the less she knew about their wine consumption the better, he thought, selecting a screw-top Chilean from the rack and going back outside.

'I don't know where to start,' Richard said.

'At the beginning. Duh-uh.' Stephie finished her glass and held it out for a top up.

'The first time I met him?'

'Yeah, that'll do.'

Richard sipped the wine tentatively, sucking in his cheeks at the difference in tannin.

'Okay,' he said. 'It was the day I left home.'

0

Although I enjoyed our walks back from the castle, they were also imbued with a hazy sense of disappointment. I wanted to stay longer, always, to see how the place looked by candlelight, what corners were thrown into sharp relief and which imperfections melted away.

Shame we have to go home, I said, as we tramped along the road towards the town. Birds were squabbling over the last haws and rosehips in the hedgerows and the light was fading, bringing an enthusiastically wintry bite to the evening air.

You know the rule, Luke said, and indeed I did. We recited it to remind ourselves: if you're caught somewhere you shouldn't be in daylight you've got half a chance of talking your way out of it; if you're caught there at midnight, you're fucked.

After a while he said, I'd like to see it some day, your town.

Don't worry, I said. It isn't going anywhere.

All the same.

I shrugged. Any time.

We jumped up onto the verge as a car slowed to pass us, a silver Audi driven by a woman with long blonde hair. It stopped a little way ahead of us.

Maybe she needs directions, I said.

No, that car's passed us before, Luke said. Last week. I recognise it.

What'll we do?

Nothing. Just keep walking.

But as we grew nearer the car drove off over a hummock in the road and away.

I think our card might have been marked, Luke said.

Och, maybe she was just fixing her make-up or something. She was looking in the rear view mirror.

Hmm. I guess we knew it wasn't ours forever, eh?

The driver wasn't the only person who'd noticed our trips out of town. The academic community lauded in the prospectus by (token Scot) Gillian from Stirling as 'close-knit and fantastically welcoming' was a hothouse. Sometimes it seemed that nothing within its parameters was private.

I saw you! Francis had crowed at me one Monday evening at the Les-Bi-Gay. Where were you off to then, with him? A romantic stroll?

Well well well, what's going on here then – Hugo had asked, after stopping his car alongside us at the Haste Ye Back sign – A bid for freedom?

As if he'd tuned into my thoughts Luke said, I was wondering about giving the pub a miss tonight.

Yeah, I said. It can get a bit much sometimes, can't it.

And the money, he said. Don't know about you, but I'm skint.

Me too, I said, having just tried to work out a budget tight enough to see me through to the next grant cheque. But I thought Mendelssohn was going to pay you for shifting his books?

Yeah, he did. A tenner, like.

Last of the big spenders.

Do you think he's gay?

Mendelssohn?

Yeah.

Yeah, for sure. Why?

Aw, nothing. Just, he was quite nice to me and I thought he was maybe looking at me.

And did he touch you on any of your private parts?

Fuck off.

I'd never have admitted it, but I was a tiny bit jealous of Mendelssohn's supposed interest. I don't mean that he should have fancied me, merely that I'd hoped for a little acknowledgement, solidarity even. Instead he maintained a distance that went beyond typical academic scattiness. Perhaps he preferred to couch his desires in admiration of more traditional masculine qualities.

So, quiet night in it is then, Luke said. Want to come round to mine? Buggerlugs is away in Aberdeen with the rugby team and I've got a little surprise for you.

Sure, I said, and that whisper of melancholia faded away. After a while I noticed the intense evening scent of flowers drifting over the hedgerows.

Smell that? I said.

He nodded. Makes a change from manure.

Meadow sweet, I said. I think.

How do you know all that stuff? he said and smiled at me, making me proud of the half-knowledge gleaned in my child-hood. Luke knew how to face off a drunken teen and score drugs but he'd never collected frogspawn or seen a fairy ring of lurid Amanita toadstools. Those, at least, would have been right up his street; he'd already had me hunting for spindly little liberty caps in likely spots round the edge of the golf course (although the expedition failed when we were shooed away by a greenkeeper long acquainted with the ways of students).

We bought some three-minute noodles and cans of beer at the Co-op and went back to Herrick, which had a listless feel to it that evening, as though everyone's attention was elsewhere. Calum and some friend from his Physics workgroup were sprawled in the TV room with a multipack of Doritos and the Alien boxed set.

We're just putting on the second one, he called.

Nah, Luke said. You're all right Calum. Ta.

Have fun, I added. In Herrick no-one can hear you scream.

We proceeded to the kitchen, which was suffused with a boiling smell, though what had been boiled I couldn't be sure. Lentils, perhaps. It was a barren room, rendered more de-pressing by the official notices about tidying up and the handwritten labels stuck to the meagre selection of groceries which lurked in the cupboard. While I slopped our instant noodles into bowls Luke rooted around in the fridge until he found a bottle of soy sauce marked 'Gemma's!', with which he doused our dinner. Unwilling to sit under the fluorescent strip light we retreated to his room, which in the absence of Max seemed if not nearly as good as the castle, palatial in compar-ison to the other options Herrick had to offer. Luke put on

some gently throbbing dance music to stifle the sound of The
Cure from the room next door, and we were onto our second
beer before he said,

You know how you were telling me about that girl?

Wendy.

Yeah. What I was wondering was, did you manage it? With
you being gay, I mean.

I looked at him. His face was serious.

Kind of, I said.

He laughed. What do you mean kind of? Did you fuck her?

Yes.

Did you make her come?

I very much doubt it.

Did you come?

I reached for another can of beer and cracked it open. After
a moment I said, It was just some kind of hormonal mix-up,
okay? A one off. I'm gay, Luke. You know that.

Did you like it?

Not particularly.

You must have. If you came.

It made me feel sick actually. God, I'd never have mentioned
it if I'd known I was going to get the fucking Spanish Inquisi-
tion.

Sorry, he said, smiling at me, so I didn't know if he'd been
genuine or just trying to wind me up. Then he said:

But if you've done it once, you're bisexual, eh?

I made an exasperated noise. For fuck's sake Luke, I'm gay,
all right? G-A-Y gay. A poof, a faggot, a shirtlifting queer . . .

Take it easy, he said, patting me on the arm and grinning as
though satisfied at getting a rise out of me. I'm just curious.

You're a cunt, I said. That's what you are.

I know, he said. But sometimes I'm very thoughtful.

Yeah right. I pretended to sulk.

I am, he said. I said I got you a surprise, didn't I?

So what is it then?

Aha, Luke said, leaping to his feet and rummaging through
the drawer of his desk. I swear that fucker goes through my
stuff when I'm not in, he muttered.

What've you lost?

S'okay, I've found it now. Right. Close your eyes.

I obeyed.

Now stick out your tongue, he said.

I looked at him with scepticism.

Go on, he said, smiling in his very boyish, innocent way.

Okay, I said, sighing and closing my eyes again. He pressed firmly against my tongue, so that I could taste a hint of tobacco from his fingertip, then moved his hand away.

Now hold it there, don't swallow.

I twitched and he said again, Don't swallow. Then he held out his index finger, on which rested a little square of paper with a purple ohm sign stamped on it. He smiled and placed this on his own tongue, and I waited for his cue to wash mine down with a sip of beer.

An SI unit, I said. Measuring electrical resistance.

Yes, he said. You did want to, didn't you?

Sure, I said. Why not.

He laughed. Just like the Host.

The Host? I said. It resonated somehow, but I couldn't drag its meaning from my sluggish brain.

You know, he said, taking a sip of beer. Like at Mass.

I've never been to Mass.

You mean you're not Catholic? he said. Weird. I just assumed you were.

I shook my head. My family were Protestant – in the non-churchgoing, non-religious sense of the word – and our town was Protestant too. Not so far from Lodge 0, with the Catholic church kept clinging to the outskirts of the town, its mysteries a safe distance from the Main Street and Town Buildings. My mum had taken Stephie and I to a jumble sale in the assembly hall of St Ninian's Academy once. As we passed through the main entrance I'd felt Stephie's little paw patting its way up my leg until she reached my hand. I assume it was the viscerally rendered crucifix that provoked her, rather than the seventies architecture. The Virgin, in her pretty blue robe, was a bigger hit. Mum had laughed when Stephie asked why they didn't have dolly ladies in her school too. I wish I could say that I'd been set all a-quiver by the sight of pouting, red-lipped Sebastian, but he wasn't amongst the plaster saints. Perhaps they didn't want to give the pupils of the Nin's any ideas.

You mean you are a Catholic? I said.

Luke smiled. Not any more, I guess. Not so's you'd know.

The next day, for the first time, I missed my ten o'clock lecture.

9

As Richard eased himself onto a stool at the bar he realised he'd misjudged the place, put the rainbow sticker on the door together with a mild recollection of the name and come up with an image of somewhere he'd choose to round off an evening. Instead, he found himself in the Last Chance Saloon. He ordered a drink in any case, embarrassed to walk straight back out the door and still, though he didn't quite admit it, imbued with an open-minded optimism about how the night might end up. It was only a few moments walk from his hotel after all, then a mere lift journey to the claret and cream anonymity of his room. And if someone from DaCapo – such as Jonathan from the art department, for whom Richard had conceived a fancy over dinner – met him on the way, it would only lead to a good-natured ribbing at the breakfast table the next day.

Not, he guessed, that many of his colleagues would be making it to breakfast. The group had splintered after the meal, various nightclubs calling its livelier members and Rupe leading a small posse towards a 'gentleman's club' which he promised would be 'spectacularly ironic'. Tuula had made a 'wanker' gesture behind Rupe's back as he retrieved the company credit card, and Richard couldn't help agreeing with her assessment as he watched Rupe herd the Sony exec, drunk Lisa who fancied the Sony exec, gauche Ben the intern and intense Malcolm the surprisingly influential blogger out of the restaurant.

Richard paid for his pint of San Miguel, marvelling that they had it on tap given the unreconstructed air of the place. Traditional in décor, just a normal corner bar with a mirrored gantry and repro Guinness adverts on the walls. You could come in, get yourself a drink, take a seat before you noticed.

That the barmaid was the only woman in the place, aside from an elderly lady with lopsided false eyelashes and a lot of jewellery sitting beside with a man who might have been her son. That a lad on a barstool had just reached round and massaged the neck of the boy sitting beside him, close enough for their thighs to touch. The way the old soaks at the corner tables were looking at the youngsters at the bar. Richard could feel their eyes on him too, almost hear their stagey little whispers. Those few youngsters that were there must have been slumming it or trying to adopt the place as some kitsch treasure; they wouldn't be regulars unless there was something wrong with them. He glanced towards the mirror to allow a quick scan just in case: not his type, not his type, quite nice but obviously part of a couple. The fantasy of parading a slim Marc Jacobs model-type past Jonathan in order to enflame his envy and awaken his previously dormant lust for Richard would have to remain just that.

'Not seen you in here before.'

'No,' Richard said, turning back to face to the man who was sitting to his left. Not his type either, never mind.

'Local, are you?'

'I live up north. Just down here for work.'

'You don't sound like a teuchter.'

'No.' Richard hesitated, drinking too much from his pint as though he was thirsty. 'I'm from south Ayrshire originally.'

The man smiled, his face crinkling into a murder of crow's feet. 'No offence son,' he said, 'But you don't sound like you come fae there either.'

'I haven't been there for a while. I must've lost the accent somewhere along the line.'

'Aye, that can happen,' the man said, his eyes darting to the door and back again. 'Get you another of those?'

'Thanks,' Richard said, though what he'd meant to say was, no thanks. He sensed that it wasn't a chat up, the man was too distracted for that. He ordered a double vodka with orange for himself, but had downed it by the time Richard's pint was pulled. The barmaid served him another without being asked.

Soon the man – they didn't bother with introductions – upgraded to treble vodkas and lemonade and showed Richard pictures of his two children. His wife thought he was working, he explained, driving a minicab. Instead he was fortifying himself, he explained, for when his boyfriend came to meet him.

'The truth of it is that I'm feart of him,' the man said suddenly, surprising Richard because he was a wiry type, with a boxer's quick shiftiness. He hadn't been swift enough to avoid the knife that had traced a pale scar over his jawline though.

'But he loves me, you know? Gave me this.' He indicated his wrist, flashing a watch through Richard's line of vision too quickly for him to discern whether it was expensive or not. The man's hands were shaking. Richard felt he should take them in his own to still them, but he didn't.

'Listen,' he said instead. 'Why don't you just go home and see your kids and forget him for tonight?'

The man chewed on his lip and said, 'I cannae, take it from me I cannae.'

Could it really be that bad, Richard wondered, or was it a poor attempt at melodrama, falling flat because it wasn't coming from some pretty young scenester in skinny jeans? But then the swing doors to the bar flew open, and what must have been the man's lover flounced in. Flouncing, Richard realised, could look extremely threatening when the flouncer was six foot tall and built like Desperate Dan.

'Right,' he announced to the bar in general, in a voice that seemed more frightening because of its affectation than in spite of it, 'Where is he? Where the hell is he?'

Richard could feel himself shrinking from the man by his side, not wanting to get involved but disliking himself for his response. His companion hopped off his stool and stood still as his lover marched up to him, hauled him to the middle of the floor and punched him in the face. He crumpled to the ground, clutching his jaw.

'You get in that car right now,' the bigger man said, then he turned on his heels and stalked out.

Richard looked towards the barmaid, expecting her to be dialling 999, but she was holding a glass to the vodka optic, her back to the scene. As the wiry man scrambled to his feet and wiped his face she called, 'Here Joe,' and held the glass out to him. 'On the house.'

He downed it in one, not looking at Richard, not looking at anybody. The bar was quiet enough now for the music to be heard, a poor remix of an early Madonna song. As it finished the man placed the glass on the bar with care, nodded his thanks to the barmaid and walked through the door.

A high-pitched cackle erupted from the side of the room. Richard looked in the mirror and isolated the source: a plump boy in a tight pink T-shirt and clunky gold chain, nudging his companions like a puppy begging for scraps. The music increased in volume and all at once the bar was filled with chatter and giggles. Richard finished his drink and met the eye of the boy he'd noticed earlier. He and his partner looked vulnerable now, as though suddenly their Ben Shermans and tank tops were insufficient armour. Richard guessed that the bar's prospective elevation to kitsch treasure had plummeted, offered a half-smile in their direction as he got up and left.

It had started raining. Disorientated by the haloes of the streetlights and their reflections on the glistening road, Richard walked a few yards in the wrong direction before realising his mistake and turning. Taxis hurled past on their way to the ranks in the town centre, and he wished he was far enough from his destination to flag one down and step in, away from the rain and echoing shouts and the niggle of threat that dogged him on the dark walk back to his hotel. When he reached its shining façade he toyed with the idea of continuing, finding someplace else where he could salvage the remnants of the evening. Then he saw a clutch of girls of about Stephie's age careening towards him, all spike heels and snarls of lip gloss, and ducked through the automatic doors into the lobby instead.

Richard looked at his face in the mirrored wall of the elevator, tilting his head to ascertain whether his pallor was the result of tiredness or poor lighting. Thinking ahead to the drive home the next day, he was glad to be heading for bed rather than the noise and crush and heat of some club, which underneath its sleeker surface might not have been so very different from the bar he'd been in earlier.

'I wish I wasn't like this,' the man had said to Richard. Richard hadn't been sure what the man meant, if he'd been talking about his character or his sexuality. Perhaps one day you had to rationalise the stories you'd told and the parts you'd played. Scrutinise the version of yourself you'd created for others, and see how it matched up to the real thing.

0

You know where I came from, I told Luke, you know the kind of place. Stunted, grey, the industry gone, black carcasses of pits on the outskirts of town where teenagers go to drink cheap, fortified wines with poignant names. Between fighting and fucking and sucking dirty heroin into their tarry, vitamin-deprived lungs. A shithole, we called it, and it was. Education the best way out, that and crime. Or, like Kenny Dodd, a swooping, swallow-like dive from the remains of the pithead to the rough, broken concrete below. Eldorado.

But Luke pressed me for the piquant details, and flattered, I obliged. Though I called myself working class, and it was true, we were part of the elite in the 'Leck, in that both parents actually worked, in jobs they hoped to keep until death or retirement did them part. My father, whose father and his father before him had held their breaths as the cage took them deep down underground, now drove up the valley to a man-ufacturing plant. Plastics, I think it was. He didn't say much about it (and shame on me, I didn't ask). My mother was not a dentist's receptionist, she worked at the surgery in an admin-istrative capacity (ditto). So no Thunderbird or smack for me. I should mention, though it seems ungrateful to do so only as an aside, that I did love my parents. They did their best, comforted me when I was bullied (though I wouldn't tell them why), gave me pocket money and no reason to cry. And yet, alone in my room night after night, fat, selfish tears would moisten my pillow. The huge, insurmountable wedge between us was of course my inversion, my deviancy, my never-to-be-confessed secret. Later I was fascinated by the tales my more out-coming contemporaries told of how their mother always knew. Mine didn't, though of course it was to be revealed with a flourish – tada! – later on.

It might seem hard to believe, but all I used to dream of was a big double bed with a patchwork counterpane like the one my granny stitched by the gas fire; the coal, like her husband, long dead. Somewhere to indulge a gentle and romantic relationship, a pure love. But no one was gay, or if they were they kept it quiet, haunted by the memory of the man who was lynched in the town down the valley because he loved other men. This in the 1980s, mind.

There was television, there were books (not many, but some, and the interlibrary loan for that first tantalising Edmund White). I knew the lie of the land pretty early, all told. Even if, when my voice deepened and my penis developed a life of its own, there was no-one to receive the fire of my loins. The shame started then, I suppose. Oh, I harboured secret passions, for a boy in the sixth year nicknamed Coco, and Mr Martin the maths master, with his tight, teacherly trousers. But I knew they must stay secret, or else.

One day, just below and to the right of the ripely swelling breasts of Mandy, 18, 34-25-36 with her frozen lip-gloss smile and neon tanga briefs, an article in the newspaper caught my eye. A city scandal, resulting in the closure of public conveniences around Glasgow. The first time I'd heard the term cottaging. Instantly I thought of the cream-painted public bog down by the railway path. Imagined that inside the door, amid the metal urinals and shit-smeared walls, there might exist a dreamy gymnasium packed with lithe lads throwing discuses. Or the Scottish equivalent of such. Clones of the porridge oats man, in his pristine t-shirt and convenient kilt.

Knowing the mindset of some of the local lads – if any of them had seen the article, the punishment delivered upon anyone spied within a half mile radius of a public toilet would be brisk and brutal – I waited until another winter evening a few weeks down the line before I casually went for a stroll. Which wasn't very casual. Both my mother and my father asked what I was doing, as I ran fingers through my hair and splashed on my aftershave (Hi Karate, can you imagine?). Walking without a dog was considered morally suspect, so I made up a story about going to see someone. This was implausible given that I didn't have any friends, but it worked out for the best as my jumpy, forced bonhomie convinced my parents that there was some girl I fancied and hoped to glimpse.

Of course, when I got there, there were no boys with bows and arrows, no gentle, thorough Greek teachers, never mind the porridge oats man. Not that night, nor the next time I went, nor the one after that. By my fourth visit, I'd given up hope. Dejected I sat in the only cubicle, reading the signs of my Armitage Shanks Sibyl. Kirsty McGill is a slag. Benny does dugs. For a good time call Stanesy's maw. More promisingly, down beside the broken toilet roll holder, smaller letters proclaimed, I need hard dick. Meet me here 7pm. Where are you now, Hard Dick? I pondered, and then I heard a phlegmy cough.

I leapt to my feet and lunged towards the urinal, whipping open my fly en route. It might have been thought poofy to bother going to a public convenience to piss when you could just expose yourself in the street, but it would have been even more unseemly to be caught in a public convenience not pissing at all.

In came a man, who nodded at me and with inebriated clumsiness, withdrew a whopping great dong from the depths of his trousers, groaning as he started a long, luxurious urination. I recognized him, the curious blue pock marks on his face. It was Mr Sim from the miner's cottages by the war memorial. I stopped peeing, but I didn't stop staring. The thing was immense. I had only seen, during unguarded moments in the PE changing room, the youthful, teenage specimen. This was positively Neanderthal. Homo erectus eat your heart out. He noticed I hadn't moved, and swiftly, with trembling hands, I did up my jeans. But I must have done something right, because he swivelled round, newly-relieved penis still out in the open, and met my eye. I backed against the wall, wanting nothing more than to run past him and away, along the railway path and home, to Red Dwarf on the telly and my mother nipping at Stephanie for being a little madam.

Well, whit are ye waitin fur?

And that was that. I sank to the ground. Mr Sim seized me by the ears to better adjust my position, and growled with pleasure as I got to work on his savoury, urine-tanged member. I soon realised the significance of the swallow or spit debate amongst the loucher girls in my year. Mr Sim unleashed such a torrent (of a consistency not unlike over-diluted Campbell's condensed mushroom soup) that it didn't go down in the first swallow, but spilled out over my chin. He sighed, withdrew, hauled me to my feet. I hadn't even got as far as thinking that he might reciprocate when he slammed me against the wall and pinned one massive hand to my throat. With the other he seized my twitching testicles through my jeans and squeezed until tears came to my eyes.

If ye open yer gub aboot this, ah'll throttle ye, ye wee pervert. Comprende?

I nodded, he released me, and rapturous, my knees soaked through with what was probably piss, I ran home. I was in love. Not with unwashed, beer-addled Mr Sim, but with my future.

10

Richard shifted down a gear as the road narrowed to single track. It was tragic, really. Not yet thirty and he'd been unable to pull in a gay bar in Glasgow, of all places. Oh well, not every trip to a city had to mean sifting through the scene in search of a quick fix. A smart little convertible flickered into sight round the bend and he pulled into a passing place to let it sweep by. Tourists coming back from the fancy hotel along the coast, he supposed. He'd never been there himself, partly out of solidarity with the locals, who were happy enough to supply it with tatties and guinea fowl (John the Egg Man's latest venture) but less enthusiastic about spending eighty pounds a head on its tasting menu. The drama in the bar the night before seemed more distant now but Richard could still picture the expression on the man's face as he'd steeled himself to walk out the door and get into the car in which his lover was waiting. It seemed absurd, here, heading for home with the sun sharpening the tips of the mountains and turning the shallows of the sea loch lucent and inviting.

When Richard had called Stephie earlier to see if she needed anything from the supermarket she'd sounded distracted, he thought, first telling him not to go to any trouble then insisting on making him a proper dinner.

'Don't worry, just keep on with your studying,' he said, but she was already listing the ingredients for coq au vin.

'And get plenty of vin,' she'd said, to which he'd managed to resist bemoaning his ability to procure any of the other main ingredient.

He hadn't mentioned that John had been known on occasion to wring a chicken's neck and sell it to his neighbours. Richard was far too daunted by the idea of plucking and cleaning the bird but Stephie, after two years of training to be a nurse, might have a stronger stomach. As he got closer to home he saw John chasing some plump hens from his vegetable patch, and decided that his squeamishness was skin deep. He was already starting to feel hungry.

When Richard pulled up at the house he could see Stephie standing in the porch, her arms folded across her chest, but by the time he'd jumped out to open the gate she had disappeared. The muscles in his legs were groaning after the long drive. As he reversed the car up the driveway he caught sight of her again in the wing mirror, walking down over the grass to close the gate behind him. She was wearing her floral blouse again, he noticed, this time with an A-line skirt and flip-flops. The bath would be ringed with leg hairs again, he surmised.

'Hey,' she said. 'How was your trip?'

'Okay thanks,' he said. 'Though I feel pretty done in now.'

'Late night?'

'Not as bad as all that,' he said, opening the boot and handing her two shopping bags then picking up the wine carriers himself. He started walking towards the house, but Stephie didn't move.

'How are things here?' he said. There was music playing upstairs, he noticed. The Velux window on the landing was flung wide open.

'Fine,' Stephie said, shaking a pebble out of one of her shoes. She'd broken something, he decided. Worse than that, she'd used his office and something had happened.

'You haven't crashed my computer, have you?'

'No,' she said. 'Of course not.'

'Thank god for that,' he said, walking towards the house.

'It's just,' she said behind him, making him turn to face her. 'It's just that, this friend of mine, see, she was just kind of passing and well, she's here now . . .'

Richard put down the wine, the noise of the bottles clinking against each other appealing despite the mild hangover he'd woken with that morning.

'When you say here,' he said.

'In the house. I made up the other bed in my room.'

Richard pressed his thumb and middle finger to his temples

and circled them slowly. 'Stephie, nobody's ever just passing, not here. Did you plan this?'

'No,' she said. 'Well, not really.'

'Oh Stephie, for god's sake. You know how much work I've got to do.'

He stepped round her and made for the house, leaving the wine on the driveway behind him.

'Look Richard, I'm really sorry, honestly,' she called after him. 'I didn't know she'd come yesterday.'

'Well she can get on the post bus and leave tomorrow,' he said. 'I'm not running a bloody youth hostel.'

As he pushed open the porch door he heard Stephie say, 'You sound just like Dad.'

He hurried to his study, firing up his computer and checking his email straight away. A message from Neil's home address, which he skimmed for gossip: Rupe refused entry to Diamond Dolls on the grounds of the age, gender and intoxication of members of his party; Lisa insisting they stopped the car on the way back to Dundee so she could be sick on the hard shoulder. Neil signed off with an arch little, *hope you had fun, whatever you got up to . . .*

Richard could still hear the music from upstairs. He got up and stood to the side of the French doors, trying to keep out of sight as he peered towards the driveway. A dark-haired girl in narrow indigo jeans followed Stephie to the car. Her hair whipped around her face as she stooped to pick up the wine carriers, creating a disconcerting Medusa effect that disappeared as soon as she straightened up and carried the boxes to the side door.

By the time Richard had left home Stephie had only just been beginning to hang out, favouring evenings spent sitting with a row of pals on the wall of the petrol station. His recollections of her friends before that time were sketchy: a proliferation of My Little Ponies being cantered round the table by Stephie and a ginger girl with a tight French plait, the drone of skipping rhymes and the thunk, thunk, thunk of a tennis ball in a knee sock hitting the wall below his bedroom window, the sound of dislodged roughcast sprinkling to the ground. Once he'd opened his wardrobe and found dolls, shorn-headed Barbies dangling by their ankles from the clothes rail, some other kind of naked plastic female with no arms rotating in a truss of parcel string between his school shirts. Laughter rang out as Stephie and her co-conspirator congratulated themselves on their macabre little tableau.

Footsteps thudded up the stairs and the music stopped mid-song, just as Richard heard a knock at the door. He rubbed his face. His eyes felt hot and teary. Not enough sleep and a long drive, the air conditioning vent blasting his contact lenses all the way.

'Yes?' he said.

Stephie stuck her head round the door.

'I'm sorry,' she said.

'Why didn't you ask me?'

'I don't know.'

'Oh Stephie, come on . . .' he began, but then he remembered her saying that he was just like their father. 'You could have warned me at least,' he said.

'I did try to put her off, you know.'

'Not hard enough, obviously.'

He wanted to say: why don't you stop apologising and take some responsibility? Stephie came into the room and closed the door behind her.

'It's not that easy,' she said. 'Loren's quite . . . determined.'

Richard picked up a ballpoint pen and started clicking the nib in and out. 'You know that I've got to get on with work, Stephie, I can't afford any more disruption.'

He saw her eyes turn limpid with tears but before he could speak she swung round and walked out, slamming the door behind her.

0

Sprawled on the grass of the Links, I closed my eyes against the sunshine of a late autumn afternoon that seemed to have forgotten all about heralding the winter. The cricket club was practising nearby, and the gentle strikes and calls of their play recalled another of those tantalising prospectus scenes. My thumb slipped from the place it was keeping in Lemmon's *Beginning Logic*.

After a few minutes, or it could have been longer, a shadow passed above me, too swiftly to have been a cloud. Suddenly I felt fingers in my mouth, opened my eyes; Luke, of course. His papery hand, prone to eczema, and a surge of unwilling arousal at his rough fingers against my tongue. And then a taste, unfamiliar but guessable. The flashing memory of Wendy, scrawny despite her diet of soggy chips and sausage suppers. I choked, and he laughed and withdrew his fingers.

Fuck you, I said, spluttering on the ground beside me. By the time I recovered he was sitting a couple of feet away, reading a small paperback.

Where've you been hiding? I said.

Had to see someone, he said, turning his page.

Yeah, I guessed that.

No, he said. I just dropped by Katie's on my way back from seeing them.

Very mysterious.

Not really. Just a kind of progress report, eh.

With your advisor of studies?

He looked up and smiled. Kind of, he said. Yeah.

I like this Wednesday afternoon free for sport malarkey, I said, struggling upright and brushing the grass from my hair.

Hmm. Luke was hunched over his book.

I reached out and flicked the nail of my middle finger at the name on the spine.

Trocchi, I said. What are you like, with your I'm-so-cool-I-study-literature texts.

He didn't lift his eyes from the page as he said, It's not a course text.

Hmmph, I said, and returned to Lemmon. When I reached yet another new rule I said: I'm bored.

Luke laid his book to one side and looked round at me.

Well, that's the trouble with small ponds, isn't it? You'd be better off in a city.

I rolled onto my back and squinted up at the clouds which were now scudding across the sky. Bored with logic. Not bored with here, I said.

Logic dictates that you'd get your end away more often in a city. And then – he splayed the spine of his book and placed it beside him on the grass – you'd be far less bored.

What do you know about it? I said, still smug from a recent tryst with a second year anthropologist after the Les-Bi-Gay social.

Oh, just what a little bird told me, Luke said, all sly.

Well then, I said, punching him on the shoulder.

Not bad for a nancy, he said, rubbing where I'd hit him. Let's just say, you'd have more choice.

Oh really?

Bit of rough trade on Calton Hill, or scouting around the unions for a pretty boy from the art college, if that's more your scene. You'd be like a pig in shit.

Charming, I said, making as if I was going to thump him again. I'd say that a pretty boy from the art college is definitely more my scene. Don't you think?

He shrugged. I don't know.

Don't you?

Only what I hear, he said, and went back to reading his book. Now if you'll shut up and let me finish my chapter, I'll buy you a drink. Maybe even more than one.

I thought you were skint?

He tapped the side of his nose. A little windfall. Now

wheesht and back to your formulas and proofs, or whatever it is you're meant to be doing.

When we got to the Union we sat at the bar rather than at a table, which was fine by me as the rugger buggers were all in after their afternoon practice, braying and yahing in those voices I'd never encountered in the flesh before I came to university. English accents of course, and that ridiculously full-mouthed Scottish which at first I thought originated some-where specific (in Perthshire perhaps, or round about Inver-ness), until experience taught me to recognise the tones of confidence and good schooling, complete acceptance that what you have to say should be uttered loud and clear. Even if it was just a tedious inventory of alcohol consumed over the previous weekend.

Stupid cunts, Luke said, as a particularly obnoxious guffaw rang out above the sound of the jukebox. The barman heard him and curled his lip into the closest approximation of a smile I'd ever seen near his face. The Union may have been run by students, for students, but even the inept management com-mittee weren't foolish enough to employ a student to manage the bar. Instead we had Michael, a forty something local with an eagle eye for underage freshers and a penchant for recycling the contents of the slops tray.

I noticed Luke's room-mate Max and his friend Hugo detach themselves from the rugger table and approach the bar, and I thought I saw Max whisper something and nod in our direction. They issued their order and the barman stomped past us on his way to the cider tap at the far end of the bar.

Why do Scotchmen wear kilts? Max say, taking no trouble to lower his voice.

I dinnat ken, his friend said, in a dreadful pastiche of the accent.

Because sheep can hear the sound of a zip a mile away.

The barman allowed the two pints he was placing in front of them to spill over the rims of the glasses.

Hello Max, Luke called over.

Luke.

The chilliness between them was nothing new, but there was

an edge to it that I hadn't witnessed before. Luke was half-smiling to himself as he drank his pint.

Haven't run into you during waking hours for days, he said. How's it going?

Oh, I'm just fine, Max said. So, developing a little sideline, are we?

His friend angled by his side, as if preparing for some tackle or pass.

Don't know what you're talking about, Luke said, lighting a cigarette. Want another drink, Richard?

Sure, I said. But it's my turn.

Don't worry about it, he said. See you later, Max.

Max scowled at me as he left, but there was nothing new there. The Les-Bi-Gay group had all the rugby boys pegged as repressed. I disagreed, inclining more to the view that they really were rampant homophobes, communal showering or no.

Thanks, I said, raising my glass to Luke. Buying two drinks in a row for someone amounted to phenomenal largesse in student terms.

Nae probs, he said.

I waited until the barman had returned to his little cubby hole at the back of the bar before I asked, So what was that all about, with Max?

Luke smiled. Oh, nothing.

I don't believe you. You look pleased with yourself.

He sighed. Okay then. At the beach party on Monday, the one you didn't attend because you were engaged in unspeakable acts with an anthropologist – he paused to take a drink and admire the look of surprise on my face – I had a bit of a run in with a girl of Max's acquaintance.

When you say a girl?

She was definitely a girl, Richard. All the signifiers were there.

No-o. When you say a girl, do you mean his girlfriend?

He thought so. She had a slightly more flexible approach.

Ah. And what's a relationship without communication.

Exactly. So now Max is pretending very hard that he didn't come looking for her in the dunes only to discover her doing for me what I hope your little brunette did for you.

Oh he did, I said, draining my pint. And not so little, as it happens.

Really?

Mmm, I said, and suddenly I was hyper-aware of Luke next to me, of the pressure against his trousers where his cock was, of how much I wanted him to kiss me. I felt it like a kick in the stomach, like something aching inside me, screaming at him, but Luke didn't notice a thing.

You gays are all the same, he said, indicating to the barman that we wanted the same again. Perverts.

You're one to talk, I said, searching in my pocket for the five pound note I was sure I still had. So, what was Max going on about when he mentioned a sideline?

Luke shrugged. Don't know. Unless . . . I got a wee bit hash for Libby, the erstwhile girlfriend. Maybe that was it.

Hmm, I said, handing the money over to the barman before Luke could pay again. Did you know this Libby was Max's girlfriend? Before, I mean?

He shrugged. Don't pay much attention to his personal life.

You bastard, I said.

He grinned. Yeah.

So I guess room-mate relations have hit an all time low, I said.

You could say that.

Well, I said. Calum didn't come back after the weekend. Glandular fever, apparently.

Glandular fever? Who's he been kissing, Princess Leia?

I don't know, I said. Anyway, there's a spare bed in mine if it all gets too much.

Luke laughed. Stay in your room, like? I'd not be able to sleep for worrying about my virtue.

Don't flatter yourself, I said, though of course he wasn't.

We stayed in the Union, soon becoming embroiled in a happy sprawl of fellow students, getting drunker and drunker as the evening wore on. I sat opposite Luke, and we talked for what seemed like hours, laughing together, discussing I don't know what. William Burroughs and Joseph Beuys and the music of Ennio Morricone; whatever it was, it seemed to throw up connections and agreement and opportunities to tease each other for failures in taste. He was looking into my eyes, a lot, but I didn't take it seriously until it crept up on me, a sense that everyone around us had faded away. I felt sure, drunkenly sure, that this was it, that something was going to happen between us. That I needed only to reach out and press my leg against his, under the table. I don't know what stopped me, though I'm glad something did. Because it wasn't different, we weren't set apart. He was like that with everyone. I don't think he even knew he was flirting, though he was clever enough to work it out if he tried.

11

Feet pounding against the road, concentrating on avoiding potholes and pancakes of mud and dung, Richard felt better. He'd had to force himself to come for a run; he'd have preferred to collapse on the couch with his laptop and play an hour or two of *World of Warcraft* (it could almost be classed as research, after all). This thought slowed his pace, so it was an effort to speed up again as he ran along the flat by the pebbled beach. Stephie and this Laurel person were in the sitting room, his sitting room. He'd heard their voices as he passed the open door of the porch, laughter which made him skulk past rather than look in on them.

Was it possible, he wondered, ever to escape these small and to anyone else inconsequential recollections that suddenly burst into your consciousness and occupied it completely? Pausing at the wooden beam where he and Stephie had sat the other day, Richard did some stretches, flexing each leg in turn, working on his too-tight hamstrings. An awkward phrase, a stupid comment, long forgotten by the person to whom it was addressed, that years later could still flood you with self-loathing. And other memories, of stronger things, if you allowed those to slip into your mind. He thought of one of his very first programming exercises, designing a virtual version of the simplest of games. Stone blunts scissors, paper wraps stone; the present should trump the past.

Richard picked his way back to the grass verge, where he jogged on the spot for a second before setting off again. Hearing a car behind him, he paused by the little bridge ready to let it cross first, then realised it was Rab in his bashed-up old Nissan.

'Richard, hop in and I'll jump you up the hill.'

'Cheers Rab, but I need to get in shape.' He patted his stomach, an awkward, clichéd gesture.

'Ah well, each to their own, eh?' He meant running of course; Richard was exasperated by his own sensitivity. 'Getting a wee minute away from your visitors are you?'

'Something like that,' Richard said.

'Tell you what,' Rab said. 'It's going to be a beauty the morrow. Get the lassies to come down and I'll let them on the boat for free. You can get some peace.'

'That's good of you Rab, I'll tell them.'

'Aye well, no skin off my nose. Joyce telt me you were up against it with that computer work of yours. See ya.' He revved the engine, lurched forward then stuck his head out the window and called, 'Haw, Richard.'

'Uhuh?'

'Too much exercise is bad for you.'

Richard heard a hoarse chortle as Rab drove off, tooting his horn twice by way of farewell. The hatchback of his car was tied down with string, unable to close over a bale of hay which had been stowed there. As well as the boat, Rab kept a few sheep – 'just for the hell of it' – and whatever he said about exercise, he was possibly the fittest person Richard had ever met. Which made him feel all the stupider for not accepting the lift as he hauled himself up the hill and home at a pace scarcely faster than a brisk walk.

He did his final stretches at the picnic table, then collapsed onto the bench. Rab had been right about the weather. The sky was clear and tinged with seashell pink and the water between mainland and islands was as glassy and calm as he'd ever seen it. He closed his eyes and waited to see if he could hear the water swilling against the rocks. After a few moments he tuned into it, and let his breathing slow to match the ebb and flow. Then he heard footsteps and felt the bench sink as someone slipped in beside him. He smelled Stephie's perfume, pictured the bottle in the bathroom, but couldn't remember the name.

'It's going to be a nice day tomorrow,' he said, opening his eyes and seeing that Stephie had put on a jumper over her blouse and was cupping a mug of coffee in her hands. 'You feeling all right?' he asked.

'Yeah, just trying to wake myself up before we get started on dinner. We had a bit of a late night last night. If you still want to have dinner, that is?' She sipped her coffee, looking up at him over the rim of the mug.

He nodded, framing an apology in his mind then rejecting it. Stephie stuck one of her feet up on the table.

'I borrowed a pair of your walking socks. Do you mind?'

'No,' he said, wondering whether she'd taken them off the clothes horse or gone through his drawers. 'I met Rab. The guy with the boat. He says if you want to go over to the islands tomorrow he'll let you on for nothing. You and Laurel.'

'Loren,' she said.

'Loren.'

'How did he know she was here?'

Richard stretched again. The cooler evening air was starting to niggle at the sweat patches on his T-shirt. 'Someone'll have seen you both. You don't get away with much around here.'

Stephie swirled the last of her coffee around inside the mug, as though she was looking for signs in the dregs. 'So it's okay then?'

Richard sighed. 'It's just for a few days, isn't it?'

She nodded, and he wondered what she'd meant when she'd said that she didn't want Loren to come. Just some teenage tiff, he supposed, then he remembered that she wasn't teenage any more.

'I'm sorry about earlier,' he said.

She reached out and squeezed his arm. 'It's okay. It is a disruption, I know it is. I just . . . well, I just needed a break and I didn't know where else to go.'

'You certainly know how to make a person feel wanted.'

She smiled. 'I did want to see you. You never visit.'

'I know.'

She wiped away a drip of coffee that was congealing at the edge of her mug and said, 'And I want to hear more, about what you were telling me the other night.'

'I was indulging myself, going into all that stuff about when Luke and I met. There's a much simpler version of events: I was at uni, with Luke. There was a sort of accident. Somebody died. We both got chucked out.'

Stephie tucked her hands inside the cuffs of her jumper. 'An accident?'

'Yes.'

'What kind of accident?'

'A girl drowned. She was under the influence of drugs. They thought she'd fallen off the pier. The sea was very cold, in winter.'

'What age was she?'

'Twenty.'

'That's awful.'

'Yes.'

'But I don't see how it could be anything to do with you.'

He hesitated. 'It wasn't.'

'And Luke, what about him?'

'Luke was into drugs. A bit. The university court put two and two together. He withdrew from his course of studies.'

'But you got kicked out?'

'I knew her, that's all. I didn't want to tell them about Luke, about the drugs. To drop him in it. So it seemed like I was . . . implicated.'

She got up and walked over to where the slabs met the grass, then looked back at him. 'Implicated,' she said, taking care to pronounce the 't' rather than letting it drop. 'But it wasn't your fault.'

'No,' he said.

The porch door swung open and Loren walked out onto the patio. 'Hey,' she said, in Stephie's direction.

'This is my brother,' Stephie said. 'Richard.'

'Hey Richard,' Loren said, wiping her hands on her jeans as she approached him.

'Hello,' he said.

'No need to be formal,' Stephie said, laughing as they shook hands.

'Okay,' Loren said, smiling and letting her hand go limp in Richard's. 'Well it's nice to meet you anyway. Thanks for letting me stay.'

'That's all right. I guess I'd better go and freshen up.'

He realised how cold he'd become sitting there in his sweaty running gear and jumped up, feeling suddenly self-conscious at being in his shorts. When he'd first come out he'd got used to being looked up and down, convinced himself that it was welcome, that it signified acceptance, approval even. When Loren gave him the once over, he couldn't judge the tone of her gaze.

0

I found Luke in a quiet corner of the Union bar, legs stretched out along the seat, pint and cigarettes on the table by his side as he read. I couldn't see the title of his book because he'd folded the cover round over the spine.

Any good? I said, slumping down on the chair opposite him and feeling mildly resentful of his afternoon of apparent luxury.

Have to read it for a seminar tomorrow. Not that I'll be able to get a word in edgeways with that bunch of Yahs.

I nodded, and he put the book down and reached for his cigarettes.

And, he said, the tutor always smokes during the class but I reckon she'd go mental if I lit up. But I should. One day I will.

Oh, I said.

He looked at me. What's up with you?

I groaned. I've been tramping round the town for hours looking for a job and there's just nothing there. I went into every bar that was open, the Co-op, the cinema, the shops. I even went down to the golf club. No luck. One café had a sign in the window but they just looked at me and said no thanks, and the Co-op said they'd keep my details on record but I'm not holding my breath.

Luke swung his legs round and sat up. Did they ask if you were a student?

Yes. Though I'm sure they could spot it a mile off.

Not too keen on us, are they? The locals, I mean.

Can you blame them? I said. Think of your seminar group.

Yeah, I guess. Anyway, want a drink?

I held my head in my hands and said, I thought you'd never ask.

When Luke had gone to the bar I gave in to a long and

heartfelt groan. At least back home I'd known the score when it came to part time jobs, even if I'd had a similar lack of success in finding one for myself. Top of the heap: Saturdays in the chemist, the preserve of two aspiring pharmacists who lived in the new houses on the edge of town, the ones with stone-cladding and faux Tudor detail. Mediocre but still desirable: early morning shelf stacking in the Co-op, for which special dispensation to miss registration was granted by the school. Lowest of the low: counter attendant in one of the takeaways. These jobs might have been perceived as vaguely disreputable because of the late hours and the dentally-challenged man who fed the deep fat fryers in the chippy and turned up in the court report of the Ayrshire Advertiser every fortnight, but I guessed it was more due to incipient racism. People queued up to order their chicken jalfrezi and peshwari naan on a Friday night, but the way they went on about Morag McGill working in the Korma Chameleon you'd think it was the last outpost of the white slave trade. As for me, by the time I reached sixth year I still hadn't found a job and my dad had exhausted his encouraging anecdotes about childhood milk rounds.

Luke returned with my pint of cider, and tried to distract me from my financial worries with tales of minor scams and shoplifting sprees, pals who pinched money from their mother's purse when she came home drunk. He was lucky, he said; his mum had given him a bung now and then, one of the perks of not having a dad.

My parents were big on me learning to work, I said. As if I hadn't been sitting there studying for all those exams for years.

What did you do? Luke asked.

You're going to love this, I said, remembering how I'd felt when I'd discovered that my dad had finally taken matters into his own hands.

Tell Richard the good news then, Mum had said one evening as we sat down to our tea. She'd seemed particularly twittery when I was helping her carry the plates through so I should've known something was up, but my interest in whatever good news I was about to hear was commensurate with the interest a sixteen year old boy shows in anything his parents say. I continued picking the fat off my lamb chops, until my dad puffed himself up and announced:

I've got you a job. You start on Saturday. Nine sharp.

Isn't that great, my mum said, twittering again. Aren't you going to thank your dad?

I don't know what I'm going to be doing yet, I said. With suitable foreboding, the theme for the six o'clock news blared from the television.

It doesn't matter what you're going to be doing, Dad said. What matters is you've got a job.

But how will Richard know where to go to work if you don't tell him?

Good girl Steph, I thought to myself, you tell them.

In a minute, my dad said, and recognising the prompt I said thank you, prodding a disc of carrot with my fork and hoping that whatever the job was, it would pay enough for me to go to the record shop in Ayr and buy the kind of band T-shirt I usually only managed after a particularly remunerative birthday or Christmas.

So what is it I'm going to be doing? I asked.

Mowing grass, weeding, raking gravel, a bit of planting or pruning maybe.

It'll be good for you Richard, my mum said. You spend too much time cooped up in your room.

Yeah, I thought, that's because we live in the shitiest town in the world and there's fuck all else to do. Being cooped up in my room meant reading, enamelling my Warhammer figurines, furtively contemplating the Hunks of the Week I'd liberated from Stephanie's discarded teen mags.

And what's more, Dad said, it's council wages.

That's more than they get in the Co-op, Mum said. And I know because I met Vivienne McHarg the other day and she was saying . . .

I nodded, my mind turning to Joey Connelly from the Catholic school, all round cool kid and seasonal attendant in the stoner's paradise of the pitch and putt hut in the municipal park. He did all right out of a council job, didn't he? So he supplemented his wages by selling ready rolled joints to younger kids, but he was a responsible enough employee to insist that they paid for a game of pitch and putt first. My mind raced as I navigated a mental map of the town, trying to figure out where I might be posted. It had to be the park. Where else was there?

You know Mr Walls that plays cornet in the band?

I nodded, still envisaging what being colleagues with Joey Connelly would do for my street cred. Then I stopped nodding.

Mr Walls that works in the cemetery? I said.

Exactly, my dad said, triumphant.

Mr Walls the gravedigger, I said.

Don't worry, Mum said. You won't have to dig graves, will he Kenneth?

My dad told her not to be stupid, but nevertheless, I lay awake in my bed that night, turning the combined mileage of poof and gravedigger, grave robber, ghoul over and over in my mind. It could run and run. Small comfort in the fact that necrophiliac was probably too big a word for Andrew Gemmell and his snide little cronies. I couldn't wait until I left school. Until then though, I was going to have to find a way of living with being the grave digging poof.

The next Saturday I scuffed my feet all the way to the cemetery but still arrived at the gate at nine o'clock sharp, if not brimming over with enthusiasm then at least possessed of a deep awareness that any reticence on my part would be reported back to my dad at the next meeting of the social club brass band. Of course I wasn't going to be a gravedigger, that was Mr Walls's responsibility and he shouldered it with a kind of sombre pride, even when he was using the mechanical digger. My first task was mulching manure into the rose beds, which was every bit as strenuous and smelly as I could have imagined, had I ever imagined myself doing any physical labour that involved shovelling shit. The only thing that kept me going was toting up my hourly wage and the prospect of countering my dad's assertion that I'd 'never done a hand's turn'. My mum had put the water on so I could have a bath when I got home, but even so, the next day I was aching all over. But at least nobody from school had seen me.

The next week was better. My lying time was almost up and

the record shop in Ayr was exerting its call. I caught myself enjoying clipping the long grass from around the headstones; it gave me a chance to read what they said, to scout for familiar names and ones that seemed more exotic than any I'd heard in the present day town. Not that it was much of a cemetery, no memento moris, nothing going back much further than the industrial revolution. By the time I volunteered to go up a ladder and scrub the bird shit from the Celtic cross, old Mr Walls was entirely won over, anticipating spending less time supervising and more inside his cottage drinking tea and watching the racing.

When the weather got warmer the far right hand corner of the cemetery became a sheltered little suntrap where I'd sit and eat my packed lunch, watching a pair of chaffinches carrying morsels to their chirruping nest deep inside the clematis that shrouded a trellis arch over one of the headstones. I'd re-painted the bench myself, thick brushstroke after thick brush-stroke.

Bugger that for a game of soldiers, Mr Walls said when I asked if I should strip it first. You'll have every wee tyke for miles in here if you bring out the solvent or the burner. Just sand it down a bit and slap fresh stuff on.

Although I didn't tell Luke the whole story, sitting there in the student union, nursing my pint of cider and worrying about money, the images flashed through my mind. How the paint had formed hot and comforting blisters as I lazed there during that last summer, before I left the town behind me for good.

12

Waking in the morning after a bottle and a half of wine, with his muscles still aching from the drive and the run, Richard had a numb pain in his head and throbbing sinuses. He could hear Stephie mumbling something on the landing, as she and Loren crossed paths outside the bathroom, and he remembered Stephie turning down the music on her iPod when he'd walked into the kitchen the night before, the way he'd felt like somebody dressed for a wedding who's ill-advisedly gone on to a nightclub. And then opening more wine as Stephie apologised and said the chicken would be ready in just another ten minutes, and then another. He wouldn't have cared about food when he was her age.

'Richard,' he heard her say at the door. 'Are you awake?'

I am now, he thought, swinging his legs out the bed and going to see what she wanted.

'Morning,' Stephie said, looking brighter than he felt she had any right to, given that when he'd retired the cork was popping from yet another bottle of wine. 'Bit rough, are we?'

'I'm fine,' he said, wondering how long Loren would take in the shower.

'Ha, I've never seen you stubbly before,' she said. 'So, we're going to get the boat today like you said, so you'll have peace to work on your elves and goblins.'

'Infantrymen and officers,' he said, guilt starting to niggle him already. He should have been at his desk earlier.

'Whatever. Anyway, I thought we'd maybe go into the village after that and get something to eat in the pub, okay?'

'Sure.'

'But I can ring you and let you know where we are in case you get fed up and want to come and meet us.'

'Don't worry. I'm sure I'll be able find you if I want to,' he said. 'But thanks.'

He opened the blinds in his bedroom and flopped back down on the bed until at last he heard Stephie and Loren leaving the house, their voices outside mingling with the cries of the seabirds. After he'd showered and shaved he pushed open the door to the spare room that they were sharing. Duvets hastily pulled up over both beds, clothes swinging from chairs, bottles and tubes and compacts mushrooming along the dressing table. He remembered pushing his trolley round Ikea, assembling the room in his mind. Collecting white throws for each bed, a sheepskin rug for the floor between them, long gauzy curtains. Despite his efforts, the residue of the holiday cottage the house had once been remained: the floral drawer liners, the abundance of satin-covered clothes hangers, the crocheted antimacassar on the chair. Lucky for him that the owner had got a job overseas and wanted an easy long term let rather than the hassle of arranging weekly cleaning and linen changes.

Richard made coffee and took it to his desk, opening the French doors and taking a few deep breaths to help clear his head while his computer started up. The boat was already halfway across to Tanera Mhor, though it would loop round the other islands before returning to dock there, allowing the tourists close up views of the seal colony and the nesting birds. If Stephie and Loren were on the starboard side looking towards the mainland they'd see the house now, although they'd be too far away to make out Richard standing in the doorway. He watched the boat for a few moments, then wandered down to the mailbox by the gate. Phone bill, the new edition of Game Developer, nothing forwarded by his mother, nothing bearing the university crest. He was on the patio before he heard the phone ringing and ran towards his study, where the answering machine was absorbing an apparently pointless stream of consciousness from Rupe.

'Pick up please Rich. Where are you at this time on a Sunday, church? Bollocks. You've probably been gored by a Highland cow or something but if not, please call back.

You'll get me at home until let me see, two or so, then I'm heading to the airport . . .'

Richard lunged for the phone, 'Rupe, sorry . . . I was in the garden.'

'I hope you've washed your hands. You do have running water up there, don't you?'

'I've told you before Rupe. The toilet is inside, the septic tank is outside.'

'Septic tank. Marvellous. I love it. Sooo, did you enjoy our little social the other evening?'

'Great thanks Rupe. Though I heard you had a bit of bother later on.'

Using light keystrokes that wouldn't be picked up by the telephone mouthpiece, Richard typed the word 'wanker' four times in a row as Rupe spoke.

'Oh . . . yah. Bloody Chris from Sony, I told him that lapdancing isn't what we go in for at DaCapo but he was like a man possessed.'

Surveying the row of 'wankers', Richard punctuated it with a 'dickhead', then deleted the whole thing. 'You'd think he'd know that kind of thing can be actionable,' he said.

'Actionable?'

'Mmm,' Richard said, experimenting with a 'bawbag'.

'God, I didn't think . . . but no, Lise was there, can't be discrimination if there's a woman present.'

'I think that's kind of the point, Rupe.'

Rupe snorted. 'No, Lise is a good sport. Not chippy. Not like Tuula,' he said darkly. 'Must be a Nordic thing.'

'Anyway,' Richard said, 'what can I do for you?'

'The thing is Rich, I'm worried.'

'Uhuh?'

'Yep. What we've got here with *Somme* is effectively a first person shooter. I mean, everyone's going to play the officer, aren't they?'

'Not necessarily,' Richard said. The strategy elements of the game were compromised by established character relations, resulting in limited options: to follow orders or not, to face court marshal or go AWOL. The most satisfying dynamic was team play, your comrades around you.

'Okay. But it's set in the First World War, Rich. Are we too old-fashioned to be cutting edge? The really big markets are out east. Think of China. They like fantasy scenarios there.'

Richard sighed. Rupe's nerves always tended to kick in around pre-production. 'WWI is totally underdeveloped, we know that. In terms of visuals, speed and playability this is going to far exceed the games that are already out there. So let's just wait for the play-testing. That'll highlight any tweaks that need done.'

'I know this is your baby, but as it is, we're not sure it's enough.'

'We?'

'Yep, that's from Lars as well. It's got to get edgier. Ex Soviet bloc's still cool. So's organised crime and hunting for war criminals.'

'Electronic Arts is already running with all that, I'm afraid,' Richard said. His sinuses felt like they were going to burst.

'Just get on the case, Richard. Lars has been in touch with Hamburg. He's interested in what they've done over there.'

'It's the same game, Rupe. They're just working with the opposing POV.'

'Well, apparently they've taken it up a notch. Look, we both want this green lit, don't we?'

'Obviously,' Richard said.

'Great. I'm back Wednesday pm,' Rupe said. 'Get some thoughts to me by then. Ciao.'

Fuck, Richard thought. He felt like returning to his bed and sleeping off the remainder of his headache, lying there on smooth sheets as he'd done as a child with flu, his duvet a buffer against the outside world. Instead he went to the kitchen, filled the expresso maker with water and tamped ground coffee down in the sieve. 'There's no place for the auteur in game design,' or so Bill, his favourite lecturer, used to say. 'It's teamwork all the way.' Richard might have pitched the idea but he wasn't doing the graphics or writing the dialogue or pulling it all together into one complete entity. The bottom line was that if Lars wanted edgy, he got edgy. His employees referred to him as 'God' in their private correspondence; not God the creator, God the publisher.

When the pot started hissing Richard poured out a stream of tarry coffee and added extra sugar. He had to kickstart his brain somehow. Deciding another blast of fresh air would help, he went outside, where the atmosphere was annoyingly sleepy and Sunday-feeling, a day for lounging with the paper and looking at the view. When he'd told Andy from his course that he'd found a great house up north and was going to head up there to finish his first commission, Andy had been appalled.

'Don't you understand? We don't go and live in the countryside. We stay in cities! And then years later, when we get civilized, we find a house in Prestwick or Troon and get big, butch dogs. Wear matching outfits and allow ourselves to put on a few extra pounds.'

Richard had laughed. 'Another small town? God forbid. I'd rather be in the middle of nowhere.'

'Just as long as it's the arse end of nowhere, eh?' Andy had said, with a camp cackle that made Richard feel embarrassed that they'd slept together, even if it had just been the once, after their final projects had been handed in.

Remembering this embarrassment, allowing it to return, generated enough anxious adrenalin to propel him back to his desk. He clicked open every file relating to *Somme*, watched the icons chase each other along the task bar. How were you supposed to make war edgier than it already was? With mercenaries, black markets, abuses of power? He began to pick through his flowcharts and mock-ups, highlighting each point where a decision could be altered, a wild card played.

By the time the light started to fade outside, he felt he was losing sight of his ideal of OFFICER, being press-ganged into making the character less complex, less moral, than he had been in prototype. Richard remembered quiet times late at night when he was studying at Dundee, the hours spent learning how programming could create new worlds, how whorls of code could twist and turn into three-dimensional characters capable of speech and action. Music playing in the background, his anxiety at his change of direction dissolving as he immersed himself in his first attempts at level design and embraced his inner geek. Was that really how it had been? Or had he been waiting, subconsciously perhaps, for the knock at the door, for the suggestion of something more exciting, more real?

0

Did you ever think you'd end up here, Luke said. There was an edge to his voice that made me think he wasn't talking about loitering in a bedroom at a party, once again courtesy of Cowley, Farquarson and Green. We were leaning against the wall by a bay window while around us fellow students cradled bottles and six packs with jealous intent. Next to me was a desk with a computer and an shelved alcove full of smooth-spined textbooks. I'd queued for an hour that morning to type my essay at the undergrad cluster, after waiting a week for the books I needed from the library. And when I got them someone had underlined even the most banal quotes with a blue biro.

There's simply no point in renting a flat, said an authoritative voice close to us. You're throwing money down the drain every month and ultimately you have nothing to show for it.

I know, said Sara, our hostess. Have some Prosecco. My parents sent a case for my birthday party, but it didn't arrive on time.

That's a very good excuse for another party, I said to her when she reached Luke and I with her Prosecco.

She patted me on the arm as if I was a favourite pony rather than just a pet homosexual, then leaned in closer and whispered to Luke, Guess what?

What, he said, smiling and raising his glass to her.

Katie split up with her boyfriend! Quite right too, if you ask me. No point in a long distance relationship.

Maybe we should just finish the bottle for you, Luke said, guiding her hand to top up his glass again. She fluttered her eyelashes, just a little, as if flirting on behalf of her friend, and called out, Guy darling, be a sweetie and open another bottle for me, will you?

Look at them all, Luke said, when she'd gone. With their flats and their cars and their fucking easy fucking lives.

I thought I saw the angry sparkle of moisture in his eyes, but he was a little drunk, and we'd halved a pill earlier then taken another when we'd arrived and seen the same old snobby faces. I reached out and gripped his arms, just above the wrist, felt the soft hair and the sinew underneath.

Coming up? he said, and I nodded. His fingers reached around my wrists in return, and we stood like that for a moment or two, talking about something else, something inconsequential.

I could see newly-single Katie glancing towards us, towards Luke. She was wearing her embroidered top again, this time with a denim miniskirt that revealed bare, tanned legs. I didn't think the tan was natural. She smiled and started to walk towards us but he turned away and said to me, You know, I don't think I like that sort of thing after all.

We both gazed out of the window at the street, dim and empty below us.

No? I said, the damp den under the bridge flickering through my mind, how afterwards I'd walked Wendy to the end of her street without either of us saying a word. How Luke had asked, did you do it, did you fuck her?

Lay there like a sack of tatties, he said. No wonder her boyfriend's dumped her.

Reflected in the window, I saw Katie walking away from us. She couldn't have heard him, with the music so loud, but the slight was unmistakeable.

Later on, inhibitions relaxed, I got caught in conversation with a nice boy called Julian, who'd also been captivated by that infamous adaptation of Brideshead Revisited.

I hope you don't mind my asking, he said, but when did you realise you were, you know . . .

Gay? I said.

Yes, he said, and smiled at me so brightly that I was sure my luck was in. All that eye contact, the way he brushed against me.

Oh, I said, I suppose I've always known.

When he said he was finding the party too hot and noisy I

agreed wholeheartedly and said I didn't want to stay too late anyway.

Will we walk together, he said, a little shyly, and in my mind I punched the air in triumph.

I'll just say goodbye to my friend, I said, nodding over to where Luke was standing with a blonde girl who appeared to be trying to corral him against the wall.

Oh yes, Julian said. What's his name again?

Luke.

Of course! Good Samaritan or Prodigal Son, what do you reckon?

Couldn't hazard a guess, I said, and Julian laughed and held my arm just for a second as he said he'd wait on me outside. When I turned round Luke had gone. I walked along the hallway, glancing into each room. In one bedroom, Sara stood with her hands on Katie's shoulders, trying to quell her drunken sobs.

What do you expect, darling, I heard her say, from someone of that sort?

I found Luke in the kitchen, twisting the cork from another bottle of Prosecco.

Are you off then? he said, excusing himself from his blonde companion. Have fun. He was looking me straight in the eye, a half smile playing across his lips.

I will, I said, determined not to look away until he did. He gave in to the smile but it was me that broke the gaze, aware that Julian was waiting for me, not wanting to miss my chance. But I hesitated and said, I saw Katie. Crying.

He sighed and looked pained. Collateral damage.

Oh, I said, and turned to go but he called me back. Yes? I said.

Will you go back to his?

I think so, I said. I knew Julian had a room in a flat, and surely that was more appealing than my wire-framed single bed in Herrick.

Is Calum still ill?

Complicated by his asthma, poor sod, I said, then caught his drift. Want my spare key? I'll take it off the ring for you.

Yeah?

No probs. Just remember, Calum's bed's the one on the left, eh?

He pulled his key chain from his pocket and clipped my spare key onto it, then squeezed my shoulder.

You're a superstar, he said. I'll knock first. Just in case.

Julian was waiting for me by the door, talking to one of his friends from choir, a toothily enthusiastic girl who didn't seem to have a clue what was going on (or perhaps she had more idea than me). Julian and I walked along the promenade in the direction of his flat, then spent the best part of an hour sitting on the bandstand in testicle-shrivelling cold while he banged on about something amorous or, depending on your point of view, abusive, that had happened at school and whether it might possibly mean he had gay tendencies. What did I think, he asked. I said something soothing, while feeling resentful and used, and wondered if Luke was getting on better with the blonde he'd been cosying up to when I left. In desperation I put my hand on Julian's thigh, in a gesture that could've been construed as simple affection. From the way he tensed and froze, I knew the game was a bogey. I walked him home as promised, and we exchanged manly hugs at the door while he thanked me for being so understanding.

A damp chill had come in over the sea and was skirling around the buildings, fingering its way under my clothes as I started walking back the way I'd come. I pulled my jacket closer around me but still chose the long route to Herrick. Walking at night was still a novelty, being ill-advised at best back home. Here I could indulge myself with dimly lit rambles over the cobblestones and down the back streets, peering between railings and in lighted windows. I never felt so close and curious when the streets were crowded, so many other lives displayed in daylight. Besides, even though I'd crashed and burned with Julian, I was trying to wear out the tingling, buzzing feeling that insisted it was too soon to go to bed, that something might still happen, a chance encounter in the magical hinterland between where I'd been and where I was going.

Three weeks before, emboldened by my 'little brunette', as Luke had called him, I'd succeeded in picking up a French postdoc who was over for a conference. He'd walked past me as I was sitting on a bench on the front one evening, watching the waves, doubled back and asked if I had a light. A clichéd pattern, I suppose, but at the time it felt deliciously Wildean. The memory warmed me as I walked. We'd gone back to his hotel, where he displayed an exhaustive – and exhausting – sexual vocabulary that suggested that pornography was truly international, describing in precise, present tense English everything we did. It had the opposite effect to the one he intended, imbuing our liaison with a childlike innocence that nonetheless I managed to overcome. He kept calling me 'Rick', which he pronounced 'Reek': this is your cock here, Reek, you would like me to touch it, Reek? Oui, Patrick, s'il vous plaît, I said, and he laughed at my accent and formal construction. After a very thorough night amid the chintz, I crept away, too uncertain of form and wary of discovery to wait until Patrick woke up.

No such luck, tonight. I heard laughter and raucous shouts from over towards The Yards, but the only person I saw was a man who might have been wearing pyjamas under his coat, waiting with his hands thrust in his pockets as an elderly bulldog sniffed around the trunk of one of the barren cherry trees on College Road. He looked as if he was on the brink of alerting neighbourhood watch so I said good evening, which made him frown. My Ayrshire accent was slipping, I knew, as I tried to be understood in tutorials, and somehow I made such pleasantries sound downright sarcastic. I cut down Minister's Vennel, doubtless arousing the man's suspicions even more. The wind whistled and swooped down between the narrow walls, and fallen leaves made the cobbles slimy underfoot. Guessing that chance meetings were likely to be thin on the ground, I picked up pace. I wondered if Luke was still at the party, or if maybe he'd gone home alone. I'd seen him accept a jolly slap on the back from Guy, who turned out not only to be whatever in line to the throne but Honourable to boot; noticed too their retreat into a corner and the interplay of folded banknote and something slipped in the pocket of the Honourable's pale blue jeans. Next to him Luke was all edgy allure, in his drainpipes and Sonic Youth t-shirt.

Soon the streetlamps I'd found so charming when I first came to university seemed to cast an eerie, moth-filled light. If Luke was already back, I'd go to the TV room. At least it would be warm there. My restlessness had transformed itself into nerves, and I was glad to emerge onto the wider street which curved round to meet the back way to Herrick. I climbed the stairs to the attic level with some trepidation, knocked lightly on my door. I needn't have worried. Luke wasn't there.

I was just dozing off when I heard the click of the Yale lock. I opened my eyes ever so slightly, saw the angle of light from the corridor shooting across the floor. I was about to say Luke's name when I heard him whisper:

It's all right, he's asleep.

There was a silent hesitation, then his voice again.

He sleeps like the dead. Honest.

The door closed behind them and I felt the darkness deepen, then his bed creaked once, and again, and there was a moist noise of kissing then a sigh. I'll roll over and mumble, I thought, as if I'm about to wake up. They'll get the message and go away. But before I had a chance there were two quick zipping sounds followed by soft thuds, as if someone had taken off a pair of boots, an almost giggle then a shooshing noise.

I thought you said he slept like the dead, she whispered. I couldn't tell if it was the blonde girl or not.

He does, Luke said. But take it easy anyway, yeah?

A second later I heard the clink of change and the drop of first one fifty pence piece then another in the slot for the electric bar fire. Small mercies, I thought, having been too frugal to feed the heater when I'd stumbled in earlier. Moving ever so slowly, I tried to get my right ear under the duvet. Nevertheless I still heard the rustle of bedclothes falling to the floor and a succession of ghastly smoochy noises. After a while she said:

Hang on. You've got a ragged nail or something.

Sorry, he said, and a little later I heard a sharper noise from her, and then he groaned, and the bed started to creak as they moved. Right, I thought, that's it. They're the ones who should be mortified. I'll cough politely then say, excuse me, but would you mind doing that elsewhere? I'm trying to sleep. The bed kept on creaking and I found myself thinking of the muscles in his arms, how they'd tauten to bear his weight.

Oh god, I thought I heard him say, so swiftly I could hardly make it out. She made a noise which was cut off as though she'd been muffled, and a new note entered the creaking as his pace quickened and one of the springs twanged in protest. I pictured the metal straining under the combined pressure of bodies, the way the wire mesh would stretch and distort underneath the mattress. Then the noise stopped and he said:

Turn over.

There was a flurry of stifled giggling, then he said:

Please.

After some disturbance and undecipherable whispering, I heard him make a noise, a gasp, I suppose it was, a sound of such startling intimacy that I felt ashamed, almost, to have overheard it. The girl said in a louder voice: No, no, I can't.

Luke said something soothing, and I heard her say no again, so that it sounded like an apology. After a few seconds the creaking started again, coupled with the twang of the spring. His breathing was very clear now, and I could imagine – couldn't help but imagine – the sweep of his back, the muscles in his thighs. Embarrassment, or fear, quelled my erection but when I heard him utter an abrupt and wordless groan it firmed again until the desire to get some kind of relief was almost unbearable. Except I knew, lying there with every sinew stretched, that there was nothing I could do.

As they quietened I realised I'd forgotten all about keeping my own breathing steady, but as I tried to regain the right tempo I must have inhaled a stray feather from my pillow because all of a sudden I knew I was going to sneeze. The sound was smothered under the duvet, but the silence from the other bed suggested it had still been audible. I made a kind of murmuring noise and shifted position, then started breathing even more deeply – and, I hoped, convincingly – than before.

You'd better go, I thought I heard Luke say, and maybe he said my name as well, though now I was tired and groggy. There was shuffling and the floorboard by the sink squeaked and this time my eyelids didn't register the glimmer of light from the corridor outside, though I heard the yawn of the door opening. My muscles were still tense, but I didn't realise it until I felt them relax with the click of the snib. A little later on I thought I heard a whisper:

Richard?

I stayed still, kept concentrating on my breathing, slow and deep.

You're awake, aren't you?

But by then I was slipping in and out of sleep, and I might have imagined or dreamed that Luke was speaking, that I heard him laugh quietly to himself. Maybe it was the same as after a nightmare; you lie there frozen, forcing your eyes to stay closed, thinking you'll never sleep again. And the next thing you know it's morning, and the night before seems intangible, unreal.

13

A new set of possibilities for OFFICER rampaged across
Richard's computer screen, ones which would allow the character to sacrifice his men to protect himself rather than vice
versa. And COLONIAL, he could now seek revenge for
injustices perpetrated by his supposed superiors. WOMAN
might be a bloodthirsty psychopath, or else unveiled and
transformed into a damsel in distress, ripe for rescue. And
why shouldn't romance blossom between OFFICER and
INFANTRYMAN? Lars wanted edgy, didn't he, and that
would offer a nice twist for the hetero gamer, take them 'out of
their comfort zone'; something which was, according to marketing, desirable within the genre. Richard scrawled a two-way
arrow between the two on his mind map. There were plenty of
means of dying: by mortar, by bayonet, by blood poisoning, by
gas, by drowning. He scored the last option out – flooding the
trenches was too complex, too thorough – and returned to the
character flowcharts, each one still lunging towards blank
white space. Escape was unfeasible: there was nowhere to
go. Even if the geographical boundaries of the game were
extended further across Europe the action would become
meaningless if an AWOL character successfully evaded the
military police and kept going, alone. It would turn into
another game entirely, one with new territories and new modes
of play.

Richard's headache had returned, though it was now more
to do with frustration than any residue of excess alcohol from
the night before. He had a sudden urge to bring up a website
he knew, as a reward for working so late, but he couldn't look
at anything like that when his sister might come back at any
moment. His sister and her friend. The only thing worse would
be his mother. He'd never forget her inopportune delivery of

his ironed school shirt, without knocking on his bedroom door. At least the magazine he'd been looking at had women in it, even if he had been trying to obscure them with his free hand in order to concentrate on the various disembodied appendages that were approaching them from beyond the edge of the page. His father had defended him, relieved perhaps by the apparent evidence of his son doing 'just what boys do, Moira'.

As Richard backed up his files he checked the time. Rab made his last journey back from the island at quarter past six, docking at quarter to seven at the latest, and it was now approaching eleven. Tourists often assumed that the proprietors of isolated establishments liked nothing more than presiding over all night binges, but George the landlord was more likely to call last orders at ten than keep serving into the wee small hours. Richard thought of the bottle of Sancerre nestling on top of the vegetable drawer in the fridge, of splashing some of the icy wine into a glass and taking a sip. But Stephie and Loren, unused to the blanketing darkness of the countryside, might phone asking for a lift home. He'd driven back from the picnic at the beach with meticulous care, knowing he was over the limit. Smashing a headlamp on the tight turn onto the small bridge was considered the most likely pitfall of driving under the influence, especially as the Northern Constabulary had recently completed their quarterly purge, but Richard had been conscious of Stephie lolling in the passenger seat and he hadn't forgotten George's nephew Davy. It was 'gey unlucky', people said, that he'd taken a corner at speed and skited on black ice. That stretch of road was unforgiving, rocky outcrops on the one side and a drop to the sea loch on the other. He'd hit his head, they said, unconscious at least before the car went into the water.

Wishing he'd left his computer on, Richard rotated the dial on the radio through a cacophony of poor reception before rejecting a sententious religious programme which seemed to be the only comprehensible option. He'd have to read, something soothing and familiar that would help him wind down. He scanned the meagre array of fiction squatting between his sensible histories and biographies. Yellowing paperbacks bought in the secondhand bookshop when he was at uni, often with an eye to Luke's taste as much as his own: Gogol and Kerouac, Camus and Ballard. Drawn to a familiar silver spine Richard plucked a book from the shelf and allowed it to flop open where the binding had broken. He skimmed the page until a line leapt up to stall him. A description of 'that faint, unrecognised apprehension that here, at last, I should find that low door in the wall, which others, I knew, had found before me, which opened on an enclosed and enchanted garden, which was somewhere, not overlooked by any window, in the heart of that grey city'. How those words had resonated in his mind, once upon a time, when he'd searched for just such a low door in the wall of his university town, ready to stoop and enter, willing himself to be enchanted.

A crash and the clamour of voices startled Richard. He could hear Stephie's voice rising exasperated into what sounded like the two syllables of her friend's name. Then, more distinctly: 'For fuck's sake'. He dithered, closing the book and putting it back on the shelf, collecting his empty coffee cup from his desk, taking care to close his study door as noisily as possible. In the kitchen he found Stephie sitting at the table looking thunderous while Loren swayed against the worktop, hacking at the foil around the neck of the Sancerre. He watched her drop the corkscrew and realised she was likely to stab herself; there was also something pathetic in her clumsiness that made him say, 'Just what I was about to do,' and take the bottle from her.

'It's been a tough day,' he said to Stephie, as if to justify his intrusion. She accepted a glass of wine and didn't say anything when he handed one to Loren as well. He'd seen that look on his sister's face before, when she'd been biting her tongue rather than answering back to their father.

'So, have you two been enjoying the bright lights then?'

Loren started pulling at a scrap of skin by one of her nails. Her mascara had run, Richard noticed, smearing down to her cheekbones. He tried again: 'Maris Arms or the Royal Hotel?'

'Well,' Stephie said. 'We started in the Maris because we reckoned the food would be cheaper and then we went to the Royal because we reckoned it'd be open later.'

'Only for guests,' Richard said.

Stephie rolled her eyes at his pedantry and said, 'Not that it would have made any difference given that we got thrown out.'

'I just wanted,' Loren said, standing up and veering towards the door, 'I just wanted to get fucked, that's all. It's not a fucking crime you know.'

Still cradling her glass, she stopped at the door and asked of neither of them in particular, 'How come I always spoil things? I just need to touch something and it's ruined.'

'Go to bed, Loren,' Stephie said, and Richard noticed that her knuckles were white where she was squeezing the stem of her glass. 'Sleep it off.'

Loren swerved around the open door and they heard her clump across the hall and up a few stairs. There was a pause, then she clumped back into the room and said, 'I'm sorry Stephie. If I could go back . . .'

'Just go to bed. Please.'

Richard avoided looking at Loren as she left the room again, listened to her tread across the landing to the spare bedroom. Stephie got up and closed the door.

'What was that all about?' Richard said.

'Who knows? She's just being self-obsessed again.' Stephie leaned against the back of her chair.

'When she said 'get fucked'?'

'She didn't mean drunk. She was managing that perfectly well already.'

'So what happened?'

Stephie gave an exasperated groan. 'I don't know, maybe it was the wrong point in her menstrual cycle or something. She was really going for it with the drink, then she spotted some guy in the hotel that she liked the look of, only it turned out he was there with his fiancée, but she'd turned in early. Let's just say, Loren doesn't like to take no for an answer.'

'Ah.'

'So she chucked a pint over him, he called her a mad bitch, she decked him, his friend had to intervene . . . oh god, it was unbelievable. I did apologise, honestly, but we were out on our ear and it's taken me a fucking hour to haul her up the road.'

'You should have called me.'

'Och, I felt I'd pushed my luck already. Besides, she

132

might've been sick in the back of the Lotus Esprit out there.' She gestured towards the window, then paused, listening for any more noise from upstairs.

'Maybe she's passed out,' Richard said. 'Should you help her into bed?'

'The way she was earlier, she's lucky I didn't help her into the fucking sea. You'd have thought fresh air would have a sobering effect.' She sighed and spread her hands out on the table in front of her, pressing her palms down against the varnished wood. 'She can't really help it, I suppose. She's had a lot going on, I guess it just comes out like that sometimes.'

What a convenient notion, Richard thought, that your behaviour could be completely outwith your control. 'At least she apologised,' he said.

Stephie started to speak, then got up and opened the fridge door. 'Got anything to eat?'

'That white bowl's got some leftover pasta in it.'

Stephie took it out and lifted the plate which covered it, peering underneath as though mistrustful of what she might find. 'Is that pesto or mould?' she said, prodding it with a fork.

'Pesto.'

'Hmmph.' She annointed the contents of the bowl with salt and pepper and returned to the table, where she speared each farfalle in turn and put it in her mouth. Richard was reminded of old school space invaders games, where a stationary shooter eliminated the opposition one spacecraft at a time. Chasing the last butterfly round the bowl Stephie said, 'She wasn't apologising for tonight.'

'No?' Richard got up and went to the fridge to top up his wine.

Without looking over at him she said, 'No. She slept with my boyfriend. We've split up now.' She balanced her fork across the top of the bowl. 'I really liked him.'

Richard stood with the bottle in his hand, moved to top up her glass.

'I'm okay, thanks,' she said, putting her hand over it.

He wedged the cork back in and put the bottle away. 'Are you okay with her being here, really?' he said. 'I mean, I can find some excuse, make up some other visitors, anything.'

Stephie nodded. 'It's fine. Really fine.'

'That's all right then. It was just in case . . .' he trailed off, not sure what he was going to say.

'Well, I would say that a friendship is more important than being in a relationship that's going nowhere with someone who's turned out to be a twat, wouldn't you?'

'I suppose so.'

They sat in silence for a moment, the house seeming very still, as if the darkness outside was pressing down on it, muffling the small night sounds of gurgling pipes and clicking appliances.

'It's either that or lose both of them,' Stephie said, getting up and rinsing her dish then slotting it in to the dishwasher. 'I'm going to turn in now as well.'

'I can make up a bed on the couch, if you want. If you don't want to sleep in the same room.'

'Nah,' she said, 'You're all right. And I'm sorry, about causing a scene in your local. Don't want to get you barred as well.'

'Doesn't matter,' he said. 'I always preferred the Maris anyway.'

Stephie came up behind Richard and put her arms around him, resting her chin on his shoulder. He patted her elbows, then squeezed back, locking her to him in a tight hug.

0

After eighteen disconsolate years, the job in the cemetery had made me feel as if finally I'd forged some connection with my hometown. Laid some claim, or had some claim laid on me. There were my antecedents, after all, lying in neat rows which I strimmed and trimmed, scooping up the clippings and dumping them on the compost heap behind the Celtic cross which listed the fallen sons of the parish. 1916 and 1918 particularly fine vintages, it seemed, of that easy-flowing red. I imagined them in uniform, not fresh-faced but already darkened and coughing from a few years down the pit. Boys no older than the century, with the lungs of sixty-a-day men. I could see the bunting strung out as the town gathered to hasten them. No conscientious objectors here, when the decision was made it was made mob-handed. Your occupation protected, essential to the war effort? Nae bother, you knew where your duty lay. Forget your sweetheart, your children, your mother, you would not be called coward in this town, even if you had to grow gangrenous and rot in the muddy blood to prove it.

By the time I deadheaded those daffs and yanked out the horsetails, well, by then the poof and the Asian were there to be vilified, and it didn't matter if your only acts of bravery took place in the Whitehill Colliery Social Club. Heart attacks, strokes and cancers had taken the place of the roof falls, explosions, and plummets down the shaft engraved on the memorial stones the Company sponsored. The ones the mothers didn't get to see, identified by stoic fellow workers who sat silent with pint after pint that night, hating their relief that it was a boy, not them. Archibald 'Erchie' Carden (Elder of the Tent of Rechabites), sorely missed. He fell a month short of his retirement, after fifty long years. Could he not live without it?

My taste for melodrama knew no bounds. I searched for grimy glamour under every piece of gravel I combed, becoming fascinated by the failed escapes. The boy from the Royal Drake. A stoker, no less, he used skills honed here, stayed camouflaged with coal dust, the whites of his eyes tired and gleaming in the red light of the fire he fed. Could he tell if the coal he shovelled was hewn and hauled by his father, his uncle, their father in turn? Did it have a distinctive patina, leave a familiar stain upon the skin? I liked his pristine white headstone with its anchor and a rope; once I made a posy from stray carnations to lay alongside it. A crush on a boy who'd died decades before I was born. Pretty desperate, I know.

By the time the summer was drawing in I could glimpse my new life in the changing light, in the first of the fallen leaves I raked up in preparation for the oldsters who ambled along after church on Sunday. The peace of the cemetery seemed to lull them, easing them into the tug of their mortality. Some relatives didn't come at all, of course; the In Loving Memory vase empty save for a few desiccated stalks, no bulbs to pop up spring after spring. It was up to me to remove the crisp poke, the snagged condom.

So my thoughts spiralled as I sat in the fug of the Drumrigg bus, heading home for the promised mid-term visit. I looked out over the fields, where furrows of dark earth were highlighted with frost and mist drifted around the trees and hedgerows. In the distance I saw a dark shape, the old pithead rising behind a small copse. Preserved as a monument, though I wasn't sure who visited it. Old men maybe, walking their wee dugs and prodding chips of pelt and fractured Buckfast bottles with their sticks; and teenagers of course, like Kenny Dodd, who'd been cremated rather than laid to rest. I missed Luke already, I realised, was jealous of his trip to Edinburgh, his plans for sweaty clubs and new drugs.

It was mid-afternoon when I got off the bus. My parents would be at work and I guessed Stephanie was still at school, or sitting on the wall of the petrol station watching the cars whip by on their way somewhere else. As I walked from the pissy bus depot along to the war memorial I felt that it wasn't my town, not any more. Apart from a handful of summer afternoons spent behind the high walls of the cemetery it never had been. These places don't adapt. Their neat, straight, stone rows, built for a purpose, seem aimless when the purpose is taken away. The net curtains yellow in the windows, withered gardens and ramshackle sheds mourn the proud hobbies of grown men; cultivating roses and canaries, building intricate ships from matchsticks and glue. This town fell asleep, the headstone would say, Jesus said come. Mr Sim's terraced cottage lay empty, I noticed, and I wondered if he'd finally messed with the wrong boy, resolved to check the cemetery, just in case.

I followed Victoria Street, taking the route of the men in collarettes and gloves whose parades were framed on the walls of the local library. Named for the empire, for success and prosperity, it climbed the hill towards the edge of the town, beyond Louisa Row, built to celebrate a pit boss's firstborn. The houses stopped but I kept going, past the Catholic church and its primary school, past the last local bus stop, until I reached the cemetery. The gate was closed but unlocked, an officious council sign announcing the opening hours. Metal grilles covered the windows of Mr Walls' redbrick cottage. He'd been moved to the sheltered housing in Drumrigg, I'd heard. Staying on after retirement wasn't done anymore, no keepers lived within the bounds of parks or cemeteries these days; besides, he'd told my dad that he'd seen enough funerals to last him a lifetime.

Well, sure enough, a late addition to the (ssh, don't tell anyone) reused plots by the back wall. J. Sim. 47 years. And at the bottom, bluntly: Erected by his brother. I was surprised he hadn't been burnt, but some small traditions lived on amongst the Baptist community out there, like the lingering suspicion that you'd need your corporal remains on the day of judgement. Even if, by their standards, your damnation was pretty much a done deal. Just visible despite vigorous scrubbing by the council graffiti task force, I discovered his epitaph: Sucks cocks.

Is it any wonder that after spending so many of my young

days surrounded by death, I developed an appetite for living? There wasn't much living to be done there, in that stultifying place, so I was poised and eager to make up for lost time later on. I just needed someone to help show me the way.

14

When they reached the shop Stephie said, 'Let's walk further. To the garage.'

'Don't you have to get started?' Richard looked at his watch.

'Yeah, but I need the exercise. So do you.'

Richard stared at her. 'But I'm always out running . . .'

'I was joking,' she said.

'Oh,' he said, looking up to where the tips of the mountains slipped through pale drifts of cloud. It wouldn't rain yet, though the sky was darker further inland. 'What about Loren?'

Stephie shrugged. 'Still asleep.'

He nodded, and they kept walking. He thought about saying something about the field system, about the ribbons of land flanked by crumbling dry stane dykes that stretched from the road down towards the sea, but he didn't know if Stephie would be interested. They passed a tough little vegetable patch, half a dozen rows of potatoes and cabbages, a hardy clutch of raspberry canes propped together against the wind and netted for the birds. Alan Campbell had two pigs in a pen, the ground chewed up under their feet, and next to that John McKinnon's boat rested under a navy tarpaulin.

'This reminds me of home, a bit,' Stephie said.

'Does it?'

'Yeah. I mean, not the sea or anything, just the grey houses and the stuff people do. Like the house at the corner before you go into the estate's got a boat outside, and some folk have greenhouses with tomatoes.'

'All that seemed to be dying out, when I left,' Richard said. 'Anyway, at home that's the older folk, isn't it?'

'The ones who read the Advertiser every week.'

'And worry that things have got worse. Most of the town isn't like that now, surely.'

The wind whirled around them and Stephie pushed her hair back from her face. 'And do you think things have got worse?'

Richard shrugged. 'I don't know. It's years since I lived there.'

'They're demolishing the school this summer.'

'Really? Maybe I'll go back to see that.'

'Yeah, they found asbestos in it, or something. But they're going to rebuild it bigger, apparently. Don't know how exactly because they've starting building houses where the playing fields were.'

'Executive homes?' he asked. They were passing the terraced cottages by the primary school. Built to house the teachers and the coastguards, these were now inhabited by the elderly and infirm despite the steep concrete steps that led up to them from the road.

'I guess so,' Stephie said.

'Who'd pay to live there though? It's not as if there's anything to do.'

Stephie shrugged. 'Maybe you've just been spoilt by your experience of the big city. On the subject of which, how was Glasgow?' She looked at him as if she expected him to start blushing.

'Fine,' he said.

'Well, did you have a nice time? You didn't really tell me about it, what with Loren and everything.'

'Nothing to tell,' he said. 'It was a work do. Boring.'

'Hmm.'

They reached the garage and got their messages, Richard introducing Stephie to Evelyn behind the counter as they paid. He felt vindicated, as if the presence of a family member proved something. Evelyn looked at Stephie intently, nodded.

'I guess news travels fast,' Stephie said when they'd returned to the road and started walking again.

'They're pretty tolerant,' Richard said. 'Can't afford for all the white settlers to bugger off home.'

'Will you stay here forever?'

'I'm only just thirty Stephie. I'm not really making forever plans.'

'Maybe you'll hit the big time and move to London or New York or somewhere. Then I can come and visit again.'

An image flickered through Richard's mind, an alternative kind of life, full of people and parties and tall buildings. A hazy figure beside him; tall, with dark hair. A lover perhaps, or boyfriend. 'I wouldn't count on it,' he said. 'It's all changing to brain training for the over fifties and sports stuff for people who can't be bothered going outside.'

'Och, but surely war's always in? I mean, it's not like there aren't any real ones any more.'

Richard sighed. 'Yes, but First World War's a niche market, something to fill the gaps between the Hitler documentaries on UKTV History. Focus groups are more interested in modern war. Iraq, Afghanistan, the Caucasus.'

'But some of them wouldn't be the same if it wasn't for the First World War, would they?'

He smiled. 'You'll be telling me who led the opening attack at Passchendaele next.'

They walked back up the hill, past the tearoom which now had a sign on the gate saying OPEN, and another promising Home Baking, handwritten and slipped in a polypocket which was pinned underneath.

'Cup of tea?' Richard said. 'Scone?'

'Nah, it's all right. We've just bought a bumper pack of Hobnobs.' Stephie said. 'And remember, a moment on the lips . . .'

'Oh Jesus, remember Mum used to say that?'

'Yeah, in between eating bowl after bowl of Special K. It's a miracle I never ended up anorexic. Though it might not have done me that much harm,' she said, slapping her hips.

'You look fine,' Richard said.

'You're just saying that.'

'No, I'm not actually. I think you inherited the good-looking gene, if our family had one.'

Stephie kicked a pebble along the road. 'Loren's pretty though, isn't she?'

Richard chased the stone Stephie had kicked and sent it flying into the ditch by mistake. 'Not especially,' he said. 'Or at least, she's perfectly fine.'

'Guys like her,' Stephie said.

'She drinks a lot,' he said, after a moment.

'Is that a non sequitur?' Stephie said, choosing a new pebble and kicking it with one foot and then the other as they walked. Richard tried to tackle it away from her but she was too fast for him.

'Not quite. I mean, some men find that attractive, I think.' The word 'men' seemed wrong, somehow, in the context of his little sister and her friends, even though they were, he supposed, women. The characters he made in games were men; soldiers, guys with guns, heroes and villains. And his neighbours too, eking their smallholdings into the hard soil.

'You saying she's a drunken slapper?' Stephie said.

'Of course not,' he said, gaining control of the pebble and kicking it extra hard down the hill. 'Ha,' he said.

'She is though,' Stephie said. 'But there's nothing wrong with that.'

'I never said there was,' Richard said. 'I just meant that she doesn't seem to have many inhibitions.'

'Her family are quite well off,' Stephie said.

'Now who's coming out with the non sequiturs?'

They followed the road back round the bay, not stopping to sit on the beam this time, and passed the ruins of the crofts opposite the beach.

'Kind of sad, I always think,' Richard said. 'So many people lived here, once. There was a whole community, shifted to the coast by the clearances.'

'It must've been hellish.'

'Yes. And then I guess some of them emigrated, in the end. Or were forced to emigrate.'

After a moment Stephie said, 'Richard, I read your letter.'

He turned away from the lichen-etched stones and the spikes of marram and lyme that punctuated the sandy belt by the road. 'What letter?'

'I know I shouldn't have but I'd thrown out some notes that I realised I still needed and when I got them out of the recycling your letter was jumbled in with them. I saw his name – Luke's – and got nosy. I'm really sorry.'

'It doesn't matter,' Richard said, surprising himself. 'It wasn't that private.'

'So what are you going to do?'

'What do you mean?'

'Well don't you want to see him again?'

'I don't know,' Richard said. 'It's not as if you can go back in time, is it?'

'Closure?' she said.

'Is that your enlightened psychological opinion or just something cribbed from a women's magazine?'

'For fuck's sake Richard,' she said. 'It isn't exactly rocket science.'

It isn't that simple either, he wanted to say, but instead he quickened his pace so that she had to hurry to stay alongside him, and they walked the rest of the way home in silence.

0

Waiters in aprons and open-necked shirts swerved around tables awash with glasses, brandishing pepper grinders and over-seasoning their banter with *pregos* and *scusis*. One caught my eye, Guiseppe (of course), with his dark stubble and hint of cologne. It was a Thursday night and the Trat – as those who ate out dismissed it – was mobbed. Professor Mendelssohn and Dr Lloyd were at a corner table, lubricating a visiting speaker or external examiner; Yahs were trying to get their dates drunk, the boys' faces glistening in the candlelight and the girls in their skimpy tops going along with it; freshers were basking in the approval of their visiting parents and showing off to younger siblings. I'd thought of bringing my own parents when they came, imagining myself a sleek and suave host (although they, of course, would be paying). But it was too loud, the clientele too removed from that of the lounge bar at their local, the Wheatsheaf Inn, the prices too far in excess of a bar supper. I glugged down more than my share of the first carafe of house red, certain that even if I picked a margarita with no extras everyone else would be indulging in three courses. I shook my head when invited to order a starter, but the warm, savoury smell from the kitchen and the dark-fringed eyes of Giuseppe as he murmured *is very good sir, I recommend,* conspired to make me order the special linguine alle polpette. Late nights, lack of funds and a desire to be skinny and angular had depleted my diet and I was ravenous. Luke was also sticking to a liquid antipasto. He leaned over and refilled my glass, draining the carafe and smiling at the waiter for another, then raised his glass to me with a sardonic incline of his head, as if accepting that it had been his idea to come along.

We'd been walking back from the castle that afternoon when

he'd said, let's go, it might be a laugh. Unlikely, I'd replied, but he'd teased me and prodded me and tried to shove me into the ditch at the side of the road until I started laughing and said, well all right then. Anything to make you happy. Maybe I was trying to prove to myself that no matter how many of these friendly little invitations were thrown our way, it was still a case of us against them. The castle had been cold, frost crackling across the windowpanes, and we'd looked wistfully at the marble fireplace, imagining a warming blaze. I think we both knew our visits were numbered, as I huddled on the chaise-longue with my knees hunched up to my chest and my breath crystallising in the air.

Yah, I heard Guy's voice raised above the others at the far end of the table. We'll be at Val for the hols. The chalet sleeps another two, why don't you tag along?

We go to Colorado usually, said a clipped, East Coast American voice. But I'm willing for a change . . .

Oh yah, said Sara Green, do come along. It'll be super.

The girl to the right of Luke was a doctor's daughter; she'd already instigated that conversation, eager to rank and file her neighbours. I lied and told her that my father was a lawyer and my mother didn't work, which reassured her. She might as well have had a set of crampons strung round her waist, she was so earnest a social climber.

Do you ski, she turned to Luke to ask.

I thought for a split second that he was going to throw his glass of wine over her, but instead he just laughed, oozing scorn. She turned back to more illustrious members of the group, obviously desperate to spear the table with an ice pick and haul herself up and onto the Val d'Isère trip. Luke plucked a piece of bread from the basket and started gnawing on it, then when he'd finished he offered me a cigarette, which allowed me to extricate myself from an increasingly tedious conversation with the girl next to me, who was trying to convince me to come and see the operatic society's Christmas show. Someone at the other end of the table snapped his fingers to attract a waiter. Most of them were offhand with the staff and although I'd tried to compensate by being over-solicitous our pecking order must've been clear to the eye.

Giuseppe and his colleagues weren't impressed. I thought of my parents again, my mum's near-pathological dislike of shellfish, my dad's oft stated belief that pasta was food for women.

Gilbert and Sullivan are irresistible, don't you think? the operatic girl said to Luke instead. And it's The Mikado. That's everyone's favourite. You will come, won't you? I'm one of the three little maids, you know.

I'd rather die, he said with polite restraint that struck me as ersatz, a sarcastic double bluff. His face was flushed, I noticed, and he was drinking faster than usual. He looked dissolute and slatternly and the more I drank, the more I wanted to touch him.

Philistine, the girl announced, her enthusiasm unshaken as she turned to recruit another potential audience member.

Cunt, Luke said. If she heard him, she didn't react. Perhaps it was her operatic training, some kind of stagecraft.

I was starting to feel a little unreal myself, appended to this tableful of people who were so emphatically not my kind of people. The horsey laughs of the girls were getting louder, as they tossed their highlighted hair in response to the boys, who were preening in front of each other as much as for the benefit of the girls, becoming more swollen with self-satisfaction with every glassful. Luke caught my eye and smiled. I smiled back and he nodded, as though in acknowledgment of an expected signal. Just then our plates were put down in front of us, my polpette and his vongole. Luke glanced around the table, where people were already stuffing pizza and garlic bread into their mouths, then looked at me again. As if of one accord, we picked up our plates and stood up. Luke paused, and I thought for a second that he wasn't going to go through with it, but then he reached over and lifted the nearest litre carafe of wine as well.

Buon appetito, he said, and we walked out.

Don't worry, he said to the waiter as we passed, the guy in the white shirt's paying.

It was cold but we walked down towards the harbour and sat on a bench to finish our meal, taking turns to slug red wine from the carafe. It might have seemed romantic, if I hadn't been with Luke, or if Luke hadn't been who he was. The tide was in, the water lapping high against the wall of the harbour. I'd seen seals there once, begging for scraps from the fishing boats.

They're all the fucking same, Luke said. Every last fucking one of them.

I know, I said, passing him the carafe. It looked absurd, out of proportion, and I was going to make a joke of it but didn't. Luke gulped down some wine, wiped his mouth with his hand and said, I hate them.

Me too, I said.

When Luke had finished eating he stood up and braced himself like a discus thrower, then hurled his plate into the harbour. It arced out across the water, the splash of its impact catching in the light from the streetlamps, sending glinting droplets of orange into the darkness.

Yours? he said, holding out his hand.

I'll do it myself, thanks, I said, tracing the logo of the restaurant with my finger. I stood up and launched my own plate out into the darkness as though I was skimming a stone, except that the edge of the plate cut through the water and it sank straight away.

What now, Luke asked.

Let's not go home yet, I said.

15

Rummaging at the back of the cupboard under the sink, Richard found his gardening gloves at last. On his way outside he saw Loren was sprawled along the couch, leafing through one of the back copies of Country Life that had been gathering dust on the bookshelves in the living room.

'These aren't mine, by the way,' he said. 'They came with the house. I've been meaning to put them away in the loft.'

'Why? They're fascinating,' Loren said. She sat up, making room for him beside her. 'Look at this. Isn't it near here?'

The magazine was open at the property section. She indicated a half-page advertisement, a glossy aerial photograph of an island.

'So it is,' Richard said. 'Just round the peninsula. When was that?'

She checked the date. 'Seven years ago.'

'Before I came here then. Wonder if they've got running water yet?'

'Imagine being able to buy an island.'

'Imagine being able to sell an island,' he said. 'That's the thing, isn't it?'

She grinned. 'I suppose it is, yeah.'

'Oh well, I'll leave you to it.' Richard wondered what exactly he meant by this, other than that he didn't know what else to say.

'What're you up to?' she asked.

'My turn to clip the hedge.'

'Sounds urgent.'

'Oh, the folk who own the house on that side,' he pointed, 'are coming up for a week. They're kind of fussy. Can't have their over-privileged kids traumatised by out of control privet.

Also, I feel as though my head'll explode if I sit in front of my computer any longer.'

She smiled. 'Want a hand?'

He hesitated. 'Okay then, that'd be great.'

'No problem.' She stretched her arms then twisted her hair into a topknot that seemed to stay put of its own accord. The magazine slithered to the floor. 'I should do something to earn my keep.'

Richard took the ladder from the shed, and sent Loren to plug in the extension cable. As the afternoon grew warmer, he felt sweat pooling between his shoulder blades and realised that he was enjoying the job, the errant manliness of operating a power tool. He sliced through shoot after shoot of privet, concentrating on achieving an even edge, and the situation with Rupe and *Somme* slipped from his mind. Luke still hovered on the periphery of his thoughts, and Richard wondered how he was spending his day. Did he have a garden, a hedge to clip? A wife, children? Loren darted around below him, scooping up armfuls of cuttings and stuffing them into garden refuse bags, her hands exaggerated and clumsy inside his heavy gloves. The clippers were too noisy to allow conversation, but every now and then he paused to ask if the top of the hedge looked straight. The drive sloped more steeply before it met the road, and the ladder didn't feel as secure as he'd have liked. Clambering onto the top rung to reach further than was safe to lop off one last shoot, he shouted down, 'There, will that do it?'

'Hang on a minute,' she said, and he glanced round and saw that she was pulling her t-shirt over her head. The ladder shifted slightly in the gravel.

'Sorry,' she said, standing back to look at the hedge. Purple bra straps showed on either side of her red vest. 'Down a bit to your right,' she called.

Richard nodded, the clippers whirring to life in his hands.

'Is that it?' he asked after a few more strokes.

'Yes, that'll do it,' she said, ducking to collect the last few clippings that had fallen. Relieved, Richard climbed down the ladder.

'Do you know what's nice after an afternoon of hard

labour?' she said, pressing the button on the four-gang to reel in the extension cable.

'What?'

'A beer. You put the stuff away, I'll bring us one out.'

'Deal,' Richard said. When she turned to go back to the house he looked at his watch. The back of four. Early, but they had been at it for hours. He'd told Stephie she could work in his study for a change, and he thought about calling in to her. Instead he sat down at the picnic table, felt the wall hot and prickly against his back. She'd said she wanted to work until six anyway. The sky had turned hazy, as though the blue had been leached out by prolonged soaking. Loren came back with two bottles of beer, and as she reached over the table to hand him one, Richard noticed the light catching the skin on her inner arms. He thought she'd scratched herself on the shoots of privet, but then the marks resolved into delicate threads of scarring, long-faded.

'Cheers,' she said.

'Cheers,' he said, watching the scars slip out of sight as she raised her bottle to drink.

'Oh,' she said, catching the direction of his gaze. 'That.'

'Mmm.'

She took another drink of beer and smiled. 'Teenage angst.'

'Right.'

'What can you do. Sometimes you just have to feel something, don't you?'

Two wrens started squabbling on the ground close to the table, conducting a territorial disagreement or picking over some scrap that one had plucked from between the slabs. Loren turned to watch them. Her face had been in shadow, her back to the sun; now her profile was sharply illuminated.

'Nice here, isn't it?' she said.

'Lucky weather. Not so nice in winter.'

'But you stay.'

'Yes,' he said.

'Do you get snowed in?'

'Not yet. The snow plough comes by, and people are pretty quick off the mark with the grit.'

'Shame.'

He smiled. 'I don't think I really want to be that isolated.'

Loren twisted round, looking towards the road and the sea beyond it.

'What must it have been like round here, before snow ploughs and gritting?'

'All fields?' he said.

She laughed. 'Yeah, I guess so. Ever regret coming?'

He circled the base of his beer bottle on the table, watching the liquid inside adjust and find its level.

'I like it here,' he said. 'Seeing the landscape change, being near the sea. It's very . . . open.'

Loren started picking at the label on her beer bottle. Without looking up, she said, 'If you looked back at your life so far, could you pinpoint when it took the twists and turns that it did?'

'Are you talking about any particular twists and turns?' he said, wondering what Stephie had told her.

'No,' she said. 'Sorry, I didn't mean to be nosey. I just wondered if you could put your finger on the moments you made the choices that mattered, the ones that changed your path.'

'You mean like when I turned into the sort of person who owns gardening gloves?' he asked, nodding towards the gloves on the table beside her.

'No,' she smiled. 'Well, maybe. I don't know what's a big deal for you. Anyway, ignore me, I'm waffling. I'll put these back in the shed.'

'Thanks,' he said. 'And thanks for the help.'

'You're welcome. It was kind of fun.'

Loren picked up the gloves and sauntered towards the byre. Her vest had a racer back, and Richard could see that her shoulders had caught the sun. He got up and hopped down off the patio onto the grass to look at the hedge. When he turned back towards the house he saw Stephie looking out the window of his study. She didn't wave. He wondered how long she'd been standing there.

0

What do you want to do then? Luke asked.

I don't know, I said. Something different. Something fun.

Although we were taking a roundabout route, hopping on and off the kerbs and jumping over puddles as we went, I knew we were heading home. There was nowhere else to go. As we walked along Trinity Wynd we saw a bin that had been upturned, skewing rubbish all over the narrow street. I sent a can rattling over the cobblestones, chased it for another kick. When Luke caught up with me, he was twirling a wire coat hanger around his index finger.

Look at you. Were you in the majorettes or what?

He aimed a punch at my shoulder but I jumped out of his way and continued along the narrow street. The light grew dimmer as the road curved, the bare twisted branches of trees overhanging high garden walls on one side, the blank façade of a church hall on the other. Spotting the opening of the lane behind the big houses, I asked Luke to hang on and jogged ahead, turning the corner for privacy. As I peed, I looked up and scanned the sky for stars, but it was murky with cloud.

When I returned to the street I couldn't see Luke anywhere. Bastard, I thought, he's just gone off without me. Then I tried to reassure myself that he'd gone for a pee as well, and he'd appear any moment, hands in pockets, whistling. I stamped my feet, gave my arms a brisk pat, as though I'd arrived early for an appointment. A car engine spluttered into life along the street, and I turned my back as the car slunk along the road towards me, hoping I didn't look too dubious loitering there alone. I heard the click of a car door opening behind me, and then Luke's voice, low and urgent.

Come on then. Get in.

What the fuck are you doing, I said, but I said it in a whisper as I slipped into the passenger seat and closed the door behind me.

You said you wanted to do something different. A change is as good as a rest, eh?

I leaned over to watch as he pressed a twist of paler wires to a darker one and coaxed the car back to life, feeling ice slipping over my back, unable to tell if it was nerves or the cold of the upholstery. He drove slowly to the end of the road then switched the headlights on and turned onto the coastal road.

So, he said. Where do you want to go?

I laughed and said, Anywhere.

Okay, he said, and put his foot down. The car leapt forward and then juddered as Luke crunched the gears.

Can you drive? I asked.

Do you want to take over?

No. My voice squeaked and he turned to look at my face.

Don't worry, he said. We'll bring it back.

I nodded, but a car was approaching on the other side of the road. He cut our speed and kept his eyes on the road. The car passed by, heading into town. Raindrops started to blotch across the windscreen, and he flicked several switches before he found the wipers.

Want to figure out how to put on the heater and de-mister, he said, waving at the panel below the radio.

So when did you learn about cars? I said, hitting a button that seemed to depict a windscreen and turning the fan on.

There was a kind of craze on the estate for a while. I didn't really get into it or anything, just rode along with the older boys a few times, eh? And then once a pal and I took a couple of girls for a ride – he effected a smooth gear change – as a prelude to taking them for a ride, if you see what I mean.

Yeah, I see.

Got them all scared and fluttery, next thing they're on the back seat. Not both at once, you understand. We took turns.

Spare me the details. What about the driving?

Oh, picked it up as I went along. Friend with a car let me practice sometimes.

Luke, do you have a licence?

Nah, course not – he swerved across to the other side of the road and then zigzagged for a moment or two – but if the police pull us, that'll be the last thing on their minds.

Hmm, I said, uncertain of his logic.

Another few cars passed us and Luke turned onto a quiet single track road, swooping over the bumps and sending my stomach plummeting. I leaned back against the headrest and watched the wipers slapping rain off the window, the flashes of trees illuminated in the headlights. A fox froze in our path, eyes luminescent as it stared at us. It was holding something in its mouth, some smaller creature, bloodied and limp. Luke hit the brake, flinging me against my seatbelt, and the fox leapt through the hedge and away.

Do you know where we are? he said.

No, not really.

Me neither.

He grinned and started the engine again. Something about the movement of the car stirred me, or maybe I was just thinking of what Luke had said. I would've liked a friend like him when I was a year or two younger. It might have been me, leaning against the bonnet, waiting while I felt the vehicle shift in time with the rhythm of his body. I recast his story, dismissing the girls and imagining myself in his role, assured enough to drive a borrowed car, assured enough to unbutton my jeans and push his head down.

That wall on the right, he said, and startled by his voice I looked over just in time to see the castle gatehouse loom up beside the road, unfamiliar for a second in the darkness, and then we were past it and away.

We've just come at it a different way, Luke said.

Was there a light on, inside? I said.

I think so. I wonder if someone's living there again.

Or it's for security.

We kept going, past the turn off that would have taken us back towards the town. The rain shrunk into drizzle, and then swathes of white mist began rolling down from the fields onto the road. Soon they were charging the windscreen, dispersing, jousting us again. It seemed magical, as if we were in another world.

Do you believe in ghosts, I asked Luke.

No.

This looks spooky though.

Yes.

We reached a junction where a cluster of trees hunched over the road. Luke stopped the car and the engine stalled, the dark rushing towards us as the headlights cut out. In an instant it felt cold again. He fiddled again with the wires under the steering column, and I heard him mutter under his breath: fuck, fuck, fuck.

Is it all right? I said.

I can't see, is all.

The engine stuttered and the headlights flashed on, illuminating the trees opposite us, an old milestone and a bench, and then it died again.

Fuck, he said again.

Take it easy.

I don't want to fucking walk home from here.

My eyes were getting accustomed to the dark, but the mist seemed to be thickening around us. I wanted to lock my door, but didn't. Luke took a deep breath, as though he was trying to calm down, but then he started muttering again, filling the silence with a litany of swear words. The ignition caught and he revved the engine.

Thank fuck, he said. Okay, where now?

Just keep driving.

How far? To Edinburgh? To Glasgow?

Anywhere. I don't care.

I felt cheated when Luke remembered the petrol gauge and realised it had dropped into red; it seemed a prosaic end to the adventure. When at last we drove back into town, my nerves started twitching again.

I suppose we could just leave it somewhere. In the supermarket car park or something.

Luke continued round the roundabout and took the last exit for the town centre.

I'm not a thief, he said.

No, I agreed. Just a borrower. Like the little people behind the skirting.

What the fuck are you on about Richard?

Nothing.

If we get it back okay, it'll be less suspicious. They might not notice for a day or two. Or know that we drove it off.

If we get it back okay, I thought.

There's no one about, Luke said, as if he'd read my mind. It's four in the morning.

He edged round the one way system, so slowly and carefully that I thought that if anyone saw they'd report him as a drunk driver. At last he turned into Trinity Wynd. The space the car had come from was still empty, thank god.

I'm not very good at parking, Luke said, stopping in the middle of the road and looking at the space. Reversing's a bit dodgy too.

It was facing the other way, I said.

You're right, attention to detail, that's the key.

I wished I hadn't spoken as he drove slowly round the block and into the car park by the abbey.

Three point turns a bit dodgy too?

Yeah. He smiled, turning the car in a big circle and nosing it back towards the entrance. Forwards though. You have to admit, I'm pretty good at going forwards.

Shit, I whispered, putting my hand on his arm. There's someone over there. Guy with a dog.

Luke stopped the engine. He's looking the other way. Waiting on the dog.

He's walking again now, I whispered.

Duck then. Make it look as if the car's empty.

The blood rushed to my head as I hunched over. I felt it throbbing in my ears, smelled the rubber of the mat in the footwell of the car. Luke had curled himself to the side, and I felt his body pressing against mine, imagined the beat of his heart even through our jackets. Any minute, I thought, any minute the door of the car will open and a voice will ask us what we're doing. And then what will we do, talk our way out of it?

Luke shifted and sat up. He laid his hand on my shoulder. It's cool. He went into the flats over there. Let's go.

When I finally slid between my cold sheets, I lay there in the dark and smiled to myself, too nervy to sleep, trying to let the excitement that was still flickering through my body dissipate into warmth and tiredness. When I went to my morning lectures the next day I felt as though I was decorated with a medal, set apart.

16

Two words. *Dear Calum* . . . That was a start, Richard supposed. *How nice to hear from you!* The jaunty exclamation mark added little veracity to the statement. He sighed and deleted it. The problem was that he was a glutton for information, wanted to dispense with the niceties and gorge on every detail. *How did Luke sound when he mentioned me? What does he look like? Does he still bite his lips, get embarrassed when he has to put salve on them? Did you guess Calum, ever, that while I was lying in that shabby little single bed opposite you I was thinking of him, how it would feel if he was fucking me, right there on the floor in front of that two bar electric fire?*

The phone rang and Richard picked up to hear Rupe's voice, distant as though he'd turned away from the receiver.

'Tuula . . . Tuula? Did she just tell me to get to fuck? Is that what she said?'

'Hey Rupe, how nice to hear from you.' As he spoke, Richard typed the words again, minus the exclamation this time.

'These Scandinavians. They're so touchy. Anyway, just a quick call to say I love this iteration. It's marvellous.'

'That's great. I took what you were saying about fun on board.'

'And it shows. This is more like the thing. Escapism, that's the key. You always get bogged down in the detail, Rich, when all we want is basic narrative. Who needs nuance when you've got guns, eh?'

'Indeed.' Richard cradled the phone on his shoulder and continued writing.

Are the planes still slicing through the sky above the university? I remember how the noise of them used to drown everything out.

'We've started talking about the sound strategy. We need effects, we need tunes.'

'Rupe, didn't we speak about keeping the sound environment natural? 3-D, vocal retrospective?'

'It will be natural, natural plus. Where's the fun in shooting people if there's no soundtrack? I'm telling you, we'll be working on the sequel by this time next year.'

I don't suppose you visit any of the old haunts, now you're a family man. The old haunts probably aren't even there anymore.

'I'm not so sure . . .'

'Hang on Rich, that's my other phone. Okay, so I'll see you on Saturday, right? We'll thrash out the details and then it's onwards and upwards.'

'Saturday? Rupe?' The tone changed and Richard stared at the receiver for a second. 'Dickhead,' he muttered, and starting typing again.

Thanks for passing on the message. No, I haven't seen Luke for years, not since we were at university, in fact. If you see him again . . .

He heard footsteps in the hall, checked the time and realised that he'd promised to take Stephie to the chemist in town.

. . . tell him I said . . .

She knocked on the door of the study and Richard, knowing that what he was writing was inferior to what he'd wanted to say, what he'd always planned he would say, finished the sentence and shouted that he was almost ready. As the door creaked open he battered out his signature, noticing at the same time as he hit the send button that he'd muddled the 'c' and the 'h' of his name.

'Sorry, phone rang, just give me a minute, okay?'

'Keep your wig on,' she said. 'I'll wait on you outside.'

Richard logged on to the *Somme* wiki and saw the Saturday meeting that Rupe had been talking about. It was likely to go on late, turn into another overnighter, the kind of thing he'd have enjoyed if Stephie hadn't been staying. And Loren, of course.

In the hall, Stephie was tying a patterned headscarf round her hair. Looking at him in the mirror, she said, 'Your neighbours arrived.'

'Oh right,' he said. 'Were they speaking to you?'

'No. We waved at them, but the man just nodded.'

'Yeah, I get the impression they think I'm some kind of oik because I don't own a Barbour jacket. So, will we go and get you stocked up then?'

'Brilliant, just hang on a minute.'

He followed Stephie through to the kitchen, where Loren was standing by the sink, gulping down a glass of water.

'Are you sure you don't want to come?' Stephie said.

'I'll be fine here,' Loren said, turning round. 'It's so warm, maybe I'll just lie on the grass and read or something.'

'Sure you're sure?' Stephie frowned.

'Yeah.'

They turned out of the village in time for the afternoon show on the local radio station and drove along the side of the sea loch to the sound of country and western classics. As the road curved Stephie wound down her window and clicked her camera phone at the changing view. Richard felt the air hurtling into his ears, clearing his head.

'Pretty nice, huh?'

'Not bad.' She grinned, and started singing along with Dolly Parton.

They split up when they reached the town, arranging to meet at a bar by the harbour when they'd run their various errands. Richard arrived first, chose a seat at a picnic table outside. A row of cars was waiting to board the ferry to Stornoway, doors hanging lazily open and passengers ambling around, smoking, leaning over the rail to look down into the water. Even the breeze was warm. Along the street he saw Stephie walking towards him, her head turned as she too looked towards the ferry. A horn sounded, followed by a distorted announcement. The passengers began returning to their vehicles, slamming doors and starting engines. Richard thought Stephie's posture straightened, as if she was imagining running, getting on the boat herself. When she reached him he said, 'You looked as if you were about to make a bid for freedom.'

'What?' He pointed at the ferry. 'Oh,' she said. 'Yeah. The boat. It just looked tempting, I guess. But where does it go?'

'That one? Stornoway, I think.'

'Hmm. Ever been?'

'No.'

'Scared the Wee Frees'll get you?'

'Something like that.'

'Silly. It's not as if they could be more judgemental than the good citizens of Leckie.' She frowned, held her hand up to shade her eyes as she looked back towards the ferry.

'So,' he said. 'Do you want a drink or will we just head back?'

She smiled and sat down opposite him. 'White wine spritzer, please.'

He nodded and went into the bar, dark in contrast to the bright afternoon. The television was playing silently in one corner, and a couple of tourists were already tucking into grilled langoustines and chips, their springer spaniel sprawled across the floor beside their table. The dog opened one eye as Richard stepped over it but otherwise seemed unperturbed. While he waited for the barman, a jovial Yorkshireman, to pour the drinks he read the specials blackboard. The words 'catch of the day' were written in large letters and while he seriously doubted that was what was on the tourists' plates he still felt a pang of envy, seeing them on holiday together, drinking real ale to his lager shandy. When he went back outside the light dazzled him. He set the glasses down and noticed that the gangway to the ferry had been detached.

'Looks like I missed my chance at escape,' Stephie said, picking up her glass and swirling the ice round to create a small whirlpool. 'Cheers.'

The horn sounded on the ferry, and it began to move slowly from the quay.

'It isn't that bad here, is it?' Richard said.

'It isn't bad at all,' she said. 'It's beautiful, today. Feels like we're on holiday.'

'Yes.' He was about to say something about work, but managed to swallow his words. 'It's nice to see you,' he said instead. 'Even with Loren here as well.'

Stephie looked at him. 'Don't you like her?'

'Actually I do quite like her. But I was enjoying spending time with you. Are you still okay about her being here?'

'Yeah. I guess.'

'I mean, it doesn't make you think too much about your boyfriend? Or upset you?'

'There's no point in thinking about him. Like I said, he was a twat. It just took me a bit longer than it should have to realise it. You could say that Loren did me a favour.'

Richard started to speak but Stephie got in before him. 'Look,' she said, pointing to where the ferry was rounding the peninsula. 'How long will it take to get to Stornoway?'

'Three hours, just under,' he said, realising that his chance to pick at Stephie, to press her into speaking, had also slipped away.

The tone of the light changed as afternoon slipped towards evening, and around them people relaxed into their drinks, secure in the knowledge that the sun wouldn't set for hours yet. Stephie raised her glass then yelped as she noticed a wasp inside it, crawling towards the splash of liquid left at the bottom. She slammed the glass down and pushed it towards Richard, who shrank back.

'What do you want me to do about it?' he said. 'I hate wasps.' But he took the glass by the stem and gave it a tentative shake. The wasp spiralled out, hovered in the air for a second as if disorientated, then swooped towards the more obvious target of three teenage girls with ice cream cones.

'At least you didn't make that much noise,' Stephie said. 'Anyway, will we have another one?'

Richard watched the girls colliding with each other as they danced away from the wasp. 'I'd better not,' he said. 'You have one though. I'll just have a Coke or something.'

'When did you get so sensible?' Stephie asked. 'You're positively parental.'

Richard sighed. 'I have to drive us home. Unfortunately.'

'And to think you told me a story about drunk driving in a stolen car.'

'Shh.' It seemed almost inconceivable now, looking at the lazy evening scene, feeling the warmth on the back of his neck. And yet after he'd told Stephie, he'd lain awake in his bed, his veins tickling as though in involuntary recollection of the adrenaline that had enlivened them that night. 'Anyway,' he said quietly, 'Luke didn't seem drunk. I can't remember what we'd been doing beforehand.'

'Even so. You could've had an accident.'

He bowed his head, a half acknowledgement.

Stephie put on a pleading voice. 'Can't we stay here for a while and then get a bus or something?'

'There only are two a day, and the last one's gone. Anyway, I'd have to come back for the car.'

'So? You don't need it until Saturday.'

'Yes, but that doesn't help us get home tonight.' Stephie let out a crow of laughter. 'What?' he said. 'What's so funny?'

'There. You said it.'

'What?'

'That doesn't help us get home tonight. You've decided, haven't you?'

He groaned. 'No. But I just remembered something.'

'What?'

'Rab. Plays pool at the Albion every Tuesday. It finishes about half ten. So, if that's a late enough night for you, I suppose we could hitch a ride with him.'

She looked at her watch. 'Sounds fine to me. Or do you want to go and play pool with him?'

'No, I don't like it much.'

'Okay. So, do you want a proper beer this time or another nancy drink?'

'A proper beer. And less cheek.'

Stephie swung her legs out from under the picnic table and picked up their empty glasses. As she turned to go into the bar, Richard said, 'Wait a minute.'

'What?'

'What about Loren?'

'What about her?' Stephie shrugged. 'She can't grudge me some time alone with you.'

0

Sunlight stretched through the plate glass windows, just reaching the library desk at which I was sitting, new fine-nibbed biro in hand, trying to forge through the problems that had been set for my logic seminar. Half my body was bathed in warmth, the other cool and shaded. I felt footsteps quivering through the floor, and then Luke hunched down beside me, looking unkempt and pleased with himself.

Have you been home? I asked, pretending to be stern.

He shook his head, then announced: I love these public school girls.

Really, I said.

Mmm.

I looked down at the truth-table I was trying to construct. I'd been enjoying myself, reaching clear answers. Everything T or F, nothing in between.

Must be that all the public school boys are shirtlifters, he said. Turns them into nymphos.

There's a fundamental distinction between truth and validity, I told him.

Would you mind belting up? The boy at the desk in front of me turned to face us. I'm trying to study.

Sorry Freddy, I didn't see you there, Luke said. I'm sure there was nothing of that nature at that school that you and Max went to, what's it called, Wykeham.

The boy scowled. I wouldn't know, he said. But if anyone did try that kind of thing, they gave it up after school. Winchester – he elongated the first syllable of the word – was not a breeding ground for pooves.

Better cancel your train ticket then Richard, Luke said with a wink. Freddy flashed me a look and returned to his books. He had the good grace to blush; I could see his earlobes turning pink.

I've got to go and type my essay, Luke whispered. Won't take that long. I'll see you at home, maybe about two? I need you to do me a favour.

I nodded and returned to my truth-table.

It was nearer three when Luke got back to Herrick. He found me in the kitchen, chatting to Sheng from my maths class as I ate more of the inevitable chicken-flavour instant noodles. I would've stayed longer in the library, but I knew Luke was planning to go away for a day or two and I didn't want to miss him.

Hey, I said. Get your essay done?

Yep, handed in. How did you get on?

I've not really broken the back of it yet.

Started the Euripides one for Mendelssohn?

Kind of. Haven't got very far though. So, what's this favour you want me to do?

Oh, nothing, eh? It's cool.

He put his finger to his lips and nodded towards Sheng, who had his back to us as he filled the kettle. We declined a cup of tea, I rinsed my bowl and fork and Luke and I went upstairs.

I hope Max isn't in, he said as we approached his door.

Wednesday, I said.

Oh yeah, rugby. Luke stood on his tip toes so that he could reach his Yale key to the lock without taking it off the key chain. Just go to your room if you want, I'll be along in a minute.

I went in and laid my books out on the desk, glanced at the problem I'd been about to start before I left the library. I scrawled *modus tollens* next to it to remind myself where to begin. There was a tap and the door and Luke came in, holding something behind his back.

You know how I said I was going away for a couple of days?

Yes.

Well, can you keep this for me? He handed me a padded envelope. Don't want Max to find it if he's rooting about when I'm away.

Sure, I said. The envelope felt heavier than I'd expected. When I squeezed the bottom of it I could feel solid lumps, but when I peered in the top there was a polythene bag containing shiny magazine wraps of what I assumed was speed. There must have been a dozen of them at least.

Oh hang on, I've forgotten something, he said, and dived out the door.

It hadn't taken Luke long to garner a reputation as someone who might bring something along, someone who might be able to sort you out. In the first week of term he'd been scruffy and stand-offish, not speaking to anyone as we stood in the corridor waiting to go into the Classics seminar room. Was he really poor, you could see them wondering, as he stuffed his notes into a carrier bag after lectures. By the time we were dressing up for the Union and being invited to parties, they'd decided he added an edgy bit of rough to their try too hard hedonism. Helped of course by the way he always had some hash, or if it wasn't hash it was grass, and if it wasn't grass it was speed, and if it wasn't speed it was ecstasy.

That's a lot of gear, I said, when he bobbed back into the room and dropped a small poly bag into the envelope.

A dozen pills, like.

I meant the rest.

Not really, he said. This and that for other folk.

Friends?

Yeah. And friends of friends.

He must have seen something in my face, nerves perhaps, masquerading as disapproval, because he said:

I'm skint Richard, even with my grant I'm skint. This is just a way of making life a little easier.

Okay, I said.

Distributing a few eighths round Herrick House hardly makes me Pablo fucking Escobar.

Yeah, I know that, I said, forcing a laugh. It's just that . . .

Oh come on Richard, get out my face, eh? If you don't want me to leave it with you I'll give it to someone else. It's no big deal.

He walked over to the window, pressing his face up close to the glass to peer down into Herrick's concrete back yard, with its rows of dustbins and washing lines that nobody ever used. I wonder if that's when I noticed that with a casual phrase, a change of tone, he could cut me to the quick. My over-sensitivity had ebbed but never truly disappeared. I looked at the floor, scuffing my feet against a curled carpet tile, trying to get it to lie flat.

It's fine, I said at last. Calum's still at home so it's no problem.

He spun round, bright and smiling again. Thanks man, I really appreciate it.

Mind and bring me back some Edinburgh rock.

He leaned over to read the time from Calum's alarm clock. Tell you what, I'll get you a present in advance. A pint on my way to the bus.

As we walked into town together I wished I'd put a jumper on under my jacket. The crisp sunshine of earlier in the day had been replaced by grey, and the damp sea air was coalescing into melancholy wreaths of mist in the vennels and courtyards.

Aye, I said. The nights are fair drawing in.

Luke smiled and held the door of the bar open for me. This'll warm the cockles of your wee Ayrshire heart then.

So what are your plans then, I asked him, knowing I had to study but not relishing a weekend without him.

Stay with my mum tonight, then I'm off to visit a friend. Back on Sunday night I think. I've got a ten o'clock on Monday.

What about the pal you're visiting, does he live in Edinburgh?

Kind of. Near, anyhow. But I'm just going to meet him in town, like. He frowned. What about you?

Staying in. I'm skint too. Don't know how I'll manage until the end of term.

He nodded, then thought for a moment and said, Richard, what can you get out the bank?

Dunno. Haven't looked. I've maybe got a hundred left.

He leaned in closer. Look, I'll tell you what, if you give me what you can, fifty say, I'll treble it for you. Promise.

What, have you got an infallible gambling system now?

No-o. But I was going to replenish my supplies anyway. So if you give me that, and I put in the same, I can get the stuff cheaper. Shift it no problem.

I suppose, I said.

Nothing heavy, just a wee bit hash, grass if he's got it, some more pills. They'll go for three times what I can get them for and we'll be providing a much needed public service.

We finished our drinks and I went to the cashline by the cinema to get the money. I pressed it firmly in his hand, as though I was placing a daring bet – 22, red – not sure that lady luck would see me through.

So will you get the stuff from this friend you're meeting? I said.

Him? Nah. Not really his thing. There's a guy on the other side of my mum's courtyard. He'll sort me out.

Doesn't he have a name?

Yeah, Spanish Tony. Except his real name's Frank.

I meant your pal.

Oh. Dan.

D'you know him from school?

Nah.

Luke ran ahead, jumped up on the first of a row of bollards, then hopped to the next one and on along the others. When he reached the end he waited a second for me to catch up, and said, still standing balanced above me, We're going to have a good time Richard. I know we are.

Walking back from the bus station without him, in the early darkness and the haar, this seemed unlikely. While I was buying biscuits in the Co-op I bumped into Rebecca from Herrick, who asked if I wanted to go to the cinema with her and Marc, but I pleaded my logic problems and waved my orange Viscounts as evidence of how seriously I intended to study. The haar turned to drizzle as I walked on, and on impulse I ducked into a call box and dialled my parents' number. I pictured the phone on the hall table, ringing out. There was no reply.

When I reached my room I put one pound fifty into the heater, as if to anchor me there for the evening. By ten o'clock I'd finished the logic exercises – and most of the Viscounts –

but I still felt gloomy. Herrick was quiet, as though everybody was either out or sleeping. I drifted to the kitchen and made a cup of tea, considered going to the television room in search of company but couldn't really be bothered. Slumped on my saggy bed, listening to the same music I'd played in my bedroom at home, it seemed that the images I'd nurtured of my future had been two-dimensional. Once again I was alone in my room, with Calum away and Luke off with other friends, better friends, and only the thought of my half-written analysis of attitudes towards moral obligation in the characters of Euripides to distract me.

If I admitted it, I'd thought classics at university might attract others of a Greek persuasion. It hadn't. Philosophy had sounded fun to me, a bookish sort, and Maths was my only concession to proper, practical study.

But will it get you a job son? my father had asked, as I toiled over my UCAS form.

Oh yes, of course it will, I said, and in a flash I was gone.

In fact university had been on the cards relatively early on, for me and anybody else that could be swept off the unemployment chart that way. My teachers, though put upon, were decent enough. Smart kids did eight O grades, three sciences, but it didn't do to exhibit too much aptitude; the line between doing well and getting above yourself was needle thin. Four or five Highers, maybe a Sixth Year Certificate or two, and those from the bought houses were out. Up, up and away: the doctor's daughter went to do medicine; the solicitor's son, law.

The non-academically minded weren't as lucky. Tolerated as troublemakers, expected to dog off or bring knives into the playground, they fulfilled their destiny as Christmas leavers, YTS candidates. At fifteen Lizzy Maxwell had to follow the words on the page with her finger and couldn't pronounce deciduous, no matter how often Mrs Boss repeated it. Wee Sammy McGuire with the bruises couldn't read at all, as far as I could see, and I don't think anyone gave a flying fuck. When he joined in chanting 'poof' at me, whilst clearly having no idea what it meant, I can't say I gave a flying fuck either.

When I was about twelve, I remember, my mother and sister and I went on days out with my gran. Tearooms in Troon, flower shows in Ayr, a National Trust country house. Ooh, how the other half live, Gran bleated, as we passed through room after luxurious room of gilt-edged porcelain and glistening mahogany. We spent longest in the kitchen and the servants' quarters though. I imagined it was because my mother liked cooking and my gran was interested in seeing the butter patters and wool carders and whatever else they had when she was a girl (when had she grown up, I wondered, the 18th century?), but later I became convinced that it wasn't that but a forced feeling of unworthiness. Afraid the tread of their shoes would soil the hand-knotted oriental rugs in the rooms above or their fingertips sully the silken wallcoverings, they took comfort in the low ceilings and institutional paintwork below stairs.

17

Richard peered out the window of Rab's car, trying to judge where they were. The tartan blanket he was sitting on smelled of dogs, and whenever they took a sharp turn the sack of pony nuts with which he was sharing the back seat jostled against him. Rab had two Border collies but no pony as far as Richard knew. Perhaps they were for the sheep. He'd been unable to get the seatbelt to fasten, and couldn't help thinking of young Davy Guthrie, the sickening swerve as the car lost the road, its final slump into the dark water of the loch. Though Davy had been well over the limit, or so Richard had heard, and Rab was teetotal. Teetotal, but a fast driver, turning his head to talk to Stephie as his foot eased down on the accelerator.

'Aye well, it's no the winning it's the taking part,' he was saying. 'But we'll thrash them the next time.'

After several glasses of wine Stephie had the kind of joie de vivre Richard remembered from the first day of the school holidays, as she quizzed Rab about the politics of the local pool league. Rab's anecdotes stirred distant memories of trick shots and penalties, gleaned from Richard's few frames in the student union or the late night snooker club in Dundee. He envied Stephie her social ease while also feeling proud. He didn't know if it came naturally or if she had to pretend confidence until she convinced herself of it.

Gorse bushes and rocks flashed by outside, and he thought again of the joyride with Luke, wondered if he should have told Stephie about it or not, if he had hoped it would provoke a similar confession from her. He remembered the sensation of abandon, of not caring, felt an answering twinge in the pit of his stomach. What kind of car was it? Had Luke been drunk? Vital points seemed to have drifted away from him, while the details remained etched on his mind as if it was a drypoint plate, poised for the next printing.

At Richard's insistence, Rab dropped them at the track that led to his own house, and they walked on up the hill. The sky was still light, although it was past eleven, and the half moon shone palely against it.

'That was fun,' Stephie said. 'It took me out of myself.'

'You're a bit evasive,' Richard said before he could stop himself, 'about why you might need taken out of yourself.'

'That's quite something coming from you,' she said, but he could hear the smile in her voice. Across the water the lights on the island were small and wavering, fragile-looking although he knew the houses themselves were robust.

'I know. I'm sorry. About disappearing on you.'

'Yeah, I know. You've said that before. But I should have got my act together to leave.'

'When I first went to university I got a grant and cheap digs. I scraped by. Second time I got a career development loan because IT was the next big thing. I was lucky. It isn't like that now.'

'But if I've painted myself into a corner, that's my own fault.'

Their voices disturbed a ewe lying in the ditch by the side of road. She lurched to her feet and ambled away, followed by two lambs who looked back as though they might be missing out on something.

'They're so cute,' Stephie said. 'I should be a vegetarian again. I should leave Leckie and become a vegetarian. That's not much of a life plan, is it?'

'You're young,' Richard said.

'But if I'm not careful, I could get stuck there for life. I'm serious. Do you know, I actually chat to the girls that used to give me a hard time at school?'

'I didn't know you had a hard time at school.'

'Just the usual. I thought I'd never see them again, and now I meet them on the bus back from Ayr and we have the same banal conversations every time. I have to pass this fucking course, and I have to get a placement and get to Glasgow.'

Richard linked his arm with hers. Her skin felt cool against his. 'You will pass.'

'Hmm,' she said. 'Right, step it up a bit, I'm bursting for the toilet.'

When they reached Richard's gate she kissed him good-night. 'Hey, that was fun. Thanks. Now, bagsie me first in the bathroom.'

She ran ahead, leaving him to close the gate behind them. He walked up the drive, thinking about what she'd said and wondering, with a slight sense of shame, whether it really was harder than before or whether she just hadn't wanted to leave badly enough. He noticed that the gate in the hedge that connected his drive to the neighbours was wide open and wondered if the Manbys had called round, possibly to complain about some overlooked piece of hedge debris sullying their garden. As he went to close it, he saw that the door of their shed was also swinging in the breeze, creaking then tapping shut. He glanced up at his bedroom window and sighed, deciding the creak-tap, creak-tap might be enough to keep him awake. Unlike Gerald to be so careless, he thought, must have been one of the kids. Some other, smaller noise made him peer inside as he went to secure the door.

The Manbys had a sleek wooden dinghy, which Gerald seemed to spend a great deal more time varnishing than he did sailing. It took Richard a moment to understand what he was seeing. Loren was lying on a tarpaulin inside the boat. Between her legs was what Richard assumed was the older of the two Manby boys. He saw the back of Loren's hand go to her face, saw her grasp the skin on the back of her wrist between her teeth. Her eyes were closed and her face looked tightened, as if she was either concentrating very hard or steeling herself against the urgent, awkward thrusts of the boy, whose jeans had slid beyond his buttocks and down his thighs. Richard looked away quickly, the first prickling of envy spreading through his body, then realised that Loren had opened her eyes and was looking straight at him. He spun round, closed the door and walked away.

Back in his office, drinking a bottle of beer that he hadn't intended to have, Richard considered closing the French doors but then decided it was too warm. He'd just pretend it hadn't happened, he decided, when he saw Loren the next day. He logged on to the *Somme* wiki and scrolled through the coding Neil had put up, realising how close they were to a playable iteration.

Hey Neil, looking good, he typed. *Will double check that bug in the Ypres chapter AM tomorrow. RE the play testers: I will buy you buckets of beer after crunch if you please pretty please find some 30/40something fathers looking for a serious game to play when the kids are in bed.*

After a while, he heard a tap on the glass door. When he turned round, Loren was already standing in the room. She was wearing Stephie's skirt, he was almost sure, the one with the ribbon stripe that he'd noticed the other day. It hung loosely on her hips.

'Hiya,' he said, and she came over and perched on the stool by his drawing board, dangling her feet down. Her eyes were shining and her lips looked puffy, as though she was suffering from an allergy.

'I'm sorry,' she said.

'What for?'

She shifted on the stool and he saw a bruise flowering across the outside of her thigh. 'I didn't mean for you to see that.'

He shrugged. 'You're old enough to do what you want. Though I'm not sure about your friend.'

'He's seventeen,' she said. 'It showed.' Her smile was disarmingly toothy and genuine, changing her face. He caught the corners of his mouth twitching upwards in response. 'Can I have a sip of your beer?' she said.

He handed the bottle to her and she took a gulp then offered it back to him.

'It's all right,' he said. 'You finish it. Stephie and I had enough tonight.'

'Yeah. I got bored without you.'

'Oh well. You found something to do.'

His eye caught a corner of the computer screen. The wiki had refreshed, showing that Tuula was online and uploading code. It was midnight, he saw, and he pictured the puddle of light around her booth in the DaCapo lab, the crushed Red

Bull cans that she never managed to get into the bin when she threw them over her shoulder.

'You know what I think?' Loren said.

He shook his head, wondering if he was missing out, if perhaps he'd go back to Dundee when the lease was up on the house.

'I think you're very good at pretending.'

'And what do I pretend?'

'That you're what you seem on the surface.'

He looked at her.

'You know,' she said. 'Workaholic, a loner, a nature lover.'

'What's wrong with being a nature lover?' Richard said. 'I always have been, ever since I was a kid. Ask Stephie.'

'Okay. But there has to be something underneath.'

'Yeah. Actually I'm a serial killer,' he said.

'My guess is that you're a bit of a kindred spirit,' she said, hopping down from the stool and putting the beer bottle down on the corner of his desk. She seemed to be standing too close to him, and he wondered, though his judgement was clouded by drink and tiredness, whether she was coming on to him.

'Unlike your juvenile friend,' he heard himself say.

'Yeah,' she said, reaching out and placing her palm over his hand. 'Like I said, that didn't quite . . .'

Before he realised what was going on, she'd taken his hand and slid it up her skirt. She didn't seem to be wearing pants and he felt hair, warm and damp, and then she isolated his index finger and pushed it forward, inside her.

'Loren,' he said. 'You do know that I'm gay.'

'Does everything have to be that clear cut?'

'For me it does.'

She was very close to him now, her mouth open. 'So close your eyes and pretend,' she said. Her muscles tightened around his finger and he thought of Luke, suddenly, how he wouldn't have hesitated, how he'd have been able to answer her.

'I'm afraid it doesn't work like that,' Richard said, withdrawing his hand. 'I'm sorry.'

'Don't apologise,' she said. 'Please.'

He had to bite his lip to stop himself telling her again that he was sorry. She turned and walked out of the room, leaving him sitting by his desk, holding his hand stiffly as though he didn't want to contaminate anything else with its touch.

0

Luke was warm and dishevelled, seemingly at ease in his skin, as if our impromptu game of football had fed some part of him that had been neglected for a while. He'd kicked a ball back to some boys, quickly become absorbed into their game until he managed to score between two bundles of discarded hoodies that marked the goal. I'd kept up, barely, and although I'd failed to challenge him it wasn't a bad way to pass a frosty Tuesday afternoon; especially viewed in retrospect, from the corner table in the Earl of Merchiston where we'd retired for a post-game pint.

Admit it, I said to him. You prefer the company of men to the company of women.

Depends on the men.

Look how well you got on with those boys.

Oh come on, wee kick about on a winter's day? That's nothing. We used to go up the Meadows all the time, join any game that was going. That and check out the talent, like.

Of course.

Anyhow, they were just boys. Nice boys who play football rather than sniffing glue and slashing tyres.

Yeah, but most of the boys around here hate students and shout wanker at them when they pass them in the street.

That's because most of the students are wankers. Except for us, of course. He looked down into his pint glass. You've offended me now.

Oh yeah?

Yeah. I do get on with women.

You get it on with women, that's a different thing altogether.

Women, men, it's all the same.

Liar. You're straight as a die. Which suggests a total lack of imagination, if you ask me.

Lack of imagination? I refute that.

How?

He laughed. In many and various ways, he said. Anyway, how can you say I don't get on with women? I'm going on a date tonight.

I snorted with laughter, choking on my pint. He slapped me on the back and said, It's not that funny.

No, I agreed. It isn't at all funny. What will you be doing, on this date?

Going to the pictures.

To see?

Something with Brad Pitt in it.

Bloody hell, I said. That sounds serious.

Well, she didn't fancy Natural Born Killers, and that's the only other thing that's on.

Who is she then?

That girl Aimee that we met on Saturday, Becca and Marc's pal.

I paused, trying to conjure up her image in my mind. Hang on, I said. The Irish one?

Yeah.

Oh, I said. He looked at me. Sorry, I added. I thought she was a bit dull.

He shrugged. Pretty, though.

Do you reckon? I said, but thinking back I recalled Luke chatting away to her, while Rebecca told me some interminable story about her brother's friend who'd gone to Berlin and ended up in a darkroom by mistake.

And it's an easy mistake to make I'm sure, I'd said, focussing on the little cross around Aimee's neck and thinking, ah well, he's on to a loser with that one. But she was laughing at something he said, and didn't seem as shy as I'd assumed.

Well she seemed to like you, Luke said. I think you did half the groundwork for me. What were you talking to her about?

She was talking to me. About how she goes to Mass every Sunday evening at the Chaplaincy, amongst other things.

Ah, he said.

You've got no chance, I observed. No sex before marriage.

She's not a slut, that's all.

Unlike you.

Unlike me. But I reckon I can give her a few impure thoughts.

Point proved, no?

You're such a cynic, Richard. It isn't just about sex.

Yeah right.

You should indulge your finer feelings sometimes. You've got a one track mind. I suppose it's because you're gay.

Luke and Aimee up a tree, I chanted. K-I-S-S-I-N-G . . .

He tipped his head back and drained his pint then shook a cigarette from his packet and tapped it on the table, as though he was afraid to sit for even a moment without a clear purpose.

Anyway, he said. Want to go to the castle? Get away from the Yahs for an hour or two?

I nodded. Carry out?

Why not? Did Dave drop by earlier?

Yeah, I said. As if I'd been playing at pharmacies, I'd dispensed three tablets of ecstasy, neatly sealing them in a tiny envelope. I wondered if the nice lady at the stationery counter of the newsagent wondered what use Luke found for these envelopes, or if she was pleased to shift some old stock. Dave the Raver had been good for thirty quid; a profit margin which – combined with the Co-op special offer on vodka – could get us drunk for the rest of the week. I opened my wallet, but couldn't see any cash.

Shit Luke, I think I've left the money back at Herrick.

No worries, we'll swing by on the way.

When we got to Herrick there were a few people in the hallway. Calum was speaking on the payphone, promising his mum that he was still feeling better. He waved at me in what seemed like an agitated way as I walked past, then continued reassuring his mum that he was taking his multivitamins. I waved back. A couple of people were waiting to speak to Parnab, the warden, who was in his little dookit of an office, issuing receipts for rent. They fell silent as we passed. Luke shrugged and we went to the stairs, acclimatising to the mild whiff of damp and school dinners as we climbed.

There was a letter pinned to the door of Luke's room.

University crest on the envelope, his name printed in block capitals. He shrugged again, digging his thumbnail under the drawing pin to remove it. I went to my door and found the same thing. They were eviction notices.

That cunt, Luke said.

Who? I said.

Max, of course. I'm going to fucking kill him.

He turned and ran, but instead of following him I sat on the edge of my bed and read the letter through. Dread crept along the follicles on the back of my neck in a way that it hadn't since school. The use and distribution of controlled substances couldn't be allowed on university premises. Parnab was doing his best, I could see that. He was left with no option: we could leave Herrick within the week, or pursue it with the university authorities, who were – he felt obliged to warn us – extremely unlikely to find in our favour given the source of the complaints and their detailed nature.

I went back downstairs, walking slowly and wondering what the fuck I was going to do. Calum was still on the phone, but he put his hand over the receiver and beckoned me over.

I'm really sorry Richard. Really. Look, there's this third year from astronomy, he's looking for someone to take over the lease of his flat. I wrote the number down for you.

Cheers, I said, bitterly, scrunching up the piece of paper Calum handed me and stuffing it into my pocket. I was angry at Luke – though much more with myself – and as I marched into town I imagined what I might say: this was your idea, you said there was no risk; if you hadn't gone off with Max's girlfriend then maybe he wouldn't have cliped on us. I wasn't sure where Luke would have gone, decided to try the Union first. When I got there I saw him soon enough. Michael the barman was throwing him out.

Get him out here, Luke was shouting. Get him out and I'll fucking show him.

A moment later Michael escorted Max out as well, and I heard him say, Sort it out between yous and dinnae set foot in here again until yous have.

I remembered the playground squabbles that used to bring kids running from all corners of the asphalt. People were gathering in an arc around Luke and Max. I saw Guy, heard him call out something about Queensberry rules.

Fucking faggot, Max spat, circling Luke.

Yeah, Luke taunted. That's what your girlfriend said. When her mouth wasn't full.

Max lunged and I could see his punch hit Luke in the face as if it was in slow motion. Blood sprang from Luke's lip and he started laughing, as though this was the release he'd been waiting for. He launched himself on Max, grabbing him by the hair. Max ducked his head down to protect it, so Luke hammered his chest and shoulders with his fist and then they tangled together, so that I had no idea who was in control, if either of them was. This was more brutal than the playground; there were no shouts of *fight-fight-fight* and no teacher or janny appeared to separate them. They hit the concrete and Max seemed to be on top on Luke but then Luke threw him off and I saw that blood was pouring from Max's nose. I heard noise then, a girl yelling and someone else shouting about calling the police, and I realised that they were really going to hurt each other.

It felt like seconds later that a siren screamed and a police car skidded round the corner. I suppose in such a small town they didn't have much else to concern them. They hauled Luke and Max apart and I moved as close as I could, wanting to go and speak to Luke, to see if he was hurt, but it was as if the police had drawn an invisible line that I couldn't cross. I heard some muttering about breach of the peace and perhaps even the word 'wanker', connected to the word 'students', but then Guy stepped forward and seemed to be introducing himself to the senior of the two officers.

That one's got a broken nose, I heard one of them say, pointing to the back of the car where they'd put Max. We'll drop him at A & E.

Luke was leaning against the bonnet of the car, his chest heaving. They said something stern to him and he stood upright, then nodded. Guy shook their hands and they got into the car and drove away. I could see Max through the window, holding a wad of tissue to his face. Guy leaned close to Luke, said a few words in his ear. Luke nodded again and

Guy slapped him on the shoulder then turned and walked back towards the Union. When Luke saw me he grabbed me by the biceps and almost shook me.

Did you see that?

I nodded and he released me. Are you okay? I said.

Yeah, he said, wiping his sleeve over his mouth. He turned back to me and grinned. I told him I'd kick his cunt in.

You broke his nose.

Yeah, he said again, and then he started coughing. He leaned forward and I wanted to place my hand between his shoulder blades to soothe him, but then he spat on the pavement at his feet. I averted my eyes, but not quickly enough to miss the red in his phlegm. He put his finger in his mouth, prodding his teeth to check for looseness, then looked up at me and said, He'll thank me for it, you know. Girls love that kind of thing.

As he stood upright a trickle of blood from his own nose reached his lip. It must have tickled, because he stretched his tongue up and licked it. Not just girls, I thought, looking at the scarlet against his pale skin, his bruising face.

Are you sure you're all right? I said, feeling in my pocket for a tissue to give to him.

I cannae tell you how good that felt, he said, using his sleeve again.

What was the Honourable Guy saying?

Dropping names, apologising.

Very nice of him to step in, I said.

Yeah well, he's having a party. Wants some coke.

Coke?

Yeah.

Oh.

Said I'd sort him out. Now let's go and get wasted.

I thought you had a date.

He caught my wrist, tilted it to read my watch. I'll phone her, he said. Call off until tomorrow. I don't think I can handle quiet and civilised right now.

On the way to the pub, I told him about the number Calum had given me, suggested phoning it and trying to arrange a viewing.

Oh man, you're a superstar, Luke said, putting his arm round my shoulder. He was still hyper from the fight and I wished I could hold him close to me to stop him trembling.

We don't know if we'll get it, I said.

Course we will. Or we'll get another one. This is going to be fantastic, Richard. Best thing that could've happened.

18

Richard looked at himself in the mirror. His eyes were still a little bloodshot from staring at his screen all day, even though he'd worn his glasses. He frowned, ran his fingers through his tousled hair, then felt an enormous smile bursting across his face. They'd done it. Crunchtime was an adrenaline rush even without the various pick-me-ups – from guarana smoothies to medical grade amphetamine – that had been circulating at DaCapo, and now at last they had a playable version of *Somme*. Neil lurched into the bathroom and slapped Richard on the back.

'So how does it feel mate? Your idea, and now it's a millimetre away from being green lit.'

'We've got to hear what the testers say. They might hate it.'

'If they hate it,' there was a pause as Neil started to urinate, during which Richard felt obliged to further scrutinise his face in the mirror so as make clear that he wasn't trying to catch a glimpse of his colleague's penis, 'Fuck them. It's a good game.'

'Thanks.'

'Rupe's already been on to marketing about a title. And guess what?'

'What?' Richard said, edging out the way so that Neil could approach the washbasin.

'He's only gone and put the DaCapo credit card behind the bar.'

'It's going to be carnage.'

'Yeah, and what do we say?'

'Play hard,' Richard said, giving him a high five and laughing as he remembered the slogan Rupe had proposed at his single, ill-advised attempt at a team-building day. Surely he must have guessed that his team would spend their entire paintball session shooting at his backside.

They went back out into the bar, just in time to see Tuula walking over to the table with a bottle of champagne. A barman hurried after her with an ice bucket and a handful of glasses.

'Don't worry Rupe,' she said. 'They only got the NV.'

Close to Richard's ear, Neil said, 'For someone who just pulled an allnighter, Tuula's looking pretty hot.'

'Hmm.'

'Oh don't worry, I know. Can't help thinking it's a bit of a waste though.'

The same could be said for Jonathan, Richard thought, seeing the art assistant talking to Lisa, who was already pink-cheeked and giggly. Neil went over and sat on the other side of her, and Richard wondered if he'd split up with his girlfriend or was just in high spirits. He wondered too when he himself had taken up running to release tension rather than other, more intimate, activities. Tuula waved at the bottle of champagne at him and he went to sit beside her.

'I was just explaining them,' she indicated Solange and Ben, who'd been hanging on to Rupe's every word, 'that I love you.'

Richard smiled. 'I love you too Tuula. You worked miracles today.'

'But we would not have straightened that bug without you. We would still be there in that fucking lab getting our eyes crossed about that fucking code if you,' she grabbed a glass, poured until it overflowed and handed it to Richard, 'If you had not worked out how to fix it. So, I love you.'

'So I take it you love Richard then?' Solange said.

'Yes,' Tuula said. She jumped up and straddled Richard, leant in and kissed him, pushing his mouth open and darting her tongue between his teeth. He allowed himself to go along with it, then she leaned back, still sitting on his knee, and ruffled his hair. Her eyes were twinkling, mischievous. 'That,' she announced, wiping her mouth, 'is how much I love my friend Richard.'

'Tuula, have you been taking drugs?' Solange said, giving in to snorts of laughter that almost choked her.

'And I tell you what Richard,' Tuula whispered in his ear, 'if neither of us get lucky here, we go out somewhere together later and see how we do.'

'Is the club any better these days?' he asked, feeling his inhibitions loosening and remembering the sticker advertising a men-only sauna he'd seen on the hand-dryer in the bathroom. She slid off his knee and sat beside him. 'No, it is shite. Thank god straight girls aren't straight as in former times.'

'This place is a lot busier than I remember. And what's with the dj?'

'Exhibition opening upstairs,' Rupe said, squeezing in between Tuula and Solange. 'Some conceptual crap, childish scribbles and misspelled slogans.'

Tuula winked at Richard. 'So maybe our chances improve.'

'Are you on the pull Tuula?' Rupe asked. 'Why not try a spot more of this to get you in the mood?'

'Cheers Rupe,' Tuula said. 'I like this retro high. Richard?'

'Okay,' he said, imagined his younger, less sensible self reaching out to him from somewhere in his memory, touching his fingertips, laughing.

'You want to come to the toilet with me?'

'Nah, you're all right Tuula, you go first.'

Richard noticed that Neil seemed to have his arm around Lisa. Team-building indeed, he thought, then realised that Rupe was speaking.

'What were you saying Rupe?'

'You know Hamburg is developing a new engine?'

'That middleware one?'

'It's done. This is a full game engine.'

'No.'

'Yeah, in the first instance it's for something about Mexican drug wars.'

'They don't need a new engine for that.'

'When has this business ever been about need? Sure, they don't need it, but they want to make something that'll work on PDAs as well as across the major platforms. They've been asking if someone wants to go over on secondment from here.'

'Oh right?'

'So think about it, okay? You did well on this one Rich, and if you go in at the ground level on this new software you can bring it back here. If *Somme* goes to sequel, maybe we can give it a more modern edge.'

'Okay. I'll think about it.'

'That's my man. An opening in Hamburg, what could be more up your street, eh?'

Rupe got up before Richard had time to reply. The noise level was rising in the bar and there was a sense of suppressed hysteria. He noticed for the first time the exposed frame of the building, iron pillars riveted to girders, hints of some industrial past. Ben slid along to sit next to him. 'This is so cool. Is it always like this?'

'No. Sometimes we're up all night and there's shouting and crying and by the time the bugs get fixed all we want to do is go and collapse in a dark corner somewhere.'

'But the bugs get fixed?'

'Yeah. Or Rupe chooses one of us to sacrifice live online to Lars.'

Ben removed his retro eighties glasses and polished them on his neon paint splash t-shirt. 'This placement has just been awesome. I know I'm a bit drunk now, but I totally feel like I'm living the dream.'

Tuula came back, her eyes glittering, and Richard patted Ben on the back before palming the small package she held out and retreating to a toilet cubicle. Hearing Ben's enthusiasm had made him think of Stephie; he was the same age as her, Richard guessed, but if Ben had landed the DaCapo placement the odds were he was going to get work in the industry as soon as he graduated. Whereas Stephie, even with an HND in Psychology, might find her ambitions somewhat trickier to fulfil. He checked his iPhone just in case she'd been in touch, thinking as he did so of Loren, and whatever absurd form of politeness or fear had prevented him from whipping his hand away from her as soon as she'd touched him. Instead there was an email from Calum, an invitation to come and stay, anytime – *but you'd get more peace in a B&B now that Kaylar's teething (still can't believe I managed to marry someone who's as big a Trekkie as I am!) . . . ran into Luke again, his number is 07774 381200 if you ever want to . . .* Richard scrolled back, thinking for a second that the first rush of the drug had made him imagine the phone number. It was still there, sharp and clear on the screen.

Richard could remember telling Luke once that he'd prefer a pretty art student to a bit of rough – or had Luke suggested that to him? – and now, an hour or so later he found himself trying his best to get a very pretty art student drunk, and not having to try very hard at all. He had an intensity that Richard found attractive, an openness about his artistic influences and pet theories that hovered somewhere between confidence and naivety, with a pleasing hint of geekiness thrown in. And then he mentioned playing football, scoring a winning goal, Richard felt himself respond to the more robust masculinity that this seemed to convey. Over at the bar he could see Tuula leaning in close to listen to a girl with an asymmetric haircut. Lisa had already gone home, helped by Neil; chivalrous to the last, as Solange had commented wryly.

I was thinking of swinging by the old place next weekend. Will you be around? Richard

Richard had to check his phone to make sure that he really had sent the text. And once he'd done that he had to keep checking, wishing he'd phrased it differently, knowing that now, years later, Luke must have other old places, and perhaps other Richards too.

'Are you waiting on a call?' the art student – Sam – asked, his eyelashes perfectly pale and very unlike Luke's, though maybe there was a hint of resemblance in the slightly girlish lips.

'I'm sorry,' Richard said. 'Just checking in. My sister and her friend are staying in my house.'

'Ah. Worried they'll set fire to the Persian rugs and drink the Margaux?'

'Not Stephie. Maybe her friend.' He almost told Sam about the pass Loren had made at him, and then wondered what it would prove. 'So where do you live?' he said instead.

'You're staying in a hotel though, right?' Sam said, with a grin that might have meant nothing at all.

'No, the company has an apartment. Rupe'll be staying there too, he's usually based in London.'

'Hmm. Let's go back to mine then. But I'm warning you, it isn't a palace.'

When Richard saw the room, like so many student dives he recalled from years before, places he'd lived and places he'd woken up with a parched mouth and the air musty with the stench of sex, he said, 'It's perfect.'

'Bring back a few memories?'

Richard nodded, though the memories were not of his time in Dundee. He recalled that as flat and grey, despite the city's pride in being the sunniest town in Britain. Working in the games department at HMV, as if finally to redeem all those rejected applications to Boots and the Co-op back home. Cooking packet pasta in his bedsit, calling round for people who were never in. Programming had been the spark that illuminated it all, and he'd never been sure whether sex hadn't featured much by inclination or lack of opportunity.

Sam put on music – something Richard didn't recognise, with lyrics in German zigzagging between electronic loops – and made cups of tea and they sat together on the couch for just long enough for Richard to wonder if he'd misread the situation after all, but then he caught the slightest tremble in Sam's hand as he put his mug down, and when he looked at Sam's face in profile his lips were parted and Richard knew that he wasn't imagining the fizz of energy between them, the urge to push it further and see where it would take them. He put his own mug down, let his leg rest against Sam's, let the silences in their conversation expand until they became replete with possibilities.

When at last Richard reached out, made an unmistakeable move, Sam responded as though he'd been constrained for too long. He kissed Richard's mouth and his face, bit the skin on his neck, a little at first, then when he moved over Richard's throat he opened his mouth wide, sucking at the flesh as though he might suddenly tear it with his teeth. Richard arched his head back and gasped, opening himself to the sensation, feeling for a second as though that alone would be enough. As Sam unfastened his belt and slid his hand inside Richard's trousers he whispered, 'Anything you want. As rough as you want.'

Later Richard found himself thinking of Loren, with her scars and her desperation, chose not to think about Sam in the same way. Instead he concentrated on Luke, the images he had of Luke from all those years ago. He ran his hand down the line of Sam's cheek and jaw, then pressed his hand over his mouth to muffle the noises that might have indicated pain as much as anything else and kept going, until everything else disappeared and he felt that he was in the moment, alone.

0

We went to Lucy's room that night, Luke and I. Diane had been trounced at pool, outdrunk at tequila, and with an eye to her safety we'd walked her home, drawing tactfully aside as Lucy held back her friend's hair while she vomited in the gutter.

Part of the appeal, I suppose, that it would happen in a narrow, single bed, under the gaze of Lucy's childhood teddy bear and the photos on her pinboard of friends, family, pet dog. A red setter, if memory serves, bounding through an herbaceous border towards a wholesome mother in gardening gloves, clipping stems with her secaturs. Luke examined the pictures with care, asking who was who amongst her school chums and those from her year abroad.

How sweet, he said, smiling his most guileless smile. Boys don't do that, put up photos of their loved ones. Boys aren't as nice as girls, are they?

She laughed and tossed her hair and lured him to admit, pretend reluctant, that there wasn't anyone he'd like to have a photo of beside his bed. Not a close family, he told her, passing his hand over his face as though even thinking about it upset him. We drank some more, lots more, and Luke trumped Lucy's soapbar with a pungent bag of pure homegrown, until we felt much older and wiser and cooler than her. Soon we were overtaken by that oddness, that almost-recognition that happens when things get out of hand and you know there's no point in going back, so it's as if you're sleepwalking, not really there. Until the morning, when it's crystal clear, and you try to layer that gauziness between your waking self and the memory that you can't afford to give house room.

There were conversations in which she tried to show off her liberal attitudes, her half-formed riot grrl feminism, but was soon left out of her depth and feeling she had something to prove. She couldn't match Luke's easy, acerbic worldliness, her attempts to hide her privilege were transparent and pathetic. He'd invite further confidences – about her house at school, her pony club rosettes – then trample over them with the lightest, most devastating footfalls. Until she lost ground, needed reassurance, realised there was one way she could get it. And so she flirted with him more, tried to win him over. Stephanie flashed through my mind, so eager to please, hiding her lovebites under polonecks.

I was sitting next to him on the floor by the bed when the first twitch of an erection started. So close that his taut, denim clad thigh was pressed against mine. I excused myself and left the smoky haven of Lucy's room, pushing through the nearest set of double doors into a corridor, long and spacey with flickering fluorescent strips overheard. Through the windows I could see trees contorting in the wind. I stumbled along, looking for a toilet, finally finding a dingy communal bathroom with no light switch that I could locate. After I'd relieved myself I hunched over the sink and drank some water from the tap, giving up when it turned lukewarm rather than colder. I mopped my face with a rough pink paper towel, the same as the ones they'd had at school.

When I crept back into Lucy's room, closing the door gently behind me and resetting the snib, they were both on the bed. Luke was lying half on top of her, kissing her, his hand up her tie-dye skirt and edging its way inside her white cotton panties. What a cliché, I thought, though even in the moment I recognised it as a detail that would stick in my mind. White cotton, with a pink scalloped trim, stretched tight over the bridge of his hand.

I'm sorry, I said. Will I leave you to it?

He rolled over. His t-shirt was all rumpled up so that I could see his scar, and below it, the firm length of his cock against those dark denim jeans. It seemed huge, eager, pulsing, ready to spring through the fabric, uncannily reminiscent of the Incredible Hulk cartoons I used to like as a child.

No, he said. We don't want you to go. Do we Lucy?

Struggling to prop herself up on one elbow, she wrenched her glazed gaze from him and said:

No, we don't want you to go.

She pulled a stray hair from her swollen lips. Luke leaned over and picked up my tumbler of vodka, held it towards me. There was a poster above the bed, I noticed, of Kiefer Sutherland in *The Lost Boys*.

I hesitated when Lucy pulled Luke's t-shirt over his head, looked away so I couldn't see what he was doing to her in return. But he met my eye when he unfastened his belt, he was looking straight at me, and I looked at his chest, bare and pale, wanted to touch it, wanted to trace his collar bones with my fingers and then my lips. When I looked at his face again he was still looking back at me, although Lucy was leaning forward to unbutton my jeans, and I thought, maybe, just maybe.

And Lucy, why did she go along with it? (Did she go along with it?) Women like to feel dirty, he'd told me once, and Lucy was the kind of girl who talked a good game, pornography as liberation and all that, the kind of girl who thought keeping lube in her bedside cabinet was a statement. She moved toward me of her own accord, or maybe he nudged her. Her mouth was clumsy and she faltered, moaning as Luke pushed his fingers inside her, but by then I was so hard it hurt and nothing else mattered. He was looking at me.

And so, and so. Let's cut to the chase. The three of us balanced on that narrow college bed, its sheets stamped with the blue logo of the university linen supplier. It's alright, he'd said earlier, Richard's gay, but when it came down to it that was the ace in his pack; she could help me, I don't know, be certain, fulfil a wish. He made it seem both safe and some kind of special privilege, awarded just to her. All the while kissing her, touching her, tender and firm. The next step was to guide her round to the idea that this was the way I was used to, the way it should be. I played my part well, it seems, struck exactly the right balance of innocence and yearning. He just pushed a little more, and a little more, to see how far she would go. All the way, it seemed, and then some. She didn't consent, not in strict legal parlance, but she didn't say no, of that I can be absolutely sure.

Do it, he said, and I did, closing my eyes and gently pressing until I gained ground.

While I stayed still but still hard in position, he eased himself in from the front. He began, slowly, to move, and I thought I would explode then expire for the pleasure of feeling him so close to me.

His pace quickened, I had to match it and I did, perfectly, wishing it could last forever. When I opened my eyes he was looking at me again, looking at my face with awful wonder in his eyes, and he smiled, as if he would have kissed me. As if he would have pressed his dry lips to mine, touched the tip of his tongue to mine. If she hadn't been between us. He reached over and stroked my hair back from my face, and his touch, his touch, the feel of him against me, his fingers brushing my throat, my lips, made me shudder and slow, and as I relaxed I saw his beautiful face contort, as if it was the sight, the sound, the feel of my ecstasy that had brought on his own, and I had to bite the inside of my cheek until I tasted blood to stop myself saying out loud what it was that I felt.

19

Richard ran the tap in the bathroom sink until the water was icy and then gulped down mouthful after mouthful until his chest burned. They'd lain together, afterwards, Richard letting his head rest on Sam's shoulder while Sam held him with one firm hand on his flank. As Richard leaned back against the wall he noticed the stained grouting around the bath, tried to steel himself to slip away into the grey early morning. There had been a moment when he had closed his eyes and felt Sam's breathing slowing, and thought he might slip into sleep and stay there overnight. And then Sam had twitched awake and Richard had swung his legs out of the bed, and even when he was dressed and outside in the deserted street, watching the gulls swoop down to peck at discarded sausage suppers, he couldn't quite shake the low throb of rejection.

After a couple of sleepless hours lying flat on his back in his room in the DaCapo flat he heard Rupe whistling and crashing around in the kitchen. Richard hauled himself up and into the shower. Just before he stepped under the water he paused, tried to catch the smell of Sam on his skin before submerging the awareness that he was washing it away for good. He'd intended nothing more than a one night stand and yet there had been a moment, standing in the doorway of the shabby student flat, when they had squeezed each other tight and kissed, and Richard thought it would have taken just one word from Sam to make him drop everything and stay.

When he got to the office he met Tuula. Her glasses didn't obscure the dark circles under her eyes.

'Hej hej Richard.' She stuck her tongue out and made a bleergh noise.

'That bad, huh?'

She nodded. 'But I had fun. And you?'

Richard felt a surge of heat flowing from his chest to his throat as he thought of the night before. He wondered if Tuula could see it, mottling above his collar. 'Yeah,' he said. 'I had fun too.'

'Ready for your alpha?'

'You bet.'

'Okay, we start with the actual Somme chapter.'

Neil came in, bearing a cardboard tray of coffees and a large paper bag, the grease spots on which indicated some kind of breakfast. 'Hey kids, here's the caffeine and the sugar.'

'You're a lifesaver,' Rupe said, emerging cadaverously from his office. 'Rich, good to see you. I take it you're not planning to disappear back to Balamory today?'

'I hadn't really thought about it.'

'Well, as soon as your hands stop trembling, get playing.'

Richard looked towards Tuula, saw her nod her head. Neil grinned, 'Let's do the show right here, eh?'

'I have worries still about that bug,' Tuula said. 'Also, Alka-Seltzer, for those who feel as bad as me.'

Richard raised his hand and she threw the packet over to him. He failed to catch it. Neil stooped to pick it up and said, 'No offence mate, but with a reaction time like that, you're going to be one of the first to fall when the shooting starts.'

'I'll just make a quick call,' Richard said, and walked over to the window. Outside it was brighter than during his solitary walk back to the flat that morning, but still grey, the Tay trying hard to sparkle in the light. Sam must have been eight years his junior, he thought, any sense of pride giving way to an uneasy melancholy about his own age. A twinge somewhere between groin and stomach seemed to plead that he wasn't past it just yet.

Sure. Let me know when.

Richard's brain, still hangover-addled, tried to recall whether he'd already texted Stephie to say he wouldn't be able to drive home that day. Sent at 07:03 am, he read, his pulse skipping over a beat as he saw the unfamiliar number. Had Luke turned into an early riser or reached for his phone while he was still in bed? Aware that Tuula was waiting for him, Richard dialled his home number. Stephie didn't answer so he left a message saying he needed to stay another night and urging her to call back. As a by-the-by he added, 'Fancy a field trip sometime?'

When he emerged from his booth several hours later, Richard was too caught up in the various quirks that had emerged in the game to check his phone. When he'd started playing it had almost been a goal in itself, something that could be achieved after an hour or so of successful gaming; text Luke, suggest the weekend. But the game had reeled him in, even with no soundtrack it had worked. There was a strange beauty to the scorched and silent landscape, to the shells blazing noiselessly, to the tarry scraps of trees that clawed the smoky sky above Mametz Wood. And there he was, Officer, loyal to the core but to his men most of all, with enough integrity to question commands from above. Only the small details were missing.

'Did anyone manage to bayonet at close range?' he asked. 'It didn't work for Officer.'

'Nah,' Neil said. 'I was Woman and I had a go on the guy in the trench next to me, but it just wasn't happening. I had to sort of bludgeon him to death instead. There's a glitch there for sure.'

Tuula turned her palms upwards. 'Okay, okay, I'm on it. But get me something to eat, somebody please. I have sugar low.'

Neil ripped open the side of the greasy bag and hooked his finger through a doughnut, which he held out to her. 'Did anyone see the bit with the cavalry?'

'Yes. It made me feel a bit sick, actually,' Richard said.

'Fucking amazing graphics though. Wait until they put sound on that, Jeez.'

'So what's the verdict so far?' Rupe asked, peering into one of the Greggs bags and then stepping back as though it contained something he hadn't expected.

Richard kept quiet, waited. Tuula, wiping sugar from the doughnut from her lips, said, 'Okay, old school weapons, no mutants, no flying machines . . .'

'Until chapter five,' Richard said, hastily. 'There's airborne bombing in five.'

'No flying machines yet,' Tuula said. 'But for me, it plays. I had to think. And it's very . . . close up?'

'Visceral,' Neil said, biting into jam doughnut and licking the filling out. 'It's like you can see who you're killing, you can see the expression in their eyes. It's cool.'

'I like the feeling of comradeship,' Richard said. 'In the trenches that was really strong. And you can base tactics on it. Decide on who to sacrifice and who to protect.'

'Yeah, it'll be good to see how that plays out in the sandbox,' Neil said, and Richard nodded.

'You want me to go into the code for the bayonets now?' Tuula asked, and Richard felt a surge of pride; that she'd asked him rather than waiting for Rupe seemed evidence that the game was all right, that she believed in it. Over at the white-board Rupe was scrawling a projected date for beta testing.

'Where's Lisa?'

'Puking,' Neil said, then coughed. 'I mean, she doesn't work on Saturdays.'

Rupe frowned, as if he'd been exposed to a belief that he found inconceivable; the existence of extra-terrestrial life, perhaps. 'Hmm. Solange, email her and tell her to get on to production first thing on Monday morning. Check the script guy's standing by. And pull those character bios off the wiki. We need some names before they cast. Lars likes names, they help him see the big picture.'

He retreated to his office and Richard heard a shriek from Tuula and turned to see her poking Neil's chest, backing him into a corner until he nodded, shamefaced. 'Bad karma Neil, bad karma,' she crowed. 'You got to work with her.'

Richard went to the water cooler and refilled his cup. Things were moving quickly, after such a long, lonely slog. Beta testing and voiceovers; sometimes these had seemed so far in the distance as to be unreachable, and now Rupe was talking as if he thought the green light was a formality. Richard felt in his pocket for his phone, coaxed it back into life.

Neighbours going ape – LOREN – can I give them this no? S x

Richard sighed, and an unwelcome flash of Loren was supplanted by the memory of Sam, an implausible fantasy of the DaCapo team going out for a drink and bumping into him again, the possibility of an encore. He hesitated over his reply but answered in the affirmative before switching off his phone and returning to his booth, where Officer was poised and waiting, his face streaked with mud and the glare of fire reflected in his blue-grey eyes.

0

Sunday morning wasn't a normal part of our week, but given the volume of music with which Luke had greeted the day, going back to sleep seemed unlikely.

You have a febrile glint in your eye, I mumbled, as he slopped a mug of coffee down on my bedside table.

He perched on the end of my bed, holding his own mug with both hands.

Nah, just surplus energy. How come you're alone? I thought you said it would be like shooting ducks in a barrel.

I could ask you the same question.

But you don't know if I am. There could be any number of new friends in my room.

Are there?

He laughed. Nah.

Well then. Don't cast aspersions on my ability to get lucky.

After a final screetch of feedback the Jesus and Mary Chain fell silent, and I closed my eyes. I was starting to feel chilly and wondered if I'd be able to drift back to sleep when Luke went away.

So, aren't you going to tell me about your big gay party? he said.

I ignored him until he started bouncing up and down on the bed, then hauled myself upright, tugging the duvet from beneath him and taking care to keep it tucked under my armpits as I sat up and reached for my coffee.

Can I help you with something? I asked.

He looked at me and let his lips relax into a pout.

Stop it, I said.

What?

You know.

After I'd taken a mouthful of hot coffee my breath was visible.

It's fucking freezing in here, I said.

Yeah, but it's nice outside. Let's go for a walk.

When we went outside we passed a staggering figure in a dinner suit, his bowtie unfurled, suckling the dregs from a bottle of Bollinger like an infant. There had been a mid-term ball the night before, and soggy corsages and scraps of ribbon lay trodden into the pavement next to discreet slops of vomit. We hadn't gone, of course; not really our scene, not even the smug Philosophy Club, with its preference for smoking jackets and vintage prom dresses, more chemical forms of stimulation. As we shivered through the graveyard I thought of how exclusive it had seemed the first time I'd explored it, with its Cambridge-born professors of Arabic and metaphysics, the great and the good whose names transposed so neatly into Latin. They'd matured well, compared to the miners and the sons of miners back home. Here was a man of 89, and another of 93.

Can't imagine us all clubbing together to commemorate old Mendelssohn, can you, Luke said.

I shook my head and we walked on, following the path that would take us down to the harbour. On the way he pointed to a small cross, perhaps made of marble though it was too grimy to tell. Instead of a name, the inscription was the outline of a dove pulling a banner that said LOVED AND LOST. Except that the lettering was worn, and the LOST looked more like LUST. I wasn't sure whether it was this, or the message itself, that Luke was indicating.

A plane screamed out over the sea ahead of us, ripping through the sharp winter sky as if it had sliced it into two trembling halves, ready to fall and smash around us. A moment or two later another one followed it, the roar of the engines fading almost as swiftly as it had come.

That noise, Luke said. It gets me every time.

Do you think they're going to Yugoslavia?

We stood watching as the planes shrank to specks and disappeared.

Maybe, Luke said. Either that or a mercy mission to

Colombia to collect the Honourable Guy's marching powder.

Is he still bugging you?

Yeah. Told him I'd sort him out once more, but then I'm getting my head down for the exams.

We rejoined the road and continued along the harbourside to the pier. The sea was grey blue, its surface rippling.

See, Luke said, a sudden gust of wind whipping the words from his mouth. Bet you're glad that you're not still stinking in your pit now.

Hmm, I said, but it did seem as if everything had been sharpened by the cold. A small white boat crept in past us, its engine chugging quietly. By the time we'd strolled to the end of the pier it had docked at the harbour wall and two men in orange overalls were already unloading creels.

Ever had lobster? I asked.

Once. You?

Nah. Don't fancy it much.

Luke grinned as if I'd confirmed something he'd long suspected of me, then turned back to face the open water. He clambered up to the flagpole and stood there, nearer the edge than I'd have gone, looking out to the horizon, where the colour of the sea deepened until it met the sky in a perfect line.

Worth it?

What? I said.

The view, twally.

Yeah, I said. Sure.

He swung round the flagpole then jumped back down onto the pier and looked up at me.

Did I ever tell you I thought about joining the Merchant Navy?

No, I said, walking back down the stone steps to join him. Why?

My mum used to say my father was in it and that's how he never came home.

Really?

Nah, don't be stupid. I heard stories, that's all, from my uncle in Leith. Fancied fucking off out of there and seeing the world.

So why didn't you?

He shrugged. Dunno, like . . . just thought I could fuck off in a different way, I guess. And here I am. Fucked off.

He sat by the bollard and took off his gloves. Although we were in the lee of the wall he cupped his hands around his cigarette to light it.

Want one?

Okay.

Here.

He gave me the one he'd just lit and took another out of the packet. We sat smoking for a moment and then he said, Look.

Up on the headland where the rocky outline of the early church lay, I saw a flash of red, then another. Students in robes, maybe a dozen of them, some flanked by parents and visitors, all picking their way down the steps in the traditional Sunday morning procession.

The parents and visitors were left behind as the students grouped into pairs and threes. After a while I noticed that Luke's gaze was fixed on one figure in particular. I crushed my cigarette out on the stone and threw the end into the water behind me. As they got closer I recognised Lucy. Luke kept staring, and I could feel my thighs tense with the cold. I wanted to move but we couldn't really, not without pushing our way through the gathering at the end of the pier. Not until they turned and went back the way they'd come.

Was it, I began, then stopped. I felt nauseous from the cigarette.

What?

Was she okay? I said. When we'd left that night, I'd looked back into the small single room and seen her perched on the edge of her rumpled bed, arms wrapped around her knees, hands clasped.

What do you mean?

The figures in red were beginning their slow progress along the pier. I turned my palms out towards him in a helpless gesture.

She was fine Richard. Unless you've got HIV or something.

I punched the top of his arm, quite hard.

That'll bruise, he said, rubbing it.

The surface of the pier was cracked and uneven, I noticed, with pebbles and broken shells embedded in the concrete. I hoped I had bruised him, because I'd hardly touched him before.

Hey, he said, and I turned to look at him, his eyes grey and steady below his dark lashes. She liked it. Couldn't you tell?

More your area than mine, I said.

He smiled. Trust me then. She'll have been thinking about it ever since, under the covers at night.

Maybe he was right. Maybe we all relive our darkest, most degrading moments for our guiltiest, most secret pleasure. My eyes were on Lucy's face when she recognised us, or rather him. Her cheeks were rosy with the fresh air, but there was no mistaking the flush that spread through her skin as she walked towards us. But she had to keep going, playing out the quirky and charming custom that their visitors had come to see. Her parents amongst them, perhaps, cameras at the ready as they waited at the mouth of the pier. Luke, leaning back against the wall, his legs stretched out in front of him, kept on looking at her. I had trimmed the edges of my memory, tried to crop the images I didn't want to see, but now I could feel it coming back. A burning photograph in reverse, details returning, clarity regained.

She held herself together well, until they turned to climb up onto the higher part of the pier wall. The stone steps were worn and damp and she slipped, breaking her fall with an outstretched hand. One of her companions hauled her up, and she didn't look back as they proceeded towards the town. At the beginning of the pier cameras were swapped, and sure enough Lucy posed between two people who must have been her parents, smiling while one of her friends took a picture.

Are you still interested? I asked.

Nah, he said. I've got Aimee, remember?

Oh right, I said. And how's that going?

Playing the long game, he said, flicking his cigarette end into the oily water of the harbour. Or maybe not playing at all.

After a few last snaps the cameras were put away and the red clad figures began to disappear behind the harbourmaster's office and on their way to lunches in restaurants and fond farewells to their visitors. Luke stood up and stretched.

Besides, he said, I think all the possibilities have been exhausted. Don't you?

20

The hedge seemed to have grown already, Richard thought, but now that it had been trimmed away from the gate it wasn't enough to screen his car from the Manbys. He saw Mrs Manby – she hadn't confided her given name – look up from her weeding and then scramble to her feet and hurry inside. Her husband had left a terse voicemail which Richard had listened to before going to bed the night before and then completely forgotten until he was looping off the main road to an isolated café designated 'Local Services'. He'd taken his mug outside and sat on the car bonnet, enjoying the open space and relief from the large and grumbling English family whose Scottish adventure seemed to have already disintegrated amidst tug-o-wars over burgers and chips. He texted Stephie with his ETA and then called Gerald Manby, who proved belligerent and unwilling to accept that it was contradictory to insist that Loren was an adult who had taken advantage of his son at the same time as complaining that she was a young person whom Richard had failed to adequately supervise. Pointing out that the boy was over the age of consent had done little to ease the situation. Richard found it hard to believe that he had only been a year older when he'd met Luke. Looking back, it seemed they'd been more mature, more formed.

Richard switched off the engine and got out of the car, locking the door behind him; a city habit he thought he'd managed to shake. He could see Gerald Manby approaching the gate, opening it and coming to a stop, arms folded over his quilted gilet. Their conversation earlier had been truncated by an expedient loss of reception, just after Richard had felt forced to make clear that there was no impropriety in having two young women to stay when one of them was your wee sister and what's more, you happened to be gay. And even if neither of those caveats applied, it was none of your neighbour's business; something which was satisfying to say, even if the line had by then reverted to the empty silence that indicated there was no longer anybody there to hear.

'Sorry I didn't call back,' Richard called. 'The signal didn't improve and I wanted to get on the road.'

'Yes well, another matter has come to my attention,' Gerald Manby said.

Richard tried to conceal the slump of his shoulders. 'Oh?'

'Alcohol and,' Manby looked around, as if even the hedge had ears, 'drugs.'

'What kind of drugs?' Richard asked, realising that a note of enthusiasm might have entered his voice as he remembered the excesses of the DaCapo night out.

'Marijuana.'

'And you think that it came from Stephanie or Loren?'

'They were the source of the alcohol,' Manby said.

This time Richard did nothing to hide his sigh. 'Well, I think it very unlikely but I will ask them about it.'

He didn't say that he thought it unlikely because otherwise, he was sure, these drugs would have made an appearance before now. Although if Loren had found her way into town, he doubted it would have taken her long to locate anything she needed. He slung his bag over his shoulder and went into the house, aware that Manby hadn't moved.

'Stephie?'

He walked through the kitchen, where plates and cups were stacked waiting to be placed in the dishwasher, and saw Stephie sitting with a textbook on her lap and her eyes closed.

'Stephie,' he said again, then noticed that she was wearing her iPod. He went a little closer, anxious not to give her a fright, but the vibration of the floor under his feet was enough to rouse her.

'Hey,' she said, pulling out her earphones and jumping up, the wires tangling around her elbow. She threw her arms around him and squeezed. 'Oh, I'm glad you're home.'

'Me too,' Richard said. 'Except for the welcoming committee.'

'What?'

'Next door. Going on about drugs or something? I think he's waiting for me to go back out.'

Stephie groaned. 'I'm sorry. Bloody Loren. I just want her to go away now, okay?'

Richard nodded. 'Did she give the boy, what's his name, something?'

'No. Well I mean like a bottle of beer, maybe. Anything else was his. He's a total stoner, apparently.' She looked at Richard. 'Don't you believe me?'

'Of course I believe you. I already said that it had nothing to do with you.' Richard pinched his temples between the thumb and middle finger of his right hand, circled them for a minute. 'Right. This is really starting to piss me off.'

As he spoke to Gerald Manby he imagined that Stephie might be watching him through the double-glazed windows, waving his arms in a silent performance of anger. Pointing behind to his house, shaking his head. Pointing towards the Manby's instead, nodding. An exaggerated, obvious mime, but one that he hoped would convince. As Manby's face reddened Richard felt his own voice soften.

'It isn't unusual for boys his age to experiment. It's probably just a phase.'

This was scant comfort, it seemed, and Manby marched off, muttering to himself. Richard turned back towards the house. There was no sign of Stephie at the window.

He found Loren upstairs. The door of the bedroom was open, but he still considered knocking. Instead he said, quite gently, 'Can I come in?'

She shrugged, so he sat on the bed opposite her, moving Stephie's pyjamas to one side.

'Loren . . .'

'You don't have to give me my marching orders. My bag's almost packed.'

Her bag was small and a tangle of underwear trailed from it as though it had burst free.

'So what's your plan?'

She laughed. 'I'm not much of a planner. You might have guessed that.'

'Are you going home, I mean?'

'Home?'

'Back to college.'

She separated a pair of socks from the underwear tangle and pulled them on. 'Don't worry; I've booked a room in a B&B for tonight. I'll get the first bus in the morning then go and stay with a friend in Glasgow.'

'I'll give you a lift to town then, when you're ready.'

'I'm sure I can hitch.'

'I'm sure you can, but I'd rather drive you,' he said. He wondered if he should insist she stay another night, whether he should drive her as far as Inverness even, and why rejecting her advances seemed somehow to have conferred this responsibility on him.

'Up to you,' she said, and stood up and began collecting toiletries from the dressing table.

Stephie was sitting at the picnic table when he went back outside. Mist or drizzle softened the outline of the islands and he could feel the dampness in the air. He perched at the end of the bench and said, 'She's going to leave in a wee while. I'll give her a run to a B&B in town.'

'Thanks.'

'It's okay. She was ready to go anyway. I didn't have to tell her.'

Stephie nodded. 'I'm going to take my book down to that jetty place and have a read. I'll tidy away her bedclothes and everything once you've gone.'

'I don't know if it'll stay dry.'

'It doesn't matter.'

Richard got up again, deciding he would have to eat something, a banana perhaps, before he got back in the car. 'Aren't you going to say goodbye?' he asked, but Stephie had plugged her iPod into her ears again.

The car outran the smirr, and by the time they passed the bay where he and Stephie had picnicked the sun was beating down. His lower back twinged as he moved his feet against the pedals and he thought a swim might sort him out, although imagining the shock of the cold water made him shiver, even in the muggy warmth. As he followed the curve of the road he glanced back towards the headland; the clouds had gathered there and he could see lines of rain. If Stephie had gone as far as the jetty she would be drenched by now.

Loren wound her window down wide. 'Do you mind,' she asked belatedly, as the breeze chased around the inside of the car.

'No,' Richard said. 'It was beginning to get stuffy. Might help keep me alert too.'

'I could have hitched.'

'Yes, you said. And I said I didn't mind.'

The road twisted more as they reached the side of the loch with all its rock formations, and Richard wondered how long he'd have to have lived there to be able to take the corners as smartly as Rab. He'd always meant to look up whether the rocks were the result of glaciations. Given that he'd never done so he supposed he wasn't that interested.

'I'm sorry,' Loren said, quietly.

Richard pulled into a passing place to allow another car by, raised his hand to acknowledge its headlight-flash thanks. He waited until they were moving again to ask, 'Have you fallen out with Stephie?'

Out of the corner of his eye he could see that Loren had turned slightly away from him to face the passenger window. Strands of her hair were dancing in the breeze.

'Did you speak to her?' she asked.

'About you?'

'Not necessarily.'

They were approaching the end of the single track road, after which it would be a quicker drive to the town. Twenty minutes, if the road was clear, half an hour if he took it easy. Someone had told him that the distance between village and town was a mere ten miles as the crow flies. He wasn't sure if that was true. He supposed that Loren wanted to tell him something, wondered if there would be enough time.

'So how's your game?' she said.

'Fine, thanks. We'll be onto beta testing in a couple of weeks.'

'Does that mean it's finished?'

He could see the sea up ahead, one of the ferries coming in from the Hebrides. 'No,' he said. 'There might still be problems. Either with the game itself or with the publisher.'

'Oh.'

'But it's looking good,' he said. 'We played it for the first time yesterday.'

'That must have been fun.'

'Yes.'

His mind flitted back to the darkened booth at DaCapo, to the moment when he'd loaded the alpha and seen the screen morph from blank blue to vivid. He thought of the eerie silence as gunfire flashed, the soundless contortions of infantry falling back into the mud. He'd dropped into the office before he'd left that morning, seen a pinboard covered in screenshots ready for marketing to decide what to leak to which forums. They looked good.

'Did Stephie tell you that she'd had an abortion?'

He kept his eyes on the road, allowed his speed to drop as a van overtook him. 'No,' he said.

'Well she might want to. If there's an opportunity.'

He wanted to tell Loren that there had been plenty of opportunities, or perhaps that now she was leaving there might be more. After a moment he said, more amiably than he felt, 'Maybe. It's up to her to decide though, wouldn't you say?'

'I love Stephie, you know. She's been a good friend to me.'

Richard nodded, letting his eyes flit to the side to see Loren's face as she said this. She was looking straight ahead.

'I'll miss her,' she said, turning to him. He met her gaze for just long enough to see that her eyes were glinting with tears then returned to concentrating on the road ahead. They were almost in the town now and he could see the new sign up ahead welcoming them to the 'Gateway to the Isles'. Some misspelling had delayed the partner sign that would offer the Gaelic translation, prompting a volley of letters to the editor of the local paper, all of them expressing their outrage in perfect English and one, Richard had noted, from a second-homer whose children were educated at the Gaelic school back in Glasgow. Still, it was nice that someone originally from Buckinghamshire should feel such a connection with the language.

'Where is it you're staying?' he asked Loren.

She stretched her legs out to allow access to the pocket of her jeans, uncurled a scrap of paper she found there. 'Seaview,' she said. 'Original.'

'It's a wild guess,' Richard said, 'but I think it might be down the front.'

He drove down past the ferry terminal, turned left onto the crescent that overlooked the bay.

'There we are,' Loren said, pointing. 'Ah well, time for you to abandon me to the chintz pelmet and hostess tray.'

He looked over at the windows of the B&B, fussy with net curtains. 'Are you sure you don't want to . . .'

'Yes,' she said. 'Not fair on Stephie otherwise. Time she had you to herself again.'

Richard nodded and swung the car round to park facing the sea wall. He switched the engine off but neither of them moved. The sea was a very deep blue, the waves forming hypnotic zigzags.

'Strange effect,' Loren said. 'Like a Bridget Riley picture. D'you think people ever get mesmerised?'

'And jump in?'

'Mmm.'

He looked at the water. 'Maybe.'

They sat in silence for a minute and then Loren said, 'This is nice, isn't it?'

'Parking and looking at the sea?'

'Like an old married couple. We should've brought a Thermos.'

'I've got a Thermos,' he said, sheepishly.

'Ha,' she said, patting him on the arm. 'You would have.'

'For when I go walking.'

'On your own.'

'On my own. Usually.'

'Ever get lonely?'

He opened the car door, but instead of going to get Loren's bag from the boot he sat on the sea wall. The breeze played against his skin and he turned to look in the direction from which they'd come. The clouds were darker now, threatening to lower and wring themselves out over the town but equally likely to swoop out over the bay and away across the waves. When he turned back Loren was sitting next to him, her legs pulled up to her chest and her hands clasped around her ankles.

'No,' he said. 'Not really. I used to, years ago. But then . . . it was almost like I got so lonely that something overloaded and burned out. And now I don't.'

'Lucky,' she said.

'I don't know.'

'Maybe it's safer that way, I mean. The sky looks amazing, doesn't it?'

'Yes.' The greys and purples were edging into black and the mass was sinking down over the peak of the mountain. 'Loren,' he said.

'Yeah?' she said, and then when he hesitated she groaned. 'Oh, this isn't about the other night, is it?'

'I just wondered why,' he began, and then he looked away to where one of the smaller ferries was docking. She swung her legs round so that they were dangling on the other side of the wall, started kicked her heels against it.

'When is there ever a why with these things?'

Two cars and a van drove off the ferry, followed by a handful of backpackers. A shaft of light bleached their hair even blonder, and he couldn't yet tell if they were boys or girls. They looked as if they came from somewhere Nordic, although he realised that the only Nordic people he'd ever known had been dark-haired and not very tall, like Tuula. He felt a pulse inside him, somewhere in his chest or stomach, and realised that part of him – or maybe most of him – wanted to stay in town, avoid any conversation with Stephie, go out and get drunk and try to pick up handsome back-packers.

'Brr,' Loren said, rubbing the goosebumps from her arms. 'I guess that's my cue to go.'

He wasn't sure if she meant the chill in the air or the backpackers, who had stopped just along the road. One of them, a boy, was pointing up the hill. Richard could go over and ask if they were looking for the bunkhouse, he supposed. Loren could come with him. Four boys and two girls, what were the odds? But instead he jumped down from the seawall and opened the boot, handed Loren her rucksack.

'Take care,' he said.

'You too,' she replied, with a hint of archness that he found mildly comforting.

'Will you be okay?' he asked, even as he wished that he hadn't.

'Yeah,' she said, and smiled wide enough to show the gap between her teeth. 'Of course. I'm always okay.'

He met her eyes for a second and didn't know if she looked grateful or sorry or ready to go to the bar that the backpackers would inevitably end up in, drinking real ales from the local microbrewery. She winked at him and turned away, swinging her rucksack over her shoulder. He watched as she loped across the road. She raised one hand and without looking back, waved.

0

This town's too small, Luke said, stretching out his arms as if to delineate the bounds of some invisible cell. I need some space.

And so we found ourselves making a gloomy trek to the castle. The damp hedgerows, the dung on the road, water pooling in the muddy fields and the Friesians lumbering and gloomy rather than jolly illustrations from a child's animal alphabet. I think we both had the sense that we'd outgrown the sparse pleasures of squatting, but perhaps we felt a duty to make a last visit, to close the chapter. Luke was wearing a 70s teal leather jacket with slim black jeans and looked thoroughly un-country. When he jogged ahead to keep warm I saw splatters of dirt on the backs of his trousers. My trainers were suede, old school, but done-in was cool and the puddles didn't look much mankier than the beer swills on the dancefloor in the Union.

Fuck me, but it's cold, I said at last.

Here, have a cigarette, he said, holding out his pack. I took one, stamping my feet to try and get the feeling back into them as he tried to find his lighter.

Remember the first time we came here? I said.

He nodded, clicking the lighter once, twice, until the flame caught. We drank cheap whisky and played truth or dare, he said.

Yeah. Well, this time I dare you to tell me a story. Something I don't know about you.

I'm an open book. You know it all.

I doubt that.

We turned past the red brick cottages and began walking along the straight road towards the fence we climbed to enter the grounds. A sign at the side of the road said WORKS ACCESS, 100YDS, and then when we reached the gatehouse we saw that a new KEEP OUT sign had been erected below the previous PRIVATE.

What the fuck happened to the right to roam, Luke said.

Doesn't apply if you're rich enough, I guess. So what will we do then?

You want your truth, don't you? So let's start with a dare.

What? I said, looking around.

Well – he hunched down to tie one of his laces that had come undone – Why should we let them stop us?

We skulked through the grounds, keeping off the road as much as possible. There wasn't any sign of the works that required access, and we started to get cockier and to speak in louder voices, even when we reached the castle and saw piles of scaffolding in the driveway. We went round the back, as we had done before, and found that our window was still unfastened. I slipped in first, feeling a familiar twinge in my chest; that flash of imagining in which Luke turned on his heels and ran, leaving me there alone. But he followed me, closing the window softly behind him. We wandered through the service corridor, trailing our fingers against the tiled walls, before following the stairs up into the entrance hall, and then up again, the grand staircase, and along the long passageway that led to our light corner room.

Smell that, Luke said, sprawled on the chaise-longue like the model in a grubby fashion plate, beginning to roll a joint. He held out a pinch of grass and, still sitting cross-legged on the parquet floor, I leaned forward and sniffed.

Strong, I said.

He grinned. You bet, he said, and then he sat bolt upright.

What, I said, quietly, because I thought I'd heard a noise as well.

Luke shrugged but he was still whispering when he said, Old buildings, they always creak, eh?

I nodded, and we sat in silence for a second. He sighed, and ran his tongue along the edge of the Rizla, but then we both heard a bang.

Fuck, he said, dropping the half-made joint on the floor.

Was that a door slamming, I said. Was it?

Dunno.

Did you shut the window?

Yeah. I think so. I don't know.

I stared at Luke, and then edged to my feet. I kept thinking I heard footsteps, but Luke stood up as well and laid his hand on my arm.

It's the wind, he said. It was something outside.

Sure, I said, but my heart was pounding inside my ribcage.

We heard more creaks, and then another, quieter noise, perhaps that of a door closing somewhere.

Shit Luke, there's someone here. There's someone in the building.

I stared at the door, expecting it to open any second, my mind racing as I tried to think what I'd say, how we'd talk our way out of this, and then I noticed the key in the lock. I leapt forward and eased it round, so that it made only the slightest click as the lock fell into place. Luke nodded at me, and then we heard the sound, closer now, of another door closing. Someone was working their way along the corridor, checking the rooms.

Luke made for the nearest of the sash windows but it wouldn't budge. I tried another but it was locked as well, the catch far too high for me to reach.

Here, Luke hissed, and I saw a chink at the bottom of the window he was struggling to raise and rushed to help him.

It's going to make a noise, I mouthed, and he held his hands out as if to say, what else can we do?

Sliding our fingers through the gap we both pulled as hard as we could, until with a grinding noise that seemed deafening, we forced the window open by about a foot. I looked back at the door, expecting someone to start banging and shouting.

Fuck, Luke whispered. This time we pushed the window from below, until at last it was open far enough to squeeze through.

Luke shoved me towards it and I slung my right leg out, looking down at the grass of the drying green below. For an instant the glossy painted posts and cracked wooden poles made me think of home. The drop was only about ten feet but it was daunting enough for me.

Go, Luke said, and I managed to get my other leg through the window and clumsily flopped to the ground. I hauled myself to my feet just as Luke landed, knees buckling, beside me.

Run, he said, and we took off, round the back of the castle and away.

Adrenaline was still flickering across my synapses when we reached the pub, despite the chilly walk back into town, and it took a hastily swallowed pint to quell it. We relived each second of our narrow escape, making more and more extreme projections of what could have happened had we been caught. Maybe he had a gun, if he'd come from the farm. Maybe it wasn't a person at all.

Some dare, eh? Luke said.

Yeah, some dare.

Want another drink?

Of course. But you're not getting out of it that easy.

Out of what?

Well, it's truth or dare, remember? You owe me.

He laughed. Okay. Now I think on it, maybe there is something that's up your street.

We were interrupted by someone I recognised as a friend of Lucy's; not Diane, but perhaps the girl who'd been beaten that night, before we started our own game of doubles. She was looking for pills, but Luke flashed a glance towards the sharp-eyed barman and gave her a hard time for approaching him in public.

Come round the flat tomorrow, yeah? he said, at last.

Aren't you in Herrick?

Nah. Not any more.

She found a pen and he scrawled the address on the back of a flyer for the dodgy club at the other end of town, which she then examined as if it was a museum quality artefact.

After my 12 o'clock lecture?

Yeah, whatever. I'll sort you out then.

Idiot, he muttered, as she walked away. What the fuck would I do if I got barred from this place, eh?

And then he sat back against the reclaimed choir stall we were sitting on and began the story that he thought might be right up my street.

21

The sky opened as Richard left the town and although he had his wipers on the highest speed it was hard to see his way ahead on the single track road. Dips and hollows in the tarmac filled with water and even a sober driver could misjudge a turn and skite across the road into rock or loch or oncoming vehicle. When at last he reached the house his neck was rigid with tension. Hopping out of the car to open and close the gate was enough to soak him to the skin. Three sheep were cowering under the overhang of the Manby's front hedge (his neighbours' obsession with privet mystified him; surely it interfered with the view of the islands). One ewe issued a miserable bleat but they failed to muster the energy to skitter away from him.

He kicked his shoes off in the hall and ducked into the utility room to peel off his sodden t-shirt and trousers. Loren's bedclothes and towels were hanging on the pulley already, as though Stephie had tried to wash all trace of her friend away. He reached up and straightened the corner of one of the fitted sheets where it was scrunched. He wanted a drink, he realised. A drink and the curtains closed and a game, nothing to do with war and nothing he'd made. One of those ephemeral Japanese things with pastel colours and compellingly repetitive tasks. Shivering, he realised that Stephie must have removed his clean clothes from the pulley, and he couldn't bear to take the wet ones out of the machine and put them on again. If he was quick he might get up the stairs and into his bedroom before she spotted him, but no, of course she was there, standing in the kitchen doorway, smirking at the sight of him in his M&S jockey shorts.

'Did you go like that?' she asked. 'Or did Loren manage to strip you off en route?'

'I've got to go and have a bath,' he said. 'Sorry.'

Stephie looked hurt, and he quickly added, 'What do you fancy for tea?'

She shrugged.

'Sorry,' he repeated. 'The drive back was hellish and now I'm freezing. That's all.'

'I'm kind of in the mood for making something,' she said. 'If that's okay.'

'That would be really good,' he said, smiling. 'Brilliant.' It was slightly too much to seem genuine, he realised, but he walked past her and went upstairs anyway, locked the door of the bathroom and turned the hot tap on full so that it overwhelmed the noise of the rain beating down on the sky-light.

When he came downstairs he saw that Stephie had decorated the kitchen table with tealights placed in glass jars from the recycling. With just these and the light above the cooker the room was dim and unfamiliar. Outside it was still raining, though not as heavily, and the sky was dark grey.

'Pretty,' he said.

'Yeah well, in the absence of proper candleholders. Want a drink?'

'I can't tell you how much.'

'Was Loren doing your head in?' she said.

'No,' he said. Stephie twisted the top on a bottle so that it crackled free. 'She was . . . fine.'

'I bought more gin.'

'Thanks, that was nice of you. Didn't you get drenched?'

She shook her head, leaning over the table to check that her measures were equal. 'Just missed the downpour.' She topped the glasses up with tonic and handed him one. Just as he took a swig she said, 'Did you sleep with her?'

He choked and it was a moment before he managed to say, 'What, on the way into town?'

'At any time.'

'Of course not. Why?'

'Experience. And something she said.'

'What?' He took another mouthful, more carefully this time.

'I don't know. It was just, like, as if she knew something about you that I didn't, or she knew you in some other way.'

'No,' he said, wondering how much Loren had told Stephie and whether he was about to be caught out. 'There was nothing like that at all.'

Stephie nodded. He wasn't sure if she believed him or not, or whether it mattered. 'She's gone now,' he said.

'Yes.'

Stephie picked up her fork and turned it in her hands as if she was checking for a silver mark, then replaced it beside her tablemat. Richard got up and went over to the oven, hunched down and peered through the glass door. 'Lasagne?'

'Yeah. Are you bored with it? It's like my signature dish.'

'No, I like it.'

'Dad still won't eat pasta.'

Richard laughed. 'He'd eat macaroni cheese. As long as it had bacon on top.'

'Yeah, you're right. And it isn't that far off, is it?'

The timer on the oven bleeped and she drained her gin and tonic before getting up to silence it. 'Open some wine, would you? I'll be mother.'

It was half past eight, he noticed. He wondered what Loren was doing, imagined her in the bar of the Albion, the fiddlers playing in the corner as she smiled her wide open smile, downed her drink and looked straight into the eyes of a backpacker with strong cheekbones and arms windburnt from long hikes and sunny ferry crossings. Feeling the gin beginning to course around his body he thought he'd like to be in that position, with those possibilities. He thought of Sam again, of their kiss goodbye in the doorway of the flat in that dingy Dundonian close. Loren might be alone in her B&B bedroom, lying on a slidey, static coverlet, flicking through the television channels and finding nothing to watch.

'Loren told me something,' Richard said. 'I didn't know whether to mention it or not.'

'Well you have now.' Stephie stopped eating and put down her cutlery.

'Yes,' he said. 'I was worried I hadn't given you any time to talk.'

She sighed. 'I wanted to listen for a change. There was this whole family thing that I missed, back then, and besides, I like hearing about how you went away and how you managed not to come back.'

'I don't think I could come back,' he said. 'But I want you to be able to tell me things as well.'

'About the abortion, is that what you mean? I assume that's what Loren told you.'

He nodded, reached for the wine bottle and topped up their glasses. If Stephie was pregnant she wouldn't be able to drink like this, he thought.

'What do you want to know? What it was like? Why I did it?'

'Anything. Anything you want to tell me.' He took a sip from his glass, then another. All of a sudden Stephie laughed, a bright peal of noise that would have shocked him if her eyes hadn't been twinkling in the candlelight.

'Oh god,' she said. 'You poor thing. You're trying so hard, and I appreciate it, I really do. But honestly, you don't have to worry.'

'No?'

'No. It was early, it was medical, it was the right thing to do.'

'Medical? Isn't it always medical?'

'What, are you thinking about coathangers now? Medical means they give you a big dose of hormones. Okay, I felt a bit pukey and it wasn't particularly nice, but it wasn't like a major trauma.'

'Tell that to the manic pro-lifers,' he said, and then wished he hadn't although Stephie didn't seem bothered. 'Oh god,' he said, slowly, remembering a distant conversation about disappointments, an accusation levelled at him by his father, lots of sentences beginning with the words 'your mother'. 'Did Mum and Dad know?' he asked.

She nodded, serious this time. 'Dad was apoplectic.'

'I can well imagine.'

'He looked as if he was about to have another heart attack. Though I'm not sure whether he was angry at me or at Russell. That was my boyfriend, Russell.'

'The one Loren . . .'

'Yep.'

Richard rolled his glass around as though he was trying to release the bouquet at a wine tasting. 'Before or after?'

'Before I realised I was pregnant. I only found out after we'd split up and I didn't want to tell him. But it's surprisingly hard to keep secrets in that town.'

Richard nodded, thinking of Mr Sim's headstone, its graffiti epitaph. 'What did he say?'

'He didn't have any right to say anything. It wasn't his business anymore.'

'What about Mum?'

Stephie smiled, and this time it didn't reach her eyes. 'Mum. Well, Mum tried to talk me into going through with it.'

'What?'

'She likes children. She'd like grandchildren.' Stephie tore off a piece of lasagne crust, nibbled at it and replaced it on her plate.

'And I'm not going to give her any?'

Stephie sighed. 'Who knows? Maybe you will.' She emptied her glass and held it out to be refilled. There was only a dreg left in the bottle.

'There's more wine in the hall cupboard, I think,' Richard said. 'I hadn't got around to putting it away.'

As he left the room Stephie said, 'Do you see how your choices might have affected me?'

The electric light in the hall seemed lurid after the candle-light. 'What choices?' he said, tugging at the door of the hall cupboard. It needed planed, or something, to stop it sticking. 'I went away, I got thrown out of university, I came back home, I went away again.'

'And I stayed close.'

Lying on top of a tangle of walking boots and a golf umbrella he found a bag for life containing a packet of toilet rolls, three tins of chick peas and two bottles of red wine. They felt a little chilly but he supposed the wine would warm up once it was poured.

'I can't believe you didn't tell me sooner,' he said, struggling to remove the cork from the slightly more expensive bottle. 'About everything.'

'My boyfriend somehow managed to impregnate me – ' she caught Richard's eye and added, ' – well, I guess it was in the traditional way. He also slept with my best friend so that I split up with him and have now fallen out with her. Amid all the hassle I fucked up my exams, and I'm terrified that if I don't get away from that fucking town I'll be stuck there forever, doing the dutiful youngest daughter thing.' The cork sprang out at last, and Richard filled her glass almost to the brim. 'So yeah,' she said, 'I'm actually not that keen on talking about myself.'

He felt there must be something he should say, laid his hand on her upper arm instead and squeezed. She put her hand over his and squeezed back. 'So, when are we going on this field trip? I fancy a change of scene.'

'Anytime,' he said. 'This weekend.'

0

It seemed that once upon a time Luke had met a man. An older man, a richer man.

Hang on a minute, I said. How old is older?

I don't know, he said. Late thirties, early forties.

And what age were you again?

Just turned seventeen.

Yeah, I guess that is older.

This man took Luke for coffee in a gallery café after seeing him wandering around some exhibition or other, sheltering from a downpour and discovering a hitherto undeveloped interest in portraiture. They struck up a conversation about the rain hammering down on the lantern light above them, how both of them were caught without hat or umbrella, how perhaps they should sit out the deluge.

Noticing the haste with which Luke scoffed one of those famous scones (I didn't know they were famous, Luke said, I mean, how famous can a scone be?) this new benefactor – *just call me Dan, please* – insisted on buying him lunch; *it's only a fucking quiche for heaven's sake.* Dan edited a fancy art magazine, apparently, and lectured part time. He asked why Luke wasn't at school or college.

Was he a paedo? I said.

Fuck's sake Richard, Luke said, d'you no think I could tell a paedo a mile off?

I stopped smirking and adopted my best listening expression, perfected during increasingly tricky philosophy of language seminars.

Two jet black coffees later and Luke had explained that he'd left school early, without the results he'd hoped for. Dan's concern was heartening, and so Luke embellished his hard luck story with an extra sprinkle of thwarted ambitions and family problems, and before he knew it they'd arranged to meet the following week to see the student show at the RSA. After that it was Dada at the Dean (I liked that one better, Luke said) and a tour of those intimidating private galleries where you have to ring a bell to get in. A few glasses of fizzy at an exhibition opening, ignoring the raised eyebrows at his sportswear, and Luke was beginning to feel that he'd been missing out on a very good thing.

Hang on, I said. When you say sportswear do you mean like a shellsuit or something?

I'm trying to tell you a fucking story and all you can worry about is whether I wore a shellsuit?

You have to admit, it is a crucial detail.

I was seventeen years old, okay? I wore Fils tracksuit bottoms. Is that acceptable?

No, not really.

Christ. The point is that no-one'd talked to me about art before. I'd lived in that city my entire fucking life and never crossed the threshold of these places.

Eventually, what do you know, one thing led to another and the young protégé ended up spending weekends in Dan's cosy commuter belt cottage.

What about your mum? I asked.

None of her business, Luke said.

But she must have worried.

I guess she was used to me going AWOL.

Luke could read what he wanted, drink what he wanted, sleep until whatever time he wanted, just so long as he acted his part. Especially when Dan's friends came for Sunday lunch – *yes, divine, isn't it, apparently they bring it direct from the family farm in Umbria* – and marvelled over this incontrovertible proof that a little nurture could kick the arse out of a whole lot of nature. Freedom and responsibility were discussed at length in the garden, chilled Pouilly Fumé splashing seductively, Ollie from the opera watching over Dan's shoulder as Luke took a can of Coke from the fridge (friendly chuckles: *I know, but I just can't wean him off it*). And Luke ignoring them steadfastly as he chose a spot in the sun, peeling off his t-shirt before lounging on the grass to read his Gide, that pretty parted lip expression of his utterly uncontrived; or was that my imagination, my own embellishment of the story?

It wasn't sexual, he explained.

Sure, I said, thinking: strictly a philanthropist then, our man Dan, wouldn't dream of demanding anything untoward of his pick-ups.

Not directly, Luke added. Not at first.

Dan's friends were male, with the exception of a few faghags, all cackling innuendo and greasy red lipstick. One of them caught Luke in the upstairs bathroom with the broken lock, tried it on.

I wouldn't be surprised if you'd led her on to begin with, I said.

He grinned. Maybe I had.

So what did you do?

I said no thanks.

My expression must have mirrored my thoughts because he said, Pots and kettles, Richard. It's not like you were a paragon when you were that age.

I flushed. That was . . . an aberration.

Luke had confided in Dan later, perhaps allowing a light tremble of his eyelashes as he tried to spare his host's embarrassment at poor Minty's behaviour. And guess whose side Dan was on? Despite his feminist pretensions, and a token lesbian at his soirees, he didn't like women very much at all. Minty was a drunk and a nymphomaniac, and Dan couldn't apologise enough.

How could you stand it, I said. Trapped in the haute homosexualité.

But I could picture it clearly, that warm summer in a secluded garden, bees buzzing, flowers blooming. Nice things to eat, crisp linen sheets. Not much of a trial, not really.

I was playing, I suppose – Luke smiled at me, as though he'd been totally immersed in the memory – playing at another life.

Well, didn't you get tired of the game?

Hmm. You can always change the rules.

Striking through the malt one evening, Luke bored with Scrabble and Sibelius, not so choosy as long as he kept his eyes closed and pretended it was somebody else. Dan might not have been a feminist, but his other liberal principles were rock solid. Solid enough to act as a fixed point from which he could extrapolate with aplomb; *well yes, when it comes down to it, of course my respect for you does necessitate that I consider you able to make adult decisions.*

What did he look like, I wanted to ask, but somehow this seemed too dangerous a question. I didn't understand where or why a line had been drawn, only sensed that despite Luke's inebriated insouciance, crossing it would snap him shut like a clam.

A week or so later, holier than thou Dan was the one getting restless. Playing with his new pet was all very well, but he wanted a little bit more. Luke hadn't tired of country life, and a promised clothes shopping trip had not yet materialised.

I guess I had to rethink my boundaries, he said, running his thumb along the rim of his glass to catch a drip.

Do you want another, I asked.

Yes please, he said. A half and a half, maybe.

Sure.

As I stood at the bar waiting to be served, I imagined the sitting room of the cottage, the cosy yet chic décor. Glancing along the optics, catching my own reflection, wide-eyed in the mirror behind the gantry, I pictured a lazy hand job; coincidentally followed by the gift of new trainers and that jacket I admired. As I placed Luke's drinks on the scuffed bar table in front of him and turned to retrieve my own, my imagination soared then dived right down. Had he let Dan push his cock between those chapped lips, had he sucked and swallowed just as I had? Except he'd have been kneeling on eiderdown where I was on grubby wet tiles.

But Dan only had Luke's best interests at heart. He scanned prospectuses and phoned admissions officers, negotiated special considerations and unusual circumstances, obtained glowing character references from friends in the arts. A few days making coffee and answering the phone for the owner of the fizzy wine gallery became a summer internship as a PA, during which he'd displayed a formidable capacity to learn as well as excellent teamworking skills. *There is a thing called clearing, we'll see what we can do.*

And here you are, I said.

Yes, Luke agreed. Here I am.

May I? I indicated his cigarettes.

'Course.

He flipped open the packet and pushed it across the table towards me. I took out a cigarette, tapped it as I'd seen him do, lit it and inhaled properly for a change. I felt the burn of the smoke, and was pleased I hadn't coughed.

Do you still see him, I was going to ask, but instead I said: Are you still in touch?

Luke shrugged. Not really. Met for coffee once. Twice, actually. I saw him in Edinburgh. He gave me fifty quid for books for this term.

Did you buy books?

He smiled and tapped the side of his nose.

So that's it, I said, rotating my cigarette in the ashtray so that the tip became a sharp red point.

Yeah, that's it. It wasn't really my thing, Luke concluded, tilting his glass and letting the whisky roll round the edges.

The violence of my feelings startled me, the urge I had to force him, to push him back against that wooden choir stall and make it his thing. Because oh god, it was mine. Yes, my own dreams had been of boys my own age, a little older, but to be so offhand about receiving a proper invert's education; a generous, liberal, middle-class shafting.

22

Richard's phone vibrated with an incoming text message. He was coasting in the slow lane avoiding the juggernauts and if he'd been alone he might have slipped it out of his pocket and risked a peek. As it was he didn't want to hand the phone over to Stephie in case the message was from Luke. He was taking a chance, he realised; when had Luke ever been reliable? He might be away for the week, or busy. There was no point in thinking ahead, in nurturing enough hope (though hope of what Richard wasn't sure) to invite disappointment. Stephie was relaxed and enthusiastic, her legs stretched out in the passenger seat, singing along to the radio and topping up her lipgloss in the sunshield mirror. Every so often Richard smelled the sugary fruit scent of whatever she used. He wanted to ask her if she was really okay, to draw her out somehow, reassure himself as much as anything else. He'd found it hard to settle since he'd returned from Dundee. *Somme* was going well, better than he'd anticipated after all of Rupe's niggles, but still Richard felt a sense of rising pressure. They needed to get through the beta test and marketing had to finalise a title and give it one last push before Lars gave it the green light. Games could fall apart at this stage, turn from team efforts full of hope and promise to lonely failures.

'This girl that drowned,' Stephie said suddenly. 'There would need to have been an inquest or something, wouldn't there?'

Richard flicked on his indicator and pulled out to overtake a caravan in front of them.

'There was an inquiry,' he said, curving back into the slow lane. 'Her parents pushed the procurator fiscal for it.'

'And what did they find?'

'Accidental death.'

'That could mean anything.'

Don't you think I know that, Richard wanted to shout, but there was a car with a trailer in front and he had to concentrate on overtaking. He and Luke had taken the bus to the neighbouring town, ended up slipping out of the court before it was over and getting straight on the next bus back. He'd thought he was going to be sick; Luke had said something about lynching. And then they'd done what they did so well. Got drunk, steadily and bitterly, in a pub as far from the university and the pier as they could manage, ignoring the locals and their sly, accusatory gaze. They just think we're above ourselves, Luke had said, that's all it is. And then, later, his accent not so dissimilar to theirs: what the fuck d'you think you're looking at?

'I know,' Richard told Stephie, when he was back in lane. 'I don't know what people expected, what they wanted.'

'Well it's better than suicide, I'd imagine.'

'It wasn't that long after the ecstasy death scares in the papers and there were traces of MDMA in her bloodstream. The sheriff commented. Made quite a big deal of it.'

'If that even had anything to do with it. She might have just slipped and fallen into the water.'

That seemed worse, almost, in its arbitrariness. Greasy stone underfoot, a sliver of stray seaweed. Dark water and no handhold on the cold stone of the pier.

'Anyhow,' Stephie went on, 'aren't there always drugs in universities? They couldn't have known where they came from.'

'It was a small town,' Richard said. 'And a smaller social circle. It probably did come from Luke. From us.'

'But the inquiry confirmed that it was an accident. What could they say?'

Neither of them was specifying who 'they' were, Richard realised. Lucy's parents with their glazed expressions, her friends with their tissues and red-rimmed eyes, her tutors blank-faced and serious. The Principal and the Vice-Principal and the Dean, who – nudged forward by the media relations officer – emphasised that it was impossible to underestimate the effect of the tragedy on the university community.

'Luke,' Richard said. 'Well, he'd . . . had a kind of relation-ship with her.'

'He'd slept with her, you mean.'

'Ye-es.'

'Hang on, what are you saying?'

'Nothing.' Richard hesitated. 'Just that they parted on bad terms. That was mentioned, in the hearing at the University Court. You see it was listed in the Acts, Ordinances and Resolutions . . .'

'Eh?'

'Yes, I know. That's what you get at an ancient university. They hold a Court of Discipline if someone has . . . let's see if I can remember it . . . intentionally and recklessly endangered the safety or health of another member of the university.'

'And selling drugs was . . .'

'Intentional and reckless, yes. Resulting in deprivation of membership of the university or of a degree.'

Richard noticed a lay-by coming up, a horseshoe off the road where two lorries were parked next to a food van. He pulled off, saying something about needing a coffee to Stephie, although it hadn't been so long since they'd stopped. While he was waiting for the woman to find a new packet of plastic lids for her polystyrene cups he checked his phone. The message was from Calum, a reply to the one Richard had sent that morning. The presence of Stephie had allowed Richard to insist he'd stay in a B&B rather than with his old roommate, and he disliked himself for hoping that the short notice wouldn't allow Calum to clear enough time to see him. His luck was in, it seemed: Calum was en route to a conference in Cambridge and would then be staying for the weekend with Verity's parents. He assumed Verity was Calum's wife, the mother of Kaylar. Richard remembered Calum's freckled face and nice nature, being tempted by his early, earnest invitations to the Sci-Fi Society and the Live Action Roleplay Club. If Richard hadn't already met Luke, he might have accepted.

'There you go pet, there's your coffees.'

'Thanks,' Richard said, turning back to the counter of the van. There was no message from Luke.

'That'll be three pound twenty,' the woman said. 'Milk and sugar's just there.'

He rummaged in his pocket for change and handed over the money, carefully peeled the lid from Stephie's cup and topped it up with milk. He was almost back at the car before he noticed that she was standing on the other side of the parking area, by a picnic table that had been inelegantly positioned next to the toilet cabin. As he got closer he saw that she was speaking on her phone and held back. She spotted him and waved, smiling, so he moved forward.

'Yes I'm studying,' she was saying. 'I'm just outside to get a mobile signal. No, I don't know. A bit longer. Of course it's fine with Richard. No, he's out at the supermarket just now Mum. D'you want me to get him to phone you? Oh, okay. Well, I'll tell him. Okay. Bye.'

She made a face as she tucked her phone back into her handbag. Richard put her coffee down on the picnic table, next to a crude – was there was any other kind, he wondered – depiction of a penis gouged in the surface of the wood.

'How's Mum?' he said.

'Asking for you.'

He nodded, wondering why they'd never been the kind of family that sent love rather than their best. Or perhaps they had been once, and he just didn't remember.

'Wondering why I'm still here. Or there, rather. I didn't tell her we were away.'

'No.'

Stephie took the lid off her coffee cup and carefully pressed it into the mound of rubbish that was overflowing from the litter bin.

'Mum and Dad, did they come to this hearing thing?'

Richard leaned against the edge of the table, looking towards the motorway with its fast and constant flow of cars and vans and roaring lorries. 'I sometimes used to think that it would have been easier on them if we'd been punished properly, both of us, charged and put on remand for possession with intent to supply or something like that.'

Stephie poured a little of her coffee onto the patchy grass, swilled the rest round in the cup to cool it. 'You were punished

Richard. You were kicked out, all that time was wasted, you had to make a fresh start.'

'But it's like . . . it's like that was another world. It was another world to me, never mind them.'

'Because they were thickos who never went to uni, is that what you're saying?'

'No, of course not. Just that they didn't . . . oh, I don't know.'

How could he explain it, the look on his mother's face as she met Dan, the way Dan seemed to be summing up Richard's father, who looked – wholly inadvertently – slightly at odds with the law himself in his funeral suit. His shoes were the wrong colour, his trousers nestled below his belly and his jacket looked cheap next to Dan's hand-tailoring and old school tie. It would have been disloyal to try to put it into words for Stephie. Richard hadn't measured up either, there had been no secret signal, no hint of camaraderie. As though he and Luke had shared nothing. Was it any wonder, how things had worked out? How could his family compete, with his mum's hesitance and his father's accent, against the fur-trimmed robes of the Senate and Dan's splendid endorsements of Luke. Guy's parents had stated a vested interest too. Their name and title were shining from a brass plaque outside the new History of Art resource centre, and the Chief Constable had attended to urge against any unpleasantness or publicity.

'It wasn't an ideal way to come out.' Richard tried to laugh. 'It was suggested that Luke and I were . . . you know. Mum and Dad hoped he'd led me astray, I suppose.' He remembered trying to tell them that it wasn't Luke's fault, the tears he couldn't quite hide seeming as shameful as anything else.

'What about Luke's mum, where was she?'

'He wouldn't let her come.' Luke had said there was no point, that she'd never find her way there on time. And that he had someone else he'd bring instead, a friend, to act as sponsor. Dan, as it turned out, who deftly tilted the blame towards Richard. He'd taken it like a man, or so he thought at the time, although his legs had been trembling under the table.

'Did you ever meet her?' Stephie said.

'Once. I chummed him to Edinburgh and we had a drink

with her somewhere near the bus station.' Somewhere with an island bar and seashell-shaped green leather booths, where Richard had bought a round of drinks that cost enough to make him panic as he scrabbled in his pockets for extra change to hand to the barman.

'What was she like?'

'Okay. I thought so anyway. Drunk.'

She'd seemed fun, knocking back her double vodka and coke and laughing with them in a way that he couldn't imagine from his own mother. But Luke's mum had been younger, with her ponytail and bright top, her jeans and her Caterpillar boots. Richard couldn't remember her name.

'Were you drunk?'

'Maybe. But we didn't show it so much. She did,' as her laugh grew louder and her words slurred and the barman started to cast glances in their direction. Luke had given her money for the cigarette machine and she'd come back with no change and Marlboro Lights rather than her usual, cheaper brand. 'And then they had a row. She touched his hair and said it was like his father's, and he went mental. Shouted at her.'

There had been something else, some conversation with a man and Luke muttering something under his breath that had shocked Richard. Stupid whore, that might have been it, and then they'd offered to walk her to her bus stop but she'd made excuses about fresh air and so they'd left her outside and gone to get their own bus home. They'd been meant to stay over-night, he recalled, to go clubbing somewhere druggy with banging techno. He'd felt relieved, on the long and dark journey home, to be drinking cans at the back of the Citylink instead.

A motorbike shrilled past, swerving past a car that was slowing to pull in to the lay-by. 'Anyway,' Richard said, standing up and stretching his arms above his head until he heard one of his shoulders pop, 'Let's get back on the road.'

He stuffed his cup into the bin, dislodging a crisp packet in the process which he didn't pick up.

'Richard?'

'This guy Dan that Luke brought to the hearing, the one he used to stay with?'

'Yes?'

'Well, he was quite a bit older, wasn't he, and you made it sound as if he was gay. And they met when Luke was seventeen, didn't they?'

Richard nodded and walked towards the car. The convertible parked next to him beeped and flashed as someone released its central locking by remote control. The Ford looked like an old rust bucket in comparison, but he knew it was solid enough to last a while longer at least. He unlocked Stephie's door first and then his own, adjusted his wing mirror for the final stretch.

An hour or two later, he found himself circling the same roundabout for the second time as he tried to negotiate the one way system that would take them into the centre of town. He told Stephie that it must be a new road layout but then remembered that he'd never driven there before. One of the exits would take him towards Herrick House, he was almost sure, though he wouldn't have walked that way. If it still existed, of course. When they went through the stone archway that channelled the traffic onto Main Street, unfamiliar shop signs caught Richard's eye. He saw that the Earl of Merchiston had been taken over by a brewery; the frontage was glossier than before, and he spotted a chalkboard offering 'Good Food!' as they passed. A packet of dry roasted peanuts and some plain crisps had been as good as it got in his day. He didn't know whether he was amused or horrified to be there, thinking in terms of 'his day'. The Italian restaurant was still there, although the name had changed, and as they drove past Stephie said, 'That place looks nice, let's go there tonight.'

'Yes. I went there once before, I think.'

He turned into College Street and said, 'Look at the numbers. Our place should be round about here.'

'There's a sign up ahead,' she said. 'That might be it on the left.'

He pulled in and checked the parking sign. He'd have to feed the meter until six o'clock, but that would be fine. His back was stiff from the drive and he couldn't figure out how he felt. If he walked down this road he'd come to the university on the right, the quadrangles and the chapel, and behind that the glass façade of the library. He could follow the lanes and vennels to the Union, the cemetery, the harbour. He wondered where Luke was: huddled over a book in the short loan study area; on a bar stool in the Mature Students' Club; tumbled in the bedclothes with an undergraduate, his hand twisted in her hair; standing at the end of the pier, looking out over the water and waiting for the scream of a Tornado F3 overhead.

'When was the last time you were here?' Stephie asked.

'The day Mum and Dad came to get me,' he said. 'The day I left.'

0

The slam of the front door wakened me. Then there was music from Luke's room, loud and insistent. I wondered if Aimee was with him; he'd spent long enough getting ready for their date, obviously hoping there would be some kind of recompense for the rom coms and chaste goodnight kisses. She'd called round for him earlier, bearing homebaking and looking as if she should have been wearing a gingham apron. I still had no idea what he saw in her, assumed it must be a challenge.

I fucking hate brownies, Luke had whispered to me before they left, scowling at the neat Tupperware container as though it had soiled our messy coffee table. In spite of my nausea at the sentiment of the gift, I'd plundered the tub three times, ostensibly because my brain needed sugar in order to complete Chapter 7 of the maths workbook.

Since we'd lived in the flat I'd become tuned in to Luke's sounds, the thump of each shoe on the floor if he came in later than me. Tonight it sounded as if he'd flung his shoes at the wall, despite the effort he'd made polishing them earlier. No voices; he seemed to be alone. Something fell and smashed, a glass perhaps. I edged out of bed, hovered undecided and then pulled on a pair of pants, expecting a rap on my door at any second, to see him flushed and penitent. I groped for the t-shirt I'd taken off before I went to bed, put that on as well, but when after five minutes or more he hadn't come I got back under the covers and fell asleep again.

The next day he got poisonously drunk. I'd refrained from knocking on his door and gone to morning lectures as usual, expecting to run into him at lunchtime at the Union, gulping down black coffee before Classics. No show, and he wasn't in class either. As I collected extra copies of the articles we'd been assigned I imagined him languishing on the couch watching daytime television. But after my maths group I bumped into Marc, who mentioned that he'd seen Luke staggering along the promenade by the West Beach, shouting at the gulls.

What was he shouting?

Sounded like poetry to me, but what do I know, I'm a social scientist.

I'll look out for him, I said.

Pretending to myself that it was concern rather than nosiness or need that drove me, I checked out the Union then walked through the town, ducked into the Earl and then the Ram's Head, where I recognised the barmaid and asked if she'd seen him.

Guy with dark hair? Scottish, about my height.

Dinnae ken, she said, bored and polishing glasses.

Wears a kind of greeny blue leather jacket sometimes.

Could be, she said. Nice looking?

I shrugged, as though I'd never given it any thought.

Shocking flirt?

Yeah, I smiled. That'll be him.

Uhuh. Had to knock him back earlier. He was in some state. D'you know where he went?

She frowned, stretched up to hang a glass from the rack overhead. No idea, she said. Here, did you read about that other student that's gone missing?

I shook my head and left before she could tell me.

Luke had probably gone round to Aimee's, and I could hardly follow him there. I tried to walk off a little of the unsettled feeling, intending to tramp the streets until the exercise warmed my blood again and the dusk made going back to the flat alone seem reasonable rather than some kind of failure. He was like an anchor, mooring me in the town, marking my place. Whenever he went away I felt less connected, no matter how many LesBiGay discos I went to and how many boys I kissed (not nearly enough).

My feet led me to the grass that bordered the east beach and a sweeping view of the sea, choppy and grey. Although I'd grown up inland it hadn't been too far from the west coast, with its bleak caravan parks and beaches of dark shingle.

People were throwing balls for their dogs, and I wished Jojo was with me, slavers and all. He'd have been burling round in excitement, waggy-tailed at the prospect of chasing his rubber bone into the waves. I moved back towards the pavement, climbed the steep path that passed by the graveyard, taking the long road home.

Luke was sitting against the back wall of the church when I found him, looking out to sea, a can of lager in his hand. His eyes were bloodshot and his lips looked parched. I crouched down beside him. He indicated the remains of a six pack lying on the ground, and I prised a can from its plastic noose and cracked it open. The chill had left the beer and it tasted sour. After a while Luke said, I don't think that Aimee and I have a future together.

He shook a cigarette out his pack and flicked his lighter at it, with no luck. I took it from him and held the flame until he got a light. His skin was pale, clammy looking. I wondered if he'd taken any pills.

I'm sorry, I said. What happened?

He slit a blade of grass with his nail and tore it into two halves, which he threw onto the ground beside him.

Ask Aimee, if you can get within spitting distance of her.

But the truth was that I didn't care about Aimee. We walked back towards Herrick, Luke putting one foot in front of the other as though it required as much coordination and strength as he possessed. The shops had closed and the streets were quiet and almost empty. The newsagent attached to the Courier office hadn't taken in their boards and the new headlines for the week's paper stopped me dead: STUDENT MISSING, DEPRESSED LUCY NOT SEEN SINCE THURS and LUCY PARENTS: HELP US FIND DAUGHTER.

Luke, I said.

Yeah, he said. I know.

They don't mean . . . Lucy, do they?

Yeah, he said again. They do.

Hang on, what happened?

He shrugged, kept walking.

What do they mean, depressed? I said, hurrying to keep up with him.

She was on anti-depressants, Luke said. They found them in her room.

How do you know?

Aimee, he said, scowling out her name.

I wonder where she is, I said.

Run away, who knows.

I hope she's okay.

She is or she isn't. Banal platitudes aren't going to make any fucking difference either way.

He started walking faster, and I jogged to keep up with him.

Do you think . . . I began but he turned and snarled at me, Fuck off Richard. I'm not in the mood, okay?

He shoved past me and marched off, back in the direction we'd come from. I stood and watched him go.

23

Richard walked past his old flat, the one he'd shared with Luke. The building looked the same, the stone still rough and older looking than it was, although it seemed he'd hardly seen it in daylight. In his memory he was always rounding the corner to see the doorway illuminated under the streetlamp that had also cast a deceptively warm light through the threadbare curtains of his bedroom window. The door itself was still ajar, and he caught a glimpse of water pooling on the concrete floor of the close, just as it had when he and Luke had lived there. He wondered if students still rented it, imagined how ridiculous he would seem if he pushed the door open and climbed the curving stairs to the first floor, asked to look around. Although the day was mild, he felt a slight shiver as he moved out of the sunlight and into the shade of the building. Now that he was alone, without Stephie beside him, the past was lagging round him, thick and airless.

4 o'clock on the pier?

Richard had liked the 'o'clock', the old fashioned lack of abbreviation. He was early, he realised. There were twenty minutes to kill. He thought about wandering around the abbey, checking out the new visitor centre, but realised that there was an admission charge and decided to save it for when Stephie was with him. If she was interested; the prospect of a run of gift shops followed by a latte and a glossy magazine had elicited a more enthusiastic response than his suggestion of the castle or the museum.

'Take your time,' she'd said when he left her to her shopping.

'It might not take any time. He might not be there.'

'But if he is, it's fine. Look, I'll tell you what, I'm going to buy something to eat and go back to the B&B. You can text me if you want me to come out, or come back and get me there.'

He'd grown used to the pleasant confines Stephie put on his activities; back by a particular time, meals at regular intervals. He wondered, not for the first time, if Luke had anyone in his life or if he was still as free as he'd always seemed. Instead of going into the abbey grounds Richard ducked right, through the gate and down the harbour road, looking for the door in the wall that would take him into the cemetery. Sudden noise split the air and he twirled round, looking up for the planes. Funny how such a terrifying sound could become almost familiar. They were returning to the base, he assumed, or he might have caught a glimpse of them firing out over the sea. Poppy wreaths were glowing scarlet against the granite of the war memorial on Main Street, he'd noticed, months after Remembrance Day. A few bunches of fresh flowers had been propped at lopsided angles between them, swathed in cellophane, but Richard hadn't gone up to read the cards that were taped to them.

He selected a bench near the highest part of the cemetery and sat down, his back to the wall. Luke might walk that way to the pier, depending on where he lived now. Although there was tension somewhere in Richard's chest – foreboding, excitement, he didn't know which – he realised that he couldn't wholly believe that he was going to see Luke again after so long. The text had come the previous evening, as he and Stephie had been eating carpaccio and wondering how the students at the opposite table could afford to go to the restaurant. She hadn't understood what it was like, Richard thought, and then she'd identified the girls' handbags on her way back from the bathroom and commented that the clientele was somewhat removed from that of the appropriately named Good Luck Cantonese, Leckie's only sit-in restaurant. He'd read Luke's message as soon as she'd left the table, checked and double checked that he'd got the sender right, ordered a jug of tap water out of a need for activity more than anything else. Something about the waiter's demeanour made Richard realise that he'd mistaken them for a couple on a date, but he swished away before there was time to correct him.

And now here Richard was, sitting overlooking the cemetery. He'd read his course books on this same bench, or so he thought, when even on warm days the flat had seemed cold. It was strange to think how much time had passed since he'd left. His parents weren't the kind of people who drove long distances and the journey back to Ayrshire had loomed over them. They'd waited in the car while he ran round the flat, stuffing his clothes in binbags and throwing CDs into his shabby leather suitcase, anxiety threatening to burst from his chest in some sprawling, irrevocable mess. He was afraid, he'd acknowledged then, of his father. Bedclothes were left in a tangle, dishes in the kitchen sink, but Richard had found himself edging open the door to Luke's bedroom, spending a moment standing there, looking at its unaccustomed neatness and imagining that if the front door were to spring open and Luke arrive, there might be an alternative.

Then a horn had sounded outside, although Richard wasn't sure if it was from his parents' car or not, and there wasn't enough time or reason for farewells. He remembered sitting in the back seat on the way home, nausea interrupted by the idea – it had been more than an idea, it had felt so urgent – that he should have taken something to remember Luke by. Though as it turned out, he hadn't needed it. Almost ten years later and the memories had come pouring back, when he pulled the covers around him and closed his eyes at night, when his feet beat their rhythm on the rough single track road, when Stephie asked him questions about what had happened back then. Those memories had never really left him. They'd been there in his lonely Dundee bedsit, and the first time he'd listened to the night noises of the house in Argyll, but they'd been at their sharpest, their most cutting, in those hellish few months he'd spent back at home. If Luke turned up Richard would punch him, square in the jaw, rather than admit how he'd felt.

Up at eight every day although sleeping was his only solace, so as not to invite comments about laziness. Nothing to do apart from packing away childish things – the Warhammer figurines, the fantasy novels that no longer diverted him – and signing on once a fortnight. When he went back to the cemetery he saw that the grass needed mowed, just as the paths needed raked and the beds weeded. No cheery annuals now, just wizened stumps of standard rose with occasional surprised blooms. When it was dry enough Richard spent hours sitting on the bench near the far wall of the cemetery, reading, thinking, trying not to think. He wasn't sure if the bench had been painted since he'd done it, only two years before. Angular letters scored in the thick, flaking colour announced: LYT, FUCK THE POPE, DARREN F IS GAY.

At times Richard looked up and half-expected to see Mr Walls ambling by, refuelling the mower or stooping to pick up a piece of litter. Once he recognised a wiry man with greyhounds who'd sometimes called by to pass the time of day. Two dead rabbits were dangling from his hand and Richard suddenly remembered that the man always used to address Mr Walls as 'Faither'. Although Mr Walls had called Richard 'son' while they were working together he'd never been able to return the compliment. Even after such a short time away – even before he'd gone, if he was honest – such things sat uneasily on his lips as they never had on his father's.

The second time he went to the Job Centre Richard saw Sammy McGuire from his year at school, and then he decided he couldn't hack it. It was either get away or climb the pithead and take the quick way down. Not that he'd manage even to get up there in the first place, or so he thought when he walked past and considered the possibility. He remembered something Luke had said – 'there's this thing called clearing' – and went to the library and scanned the papers, waiting for his slot on the one computer with dial up connection. His parents hadn't been keen, but he'd made some phone calls while they were out at work, emphasising the personal reasons that had made him drop out of his first degree course and his high marks in maths and logic. He had something to prove, though he wasn't sure what.

When Richard got to the pier he walked along to the end, sat on the big concrete step beside the harbour light. Rust stains ran down from a rivet embedded in the stone beside him. He looked at his phone, half-expecting a text from Luke cancelling their meeting, though that had never really been his style. They hadn't had mobile phones then, they'd seemed a businessman's affectation, something that only the norms needed. Luke arrived in his own time or not at all, and there was never any warning of which; Richard had sat alone in bars lingering over a pint and pretending to read the paper plenty of times. He felt the memory of a movement in his fingers, an answering call in his lungs. Although it had been years since he'd smoked the urge for a cigarette was almost overwhelming. He checked the time. It was five to four.

0

I pulled my knees up to my chest and felt the lumpy chaise-longue shift beneath me. Luke was hunched down by the fireplace, scrunching scraps of old newspaper together and stuffing them in the grate. He held a match to them, let the flame caress the yellowing edge of paper until it turned brown and then black. Although we'd found the shutters closed and fastened it seemed a risk and hardly likely to warm us, but I couldn't muster the energy to care.

There's nobody around, Richard, he said, as if I had protested. The workmen have gone home, if they were even here, and the gatehouse was all shut up. The place is ours now.

I don't know why we came, I said.

Because it's better than sitting at home with the curtains drawn, Luke said, and with a whoosh the flames leapt up, wrapping themselves around the old wooden coathangers he'd stacked on top and then dying as quickly as they'd flared. He sighed and began to shred more newspaper.

The post-exam vacuum of the Whitsun term had been filled with talk of Lucy, missing. And now that she was found the whole town seemed to be buzzing with the news. I'd been sick when I heard, in the gutter outside Mr Singh's shop. He'd always seemed a benign presence when I went to buy cigarettes or a pan loaf, but he looked disappointed when he saw me doubled over and retching while Calum stood to one side, dismayed at the effect of his news.

How did you get it going, I asked Luke, staring at the blaze.

He scrambled to his feet, his shadow leaping against the wall behind him and wavering in the firelight. He was holding a tin of lighter fuel.

I looked at it, uncomprehending, and then he pulled the nozzle open again and turned in a slow circle, the lighter fuel arcing around him onto the floor. I jumped up and tried to take the can from him but he managed to twist out of my way, splashing it faster, until I grabbed his arm and tried to prise the tin from his hand. He shoved me down and the chaise screeched across the floor as I fell against it but I held on to him, toppling him over as well, until we were grappling for possession of the can. I forgot, I think, who it was I was struggling against and why, got lost in the physical sensation of the fight. We were too close and tangled up to hit or even kick each other, but I managed to lean on his arm and almost got the can off him before he ducked in and somehow yanked the nozzle open with his teeth.

It's empty, he said, as the last of the lighter fuel seeped into the horsehair of the chaise. It's empty now you stupid bastard.

He turned away and spat on the floor, and I gave him another shove. I was still sitting on his legs, kind of, my knees sore against the floorboards, and I wasn't sure whether I was going to punch him while I had the chance or burst into tears.

You're a cunt Luke, I said.

He pulled one of his arms free and for an instant I thought he was going to strike me, but he opened his palm as if to prove that it was empty and wiped his mouth instead. My breath seemed to be rasping, with the exertion and the stench of the lighter fuel. Luke was panting too, and I realised that he was looking at me and that our bodies were touching. This was the moment, my chance, to reach out and push the hair back from his face, to lean in and kiss him. He was still looking at me, waiting, as though he expected me to hit him still, and then he frowned and I saw the expression in his eyes alter, like the changing scene through the window of a train. My gaze broke and I adjusted my weight, moved my hand from where it was pinning his shoulder to the hard frame of the chaise-longue. He clambered to his feet.

Don't you get it Richard? he said. I've got to do something.

I got to my feet as well, backed away from him. His fingers were black with newsprint, I noticed, as he delved into the pocket of his jeans and pulled out a small box of Bluebell matches. As he struck the match the fire in the grate seemed to surge. He held it over the chaise-longue and then dropped it, grabbed his rucksack just in time and jumped back as the lighter fuel caught. A spark must have hit the floor too, because then we both leapt out of the way, into the doorway.

I hadn't thought it would burn like that, that the fire would slip and fizz along paint and plaster and tinder-dry wood with such ease. But it did. It burned until the chill air inside the castle thickened and warmed. We retreated along the corridor, Luke throwing open each door as he went. There's no going back now, I thought I heard him say, but his words were swallowed by a noise like a small explosion; the end of the lighter fuel canister. We ran down the stairs and along the cool tiled passageway towards the window we'd climbed through, the one he'd smashed with a brick to get to the lock. He eased it open and stood back to let me scramble out first. I stood up and dusted the moss and grit from my hands, giving Luke space to climb through, but he didn't follow.

Wait on me, he shouted, running from the room, his rucksack flapping on his back.

I pressed my face up to the glass, ready to go back in and get him, scared now even though the castle was screened from the nearest house by woodland. If someone did come, I didn't want to face them alone. I could hear the crackle of flames, I thought, although it might just have been the trees shifting in the breeze. At last I heard the sound of running footsteps and Luke appeared and launched himself out through the open window. We ran over to the edge of the trees, where a rise in the ground gave us a view of the castle.

We stood there watching the window panes glint orange as though caught in the gleam of a streetlamp. The castle looked inhabited again, alive. Then came a bang, a sudden shatter, and we saw the first flame dart from an upper window, flicker and swell in the dusky air.

Look, I said, pointing to the other side of the castle, towards the terrace where we'd peered through the French doors and into the room we'd thought must have been a ballroom. The windows were glowing there too, as though all the wall sconces were lit and the candlelight was dancing in the mirrors above the mantels. Luke nodded, and I realised that he must have had more lighter fuel in his bag. We kept watching, exhilarated, and if the fire was an act of mourning I think it was for ourselves rather than Lucy. At last we heard a distant shrill of siren come to call time.

That's it, Luke said, his voice soft. It's over.

I felt his arm around me, his hand fleeting on my upper arm, and then we began to walk home across the fields, our clothes and hair reeking of smoke, and I knew that he was right, that we couldn't go back now.

24

Luke wasn't coming, Richard knew it. He'd leave Stephie a while longer then phone her and suggest that they met in a pub. That place they'd passed earlier, the one with the plate glass windows that looked like a wine bar. Somewhere clean and free from the patina of the past. She'd be disappointed; he guessed she'd been desperate for a glimpse of Luke. Richard tucked his feet up beside him, thought of sitting on the sea wall with Loren. The water here was greyer than it had been in Argyll, and instead of zigzags the waves were slipping into dully hypnotic curves. The lease on his house was due to expire at the end of September and although he expected he'd be able to renew it there was no obligation to do so. Rupe had mentioned Hamburg to him again, and Richard thought of the docks there, how he imagined the water to be greyer still. When he turned to glance along the pier again Luke was almost in front of him.

'Hey,' Richard said. Although he recognised Luke straight away – his slimness, his close-fitting jeans – he was unfamiliar too. A new style of jacket, not seventies any more, and his hair was different, still dishevelled but cut closer in a way that accentuated his cheekbones.

Luke grinned. 'It's been a while,' he said, and with that glimpse of white teeth, the hint of dryness on his lips, that gently mocking expression when Richard looked into his eyes, with all of that he was just the same.

'Yes.' Richard moved along a little so that there was space for Luke to sit down. Luke patted his pockets, a gesture that seemed achingly familiar. He held the cigarette packet out to Richard, who shook his head.

'No one smokes anymore, eh?' Luke said, and Richard could hear the east coast in his voice. He watched Luke lean his head back against the stone behind them, saw his Adam's apple outlined as he inhaled. He turned away to blow out the smoke but even so Richard caught the scent of it. Luke must have noticed. 'Changed your mind?' he said, and dug out the packet again.

Richard shook his head again. Over in the harbour two men in overalls were working on a boat, doing something with a welding tool. Sparks sprinkled out, brilliant for a second and then fading before they hit the water below.

'So what was it like, coming back here?' he asked.

Luke sighed. 'The lecture halls are the same, unless they've got new seats or whiteboards instead of black. The library's the same. I'm very studious now.' He smiled again, and Richard noticed his blue-grey eyes, the swiftness with which their mood flickered. 'Here's hoping it's paid off.'

'Is that . . .'

'Yeah, that's me done. Finished my finals. Only a few years late, eh?'

Richard nodded, thinking of all the things he'd rehearsed to say, about himself, about his successes. 'I heard that Lucy's parents set up a scholarship fund.'

It sounded brutal but Luke smiled, or at least Richard thought he was smiling; he'd looked away towards the men on the boat again, following the clang of their tools, their indiscernible shouts. 'I didn't apply.'

'No.'

In his darkest, most paranoid moments he'd imagined Luke with Lucy on the pier, sitting exactly where they were now, or standing maybe, her drunk and pliable in Luke's arms, full of the pills her friend had bought from him, the ones Richard had counted out and tucked up in a little brown envelope which he'd licked and sealed and handed over. It would have been easy to edge her to the brink though harder, surely, to walk away. He wondered why Luke had suggested meeting there, on the pier, but such thoughts seemed out of place in the afternoon. Even though the sun was obscured by a fine layer of cloud the sky overhead was bright. A group of tourists was standing by the harbour, listening as a guide pointed up towards the abbey and then out to sea.

Luke ground his cigarette out on the concrete. 'Do you want to go and get a drink or something?' he said.

Did you ever think of me, Richard wanted to ask, in all those years? 'Okay,' he said. 'I've got to meet someone later though.' It sounded priggish, he thought, and he hoped that Luke wouldn't ask who he was meeting.

'Sure,' Luke said, getting up and stretching. His cuffs were frayed, Richard noticed.

As they walked they spoke about Calum and various lecturers who were still around, as though the movement had somehow liberated them from the initial awkwardness of their meeting. Richard mentioned his job, aware of his own façade and sure he could detect the same reticence in Luke as well. It was as easy to recognise students as Richard supposed it always had been, although he was struck by how boring their dress sense seemed in comparison with some of he and Luke's more outlandish peers.

'Where do you go now?' Richard asked, as Luke took a left off College Street and followed the narrow street down to the square by the church. They might bump into Stephie here in the touristy heart of the town, and he felt already as if he was straddling past and present.

'Do you want to go to the Union or the Earl or somewhere, for old time's sake?'

'No. I think it would be unbearable.'

'Yeah, the students are just the same. Only younger, or it seems as if they're younger than we ever were.'

They walked until they came to a bar that Luke said wasn't bad, one that seemed to cater more to locals than students or tourists. Richard thought about insisting on paying for the drinks but didn't want to seem patronising.

'So what did you do, afterwards?' he said, once they were sitting at a table made from an old Singer sewing machine. It was early to be drinking and he'd been unable to eat at lunchtime. He felt the effect of the first few mouthfuls like a friendly tug on his arm, a promise.

Luke understood what he was asking straight away. 'Went back with Dan. Do you remember him?'

Richard nodded.

'Yeah,' Luke said, turning his glass in his hands. 'It wasn't the best decision I've ever made.' His lip curled upwards into a half-smile.

'No?'

Luke let out a harsh bark of laughter. 'No. Let's just say that I . . . couldn't afford the rent. So then I went back to Edinburgh, to my mum's. Ran into a few old acquaintances, went off the rails a bit.'

'But you could have stayed. Come back after the summer, I mean. Finished your degree.'

'There didn't seem much point.' He met Richard's eye, his gaze direct below his long eyelashes. There might have been an apology there, or not. 'Maybe a few of my decisions weren't my best ones.'

Richard looked down at Luke's arms on the table, the host of dark hairs against pale skin. An image darted through his mind and he tried to chase it away, but felt an answering kick in his body just the same. After all this time, he thought. It's still there. His phone buzzed with a message but he ignored it.

'It's okay,' Luke said. 'Check it.'

Richard had expected it to be Stephie but it was from Rupe, a video message. Traffic lights changing from red through amber to green. It stopped on the green light. He forced himself to smile, tried to feel relief as he pressed the off button.

'Good news?' Luke said.

'Yeah.' This time the smile felt easier, although there wasn't the elation he'd expected. 'Really good news. Want another drink?'

Luke nodded and Richard went up to the bar. *Somme* had been greenlit, it was going ahead. An entire game spun from just one quote he'd pulled from a history book, neglecting to jot down the name of the soldier who'd said it. An old man at the time of the interview, still proud of his dress uniform, living for reunions with the handful of veterans still left. 'I lived my whole life between the ages of eighteen and twenty-one,' he'd told the tape recorder. 'The rest is just the credits.' Richard caught his own reflection behind the gantry, distorted behind rows of glasses like something in a hall of mirrors. While the pints were being pulled – Guiness, extra cold; as soon as Luke had said it Richard realised it was what he wanted too – he stared at the fragments of his face, trying to catch sight of something that he'd recognise as his past self.

'So,' he said, returning to the table. 'You went off the rails. And then . . .' The cold glasses in his hand made him want to let go, to get drunk, to see if it could ever feel like it had back then.

'I got back on the rails. Sorted myself out. Came here.'

'Why?'

'It was easier. The different degree system, you know?'

'No, I meant what made you sort yourself out.'

Luke held out his hands, another familiar gesture. 'Dunno. I've fucked up a few times, I guess. Didn't want to do it again.'

His knuckles looked rough, and Richard remembered how much Luke had hated his skin's propensity to crack and burst and scab. Once he'd stretched his palm open and Richard had watched as red fissures appeared, a pattern the size of a fifty pence piece etched in raw, moistening flesh. Luke's face had been vulnerable, all of a sudden, as if he was asking for it to be made better. Richard couldn't remember how he'd reacted, what he'd done.

'So Calum's married with a kid, then,' Luke said.

'Yes. A kid named after a character in Star Wars. What about you?'

'What about me?' Luke said, grinning.

'Kids?' Richard said. 'Girls?'

Luke shrugged. 'There are always girls, aren't there? But . . . well, maybe I'm just not very good at relationships.'

'Me neither.'

'But you've got to meet someone tonight.'

Richard looked at the clock above the bar. Time seemed to have moved quickly. 'Yes,' he said.

'Bring them along.'

'It's okay. And it . . . isn't anything like that anyway. Thanks though.'

That morning he'd taken Stephie around the old part of the university, into the chapel and through the quadrangle. He'd seen for the first time the little wrought iron memorial bench, erected to Lucy, in memory of 'her cheerful smile, her caring nature and her love of life.' Luke must have walked past it several times a week.

'Do you ever think . . .' Richard began but Luke spoke at the same time:

'They rebuilt the castle, you know. Turned it into luxury apartments for posh golfers. You'd never know to look at it.'

Richard thought of the images he'd seen in the paper, the castle roofless and charred, its windows broken. *Vandals strike.* Then he thought of Luke walking there alone, wondered if he scaled the fence or strode through the gates, head held high. And what had he found? Security cameras, automatic lights, fancy cars in the drive; the same, but not the same. He must have wanted to remember, to touch the past, rub it between his fingertips and feel it once more. It's over, he'd said all those years ago, and yet he'd gone back anyway.

'What are you going to do,' Richard said, not sure what he was asking.

Luke's face was closed, distant. 'Stay here, finish this pint, have another one.'

Richard nodded. It wasn't enough, not yet. He didn't know if it would ever be enough. 'Can I have a cigarette?' he said.

Luke nudged the packet across the table to him, felt for his lighter. Richard took them and went outside, where he stood next to the etched glass that concealed the interior of the bar. The sky was blazing pink and red, like a west coast sunset. He reached for his phone, switched it on again.

Stay out. I have date with SATC reruns. Love u. S x

He felt disembodied, as though part of him was elsewhere, held the cigarette in his hand but didn't light it. The stone slabs of the pavement were glowing in the light, and he knew he should walk away, follow them back to his B&B, back to Stephie. He took a few steps but couldn't contain the memory of walking along those gilded pavements with Luke, back to

Herrick, back to the flat. Transitory moments, replete with the sheer and not-quite-certain potential of what was to come. Richard wanted one of them back, just one, to experience again a hope so fierce that the sins of the past were cleansed, the gleam of the future untarnished. He turned and walked back to the bar, pushed open the door.

Acknowledgements

I am indebted to the Hawthornden International Writers' Retreat, at which the idea for this novel was conceived. Many thanks are also due to Creative Scotland (previously the Scottish Arts Council) for a Writers' Bursary that bought me time and space to write. Finally, I am grateful to the K Blundell Trust whose grant helped me out in tight times.

Early extracts from this novel were published in *The Antigonish Review*, *Bordercrossing Berlin* and *Gutter*.